the
TONGUES
of
MEN

the
TONGUES
of
MEN

John Schultz

BIG TABLE PUBLISHING COMPANY
Chicago

For Annie

Some of these stories first appeared in the following
magazines and the author wants to thank the editors for
their kind permission to reprint them in this collection:
Big Table, Chicago Review and *Evergreen Review*. "Custom"
originally appeared in the collection of novellas, *3 x 3*
(Grove Press: 1961), reprinted as *4 x 4* by Grove Press in 1967.
The author thanks the publisher of Grove Press for
permission to reprint the novella.

ISBN# 0-9667557-0-7

Library of Congress Catalogue Card Number: 69-13382
Reprinted 1998

CONTENTS

I

WITNESS
CUSTOM
MORGAN

II

THE HICKORY STICK RIDER
EENIE MEENIE MINIE MO
DALEY GOES HOME

III

VISIT TO MY GRANDFATHER'S GRAVE ALONE
ECHO
JESSE HAD A WIFE
THE OFFENDING PARTY
GOODBYE

WITNESS

I could not for the life of me remember if Uncle Jack
ever had any reason for killing the stranger. Crimes of passion
are sloppy. Jack was not. His was the snake strike of
conviction. But not one of us knew his reason, and he would
not tell.

We were pressing eagerly around him on the porch of the
general store. Our backs shivered against the damp March
air. He squatted on one heel. Come from a long time alone
in the woods, *yet* his jokes played on us. His tongue in his
cheek restrained his grin. Beside him, high as his head, rose
a heap of new bought things. Harness, nails, a round of
cheese, side of bacon, bottles, candy, sacks, bullets, and other
paraphenalia. Our storekeeper completed the trade with
money. Jack's hand took the money and wrapped it into his
rear pocket. The movement was not soiled by a single glance
from his talking, laughing face and eyes. The storekeeper,
with firm lips and a forward look, retreated. He locked the
door behind him so he could count and pack the burden of

fur under which Jack staggered into town. Our storekeeper worked in cheesy air.

Before Jack went into the woods, I walked at full height under his arm. Now I was closest to him, right at his elbow. He had not yet seen me. The earth and air I occupied seemed taboo to his eyes. He did not talk to me, he talked *about* me to others. He laid one hand on top the heap as if on someone's shoulder. He shook it and laughed as he once teasingly shook me. It measured the success of his winter in the woods. His smells of sweat and cured fur sang in the nostrils. I remembered the fresh kill. I turned my face to the cold wet air away from him and the crowd.

Off the end of the porch, over the buildings far down the street, the steeple of my father's church poked up, its shingles shaggy. I set my lips against it. Yet an equally shaggy emotion thrust up in me, brushing the back of my eyes.

The crowd yammered around Jack like the hounds when he fed them. When someone did not understand what Jack said, I was asked, "What was that? What did Jack say?" I leaned more against his presence, and my inside self strained backward. "What did you say, Jack?" His lips would tell me wryly from the side of his face, though his eyes could not find me, and I would relay it to them.

With one hand Jack doodled on the porch floor with his jackknife. His gauntly active cheeks and thin lips, smiling with long sour-colored teeth, meant only conversation could occupy his mind. A mind in his head, a mind in his hand, that possibility frightened me.

Jack filled into the rare honeyed mood. He sliced thick pieces of cheese and passed them around, and then fed himself. He screwed open a bottle, and that went from hand to hand. In the street passersby stopped, veered, attracted to his mood. Around him the buzz of byplay, talk and mastication, climbed.

Suddenly from right to left a stillness cut across the porch.

The stranger walked straight down the very center of the street. He passed even women without tipping his hat. Over his face the broad brim projected a rounded shadow. His white shirt, showing through the open coat, formed a rectangle from belt to neck. Warning enough was the cocked readiness of his wrists and elbows. Yet we did not know his reason either.

We parted around Jack, backing up against the wall of the store, and exposing him to the street.

When Jack's eyes met the stranger, his hand bent the jackknife shut against his thigh. I saw the clean blade glimmer and bury itself in the bone handle. Jack slipped it into his pocket. Something significant in the action, its almost ritual smoothness, impressed a sadness on my mind. That knife skinned by the thousands over the years everything from squirrels to bear and wolf. It helped in the cooking. It carved playthings for me. My mouth had accepted food speared on its tip.

He stepped in one stride off the porch, so surely, so quickly, we thought he must know the stranger. But Jack's right hand, which would have reached to shake hands with a friend, leaped instead to his pistol. In one startled, static moment, I saw Jack's pistol drawn and levelled and the stranger's pistol half out of his holster.

As a stone shatters the reflection in a pond, one shot shattered the scene in our eyes.

Nothing made sense—not until, standing half out of our shoes, we saw the stranger pitched onto his side in the mud, his knees pumping as if he had been kicked in the balls. His black hat was rolling on its brim. The hat toppled. It squatted crow-wise a few feet from the stranger's white thin hair, his pale skin and wild pale eyes. Jack towered next to the hat, lean in the downward thrust of his cheeks and limbs, his clothes flapping, his hand with his lowered pistol ready by his thigh. The stranger galvanized into the last convulsion. It collapsed. The body lay more mysterious than it had ever been in the few seconds it lived and walked in our sight. After a moment, Jack spat into the face. The pale open eyes did not blink. A March breeze stirred the down-white hair.

It chapped our lips. Around Jack the air darkened. His eyes reflected glints from the darkening.

I did not think, I *saw* myself take one step away from the wall toward him. My suggestion rippled along our line, it wavered. I knew Jack would act honorably, I stepped forward again. The line firmed. We edged off the porch. We encircled him.

He offered his pistol butt-first to the nearest man, whose stunned hands grasped it as a baby would grasp a rattle.

Women spanked the bottoms of small children and sent them scurrying home.

Not a hand guided Jack as he walked himself silently to the jail. It looked as if he were leading us.

I looked back once. A fat face and spread fingers pressed against the inside of the store window—our storekeeper. The heap of Jack's new bought things squatted alone on the porch.

A mongrel hound, loping down the street, footed up to the stranger's body, yapped, and jumped away. It ran onto the porch, and crept up to the pile of smells. It began snuffling and lapped the shaved cheese and the puddle from the broken bottle. No one else could use the heap. I justified the dog to myself with a smile.

Three men returned to check the stranger's belongings and bury his body. There was only a little money in his pockets.

Jack was tried in jail, and sentenced in jail.

All the chairs, windows, and doors were packed with faces. He stood in the center. The only person missing was my father and I did not mention it. No one touched Jack. He said hardly a word. But first he stated with the straightforwardness of the insane,

"I have saved everyone of you."

We did not laugh at him. We simply called upon him timidly to explain his murder and his strange remark.

"Was it an old grudge, Jack?"

"Did you know him from somewhere?"

"Was he that damn dangerous?"

"I have saved you."

He said it with a friendly smile. I even expected to see his tongue tucked in his cheek. He leaned backward against

the table, cleaning his fingernails with his knife. No one
thought it necessary to take the knife away from him.

He had loved me, my uncle, and I him. I started toward
him with my arms out. I tried to make light of it all.

"Jack, this is funny. Just tell us your reason. That's all we
need to know."

"You saw me do it. You know I know what I do."

The hardness in his eyes hammered at me. He was more
strange than the most forbidding stranger I had ever seen.
We were stung with fear of him. We drew back.

"Jack," I said, "it is too late to say judge not."

"I have saved you."

Heads wagged and tongues clucked. The vote was taken.
With not a breath of delay we agreed on the sentence. He
was to be hanged. Every man of us was possessed with an
urgency to get rid of Jack. It would be done despite my
father, whose church had civilized this part of the country,
despite the raw March weather, despite anyone and
everything. I fled the crowd.

I raced to be the first to reach the hanging house on the
hill at the edge of town.

The very second I rushed past my father's church, the bells
in the tower that soared above the trees announced the news
of Jack's imminent hanging. They had no *right* to ring as
cheerily as the bells on Christmas Day.

The highest gabled window of the parsonage nosed against
the sky. A pale shadow faded upon the window, like freezing
breath. Father was toiling in his undershirt in his study. The

pine hedge behind the church and parsonage hid the
hospital. But pine limbs, lifting and brushing and busying
themselves, exposed glimpses of the hospital windows. From
the moment of my father's arrival he must appear to approve.
If he attempted clemency, there would be no end to the
burning gossip. I *insist* the bells had no *right* to ring so
cheerily.

I took up a post midway on the slope. Hands on my hips, I
was a foreman waiting for his crew. Behind and above me,
hanging house and hill together loomed like a human shadow
lying hugely upon a wall. I remember the spot where I stood
because of an abandoned singletree half imbedded in the
ground, or half washed out, next to my right foot. I could
almost believe it had been waiting for me for years. Its iron
fittings were crusted with rust. I am not superstitious. My icy
feet sank slowly into the mud. I trampled them to keep warm.
I trampled to stay free of the sensation of sinking forever.

Already the procession of townsmen followed Jack at the
bottom of the hill. Already Jack was pushing the huge barrel
up the hill. His arms and legs worked leanly, protruding from
the bright rope coiled between his shoulder and hip. Once
his feet slipped violently and threw him on his knees against
the barrel. His elbows hit like hammers against it. I winced.
No one stepped forward to help him. With the care of a
craftsman, he pulled himself back together, not an ounce of
energy lost. He was Jack of all trades, and wise man in the
wild. I added the title of unreasonable murderer.

He turned the barrel so it would not roll downhill. He

took the knife out. He whipped the blade open. With savage carelessness, he cut both shoes off his feet. The naked toes sank in the mud, seizing a grip. Not a trace of blood showed. His back was turned to me. I did not see what other chore he performed with the knife. But I saw that his gaze drilled into the crowd. One by one they looked down.

"I have always been able to do what I wanted to do," he said. It was as if what he wanted done was right because he wanted it.

His protest had no effect. He turned to his journey. Near the top he leaned on the barrel to get his breath. The crowd instantly stopped. They preserved the pure distance. When he finally spun the barrel on its rim through the black doors, they gathered around the hanging house like hunters around the hole where the fox has hidden.

I leveled my lookout on the open field. It led back to the toy-like cluster of houses around the church spire on the horizon. I would be the first to intercept my father.

I peered up the hill to reassure myself. Above the craning heads of the crowd, I saw Jack, from the belt up, inside the hanging house, head patiently bowed in the noose. For the first time he waited for what someone else had to do. He could not bless himself. But it wasn't that. It was the blue denim workshirt, with clean unironed collar wrinkling and curling inside the noose, that so tenderly, as if with strange memory, lightly stung my eye. How strange I thought, that to my Uncle Jack this should happen.

The crowd stirred. They hissed. They shifted from foot to

foot. They made impatient moans. I shouted to them to stop. They whined. They stopped on tip-toe when a stillness struck the hill. It resounded as the toll of a bell.

A dark thing came swiftly increasing in size across the field below. The crowd's shameless giggling trembled the air. I straightened. I trembled with determination as the air trembled with giggling. I was prepared to outwit both my father and them.

Onto the scene he would burst with passionate misunderstanding. Inflexibly frantic he would hurl to one and all senseless useless indignant questions.

Now I saw that he was coatless and tieless. But the collar was buttoned. It gaped nakedly without the tie. For him that was like having his fly open.

On the far side of the drainage ditch at the foot of the hill, he skidded to a halt barely in time. His arms beat the air for balance. The unbuttoned cuff on his left wrist flapped like a wounded wing. He did not know how ashamed his son was that his father did not know how to take a run at a ditch before jumping it. Finally his sense of superhuman emergency hurled him across the ditch. He did not look well running. He looked worse jumping.

He floundered in the brush. He rose. His glasses were still positioned perfectly on his face. His frantic angry questions were increasingly audible, just as he increased in size, scrabbling up the hill. The crowd expected a dramatic plea for clemency. I sprang.

At last it had come to this, that *I*, not he, would be the one to manage for both.I had it planned. I must see him safe and sound, through my life and his, all the way to the grave.

I met him. I stopped him. His verbal turmoil seared me with the old chagrin.

"What is POSSIBLY going ON?"

"Sh-h, Father. You will hurt your heart."

"What IS going ON?"

When he said Why he meant No. He meant that it cannot, *must* not, *will* not, be. He *fired* questions. His aim was uncommonly bad. His tight lips and tight teeth vibrated.

"You must listen to me, Father. We must be quiet. Like in church."

"Church. This IS not Sunday. Can't my own son answer me WHAT?"

The corners of his mouth went pale into the rough red of his cheeks. He was an emotional tower of Babel. But good! He recognized me. It is not easy to manipulate the totally insane. His emphatic switch from object to verb and back to object again was predetermined. If his confusion confused people, he could control them all the easier. I was not deceived. His suspicions were enemies breaking in at night to him. I answered him heartily, even boisterously.

"It's Uncle Jack's *hanging*, Father. We have to go quietly."

"Jack? JACK? What is Jack doing here?"

That was his brand of cunning. I could wrap it around my purpose like cold honey around a spoon.

"Jack here?"

I laughed as if it were some joke, so outrageous its very

daring commended it. I assumed a teasing tone. I slapped him cheerfully on the shoulder as I had never done before and as he had never done for me.

"Shush, Father. It will be over soon. And we will be together as if it had never happened. But right now, Father, we must be quiet. Like in *church*, Father. We can do that, now can't we?"

His fists beat against either thigh, like an exasperated child.

"I ask YOU what is Jack doing HERE?"

I laughed patiently. My laugh tacitly communicated that he was still telling a joke, an inside joke.

"It's up to us, Father. If we only try."

I wrapped my arm around his shoulders. I held him, man to man, son to father, interjecting small hearty laughs between his protesting questions, as I had never done before. Behind his glasses his mammoth eyes shifted fearfully unsure. He sighed, "I just do not understand."

It heartened me. I flung up my hand. I would leave no doubt. I pointed a finger, that no will-power on earth could stop from trembling, up the hill over the heads of the dark crowd into the hanging house door, where, calm and straight, my Uncle Jack stood on the barrel, his head bowed in the noose. I spoke secretively. Delightfully I shivered.

"Don't you *see*, Father?"

Blobs of light, playing on his glasses, hid his eyes. Sometimes I was forced to think that his glasses caused him to see tall, skinny men as roly-poly and lovely women as twisted witches. I could not guess ahead of time what he would see now. He made exhausted deprecations with his hands. My heart quaked with laughter. He was still concealed in his clever misconception.

I was not flattering him by calling his frantic qualities cunning. I insist. I spied on him with a hunter's trained eye. His inner self huddled tenderly, secretly at a distance, in need. It dogged after his clumsy Cunning. It haunted the dark field to glean the unspeakably stingy crumbs. I was the more able hunter. I would substitute for his Outer Cunning. Become his right hand! To preserve his pride, a first necessity, I would never let him know what I was doing. But I would spread a richer gleaning, and the crowd of our neighbors would never hear or see such things to gossip about again. That was my plan.

He stated as if it were painful making the simplest question clear to me,

"It's not that Jack is here. You know how I feel about Jack. He is a very fine fellow. I just wish to understand. Is that clear, my boy? Is it so difficult?"

Now was not the time to hide my jubilance under a bushel. "Yes, Father! Everything is just dandy! You don't have to worry about a single thing! Not anymore!" I clapped him on the far shoulder. Pumping that arm I bumped his near shoulder against my chest several times. It approximated hugging. Understanding what he wished to understand, exactly what I wished him to understand, he suddenly embraced me, both arms clasped extravagantly around my back. He cried.

"We have never been like this before! It's the best we've been, ever!"

He would not plead for clemency. We walked enthusiastically together, arms around each other's shoulders, up the hill to meet the first test.

The first, however, came from him. Under my arm he became apprehensive. His eyes were active behind his glasses. He struck his fist into his palm. It was a play-act of determination. He said,

"I think I can save Jack!"

I gave him the astonished look of the lawfully perplexed. "Father," I said heavily, "Jack killed."

He sighed. His gaze scattered away from me. It was that easy.

"It is a blessing," he said, "that your mother was spared seeing her brother come to this. Jack was always her favorite, you know."

"Yes, Father. I remember."

"It is a blessing. You know I liked him too."

"Yes."

Whispering pardons we pressed through the crowd. Our neighbors welcomed us in the quick chin-ducked way our people have at church and funerals. We arrived at the inner edge. A clear view went before us.

I waited for Jack to look up at me. He stood as still as a stalk in a windless field, with his face down, in all the dim, empty space inside the hanging house. His turned-back collar showed the pallid flesh next to the sunburnt triangle that made his neck and head like solid bronze. Many of those burning days were spent with me. The only day when he was not with me was the first day. My mother could never get Uncle Jack to come to church. Yet he enjoyed the books my mother snitched for him from father. I remembered a better man than the uncle who shot down a simple stranger. Without grace, he had stalked naked woods and fields. My jaw hardened. A breeze blew from nowhere into the musty hanging house. His pants legs flapped around his stick-thin ankles on the barrel.

Now my father faced the nearly accomplished fact. He clutched my hand with passionate energy. Softly mindful of the crowd at our elbows, he said,

"We were never so close! I am happy for you, my son! For us!"

He had never before called me *My son!* I am sure my face was white.

"Sh-h, Father."

Then he said, with frightening strength, "It is all right! It is all right, my boy!" And I thought our new arrangement would fail on its first day. But the crowd, edging up to the crucial moment, was concentrated on Jack.

I was taller than father by several inches. I spied down on his face, while he stared ahead at Jack. I saw, over the top behind his glasses, that his eyes were much smaller than they appeared from the front, as small as his secret tender hidden cringing inner self. And I pitied him, so deeply and fully that we could never speak truth. I cunningly agreed with something he had spoken before.

"Yes, Father. This is certainly the best ever with us."

"Pray," he said, "and God will not let it hurt you. He will let us be all right. Pray, my boy."

I sang the snake between us to sleep. I said,

"Tonight, Father."

"We welcome you, my boy. God welcomes you."

Tonight, alone at last in the long black wind, I would go on my knees. I would welcome the comforting chill. It would hypnotize my humming bones.

Impatiently the crowd sighed and stirred. With a kind of clumsy humility my father squeezed my arm above the elbow. "Poor Jack. We must be just with him, my son."

That was keeping it in the family. My mother died of an unmentionable, incurable disease two years ago. In my father's words she passed on to a fine place. I could see my mother in her haggard last days, with her large glowing eyes, standing at the back door near the pump, where hollyhocks towered in bloom around the stone step. She was handing a paper sack with a book wrapped in it to Jack. Jack gave her a sly, teasing smile. After mother died Jack lost his joking way. If he looked up at me now, it would be like passing the book concealed in the paper sack. I stood in the stares of the crowd as the fox in the tightening circle of snapping dogs.

The black book appeared in my father's hand. He believed that his gestures reflected admirable decision. Hastily he stepped free of the crowd. Solemnly he walked a few steps into the hanging house. He clambered up the ladder erected there, until his head was so close to Jack's they could whisper without being heard. His feet and hands fretted on the

23

ladder rungs for balance. His sharp in-drawn hisses signified his unschooled fear of heights. On at least one front our new arrangement had already failed. The crowd had seen.

We heard the last words faintly, my father's precise nervousness, Jack's slow soft clarity. I kept my eyes steadily upon Jack. My eyes demanded that he look up. But only a bald spot in the thinning black hair on top his bowed head looked at me. It was not as if Jack would die a sad, young death.

". . . repent . . ."

My feet kneaded the ground.

"Repentance," Jack said, "is for those that have sinned, sir."

Before the rightness of every man's fate as a sinner, it was blasphemous! I can testify to the general cold constriction in the bellies of our neighbors. He would in the end put childishness behind him and come to the faith, they had said with a smug sigh, as if it were a pity he did not earlier take up the service of their great dreary ways.

"Unless I believe, I cannot sin."

Now there was sound theology. The crowd croaked. But my father was accustomed to such dialogues.

"Unless you have sinned, Jack, you cannot believe."

"Then I cannot."

"Jack, that is a terrible sin."

"I have saved everyone of you."

There it was again, that directness of the driven mad.

His strong, soft confidence sweetly coated his words. The

24

crowd swallowed his words wholeheartedly, only to be
suddenly galled by their poisonous pain.

"... make peace, my son ... with your Father make your
peace ..."

"My peace was made when I ..."

As if probed by an icy finger my heart jerked. I had thought
that he was going to say, "My peace was made when I
killed." Father shook clownishly on the ladder. I was not
ashamed. I was grateful for this deft interruption.

"... Jack ... for our sake ... for your soul ... my wife
... your sister ... Jack ..."

Father loudly singsonged various verses from the Book. The
crowd eased. They rocked rhythmically on their heels.
Carried by the cadence of the reading they were safely asleep
to the meaning of the words. My feet squirmed in the gravel.
I successfully silenced them. But I could not find what was
rightly inconspicuous for my fidgeting hands. They were
slippery as quick fish, and so white and clammy cold. Finally
I snared them flat on my thighs.

Father spoke a responsive prayer.

"Our Father ... have mercy ..."

The crowd swayed. Their body heat stifled me. They
mumbled responses at my elbows and behind me just as they
assumed Jack responded in front. I was packed in human
wool. Clear air chilled my front, where I faced father and
Jack.

Father finished one prayer and began another. My guts
clinched as if grasping a ball of cold iron.

"Speak after me, Jack . . . Our Father, Which art in
Heaven . . ."

Jack was not scheduled for my father's fine place, where
father directed my mother to go. Jack would stalk a burning
field, shaking and slapping off flames that leaped like cats
onto his back, his face grimly grey and disputing them.

Now they could not hear Jack's confidence, and they
believed what they wished of his quiet, humble stance. His
record would close as they wished. Their smug fantasies were
efficient. Only I would be certain, along with father, of his
awful, isolated truth. And the hanging house, enclosing the
two men, echoed grandly.

". . . Thy kingdom come . . . Thy will be done . . ."

When father finished, my hands and feet were released.
He lifted the book. He pressed its apex against Jack's forehead.
A red, pinched mark sprang into sight, fading slowly.

A blundering, theatrical insult! But the crowd missed. The
shuffling and sighing I feared was boredom, as after church.
We heard a tongue-in-cheek chuckle from Jack. It was kept
in the family.

"God go with you, my son," my father said to Jack.
My son!

He stepped carefully off the ladder as he would step down
from the pulpit, so as not to disturb but to deepen his
benediction. He folded the ladder noisily. He maneuvered
with it. It banged against the barrel, shaking Jack. Jack
recovered smoothly, standing straight again. Then the
unfamiliar ladder boomed against the wall. Father cursed it.

Evidently the ladder misunderstood him too. At last he laid its full length on the ground against the wall. The crowd's rigidly bowed heads denied the shame, as when a child laughed or cried during prayer. I was a prisoner of their thoughts. My feet worked, moving over to make room for my father. He cleverly clipped his hands together and looked down.

Now Jack was alone. His collar twitched. My neck stiffened against turning to search for the source of the breeze.

Our customs recognized the true nature of the law. We stood around until someone was forced to step forward and kick the barrel out from under the victim. Sometimes the spirit of belief in the criminal's guilt failed to carry a believer forward as executioner, and then the criminal went free. Many might be coerced now by Jack's former popularity, despite the flagrant cruelty of his blasphemy. Some who had stepped forward described the moment as *ecstasy in faith*, completely powered by predestined grace.

Hurried whispers hissed here and there. *How strange* that none stepped forward. Whispering cleaned their hands.

Jack still did not look up. Self-righteous! He knew his eyes would be strikingly strange. Anger iced my hands.

Two long steps carried me toward him. I doubled my knee to my waist. I punched my foot flatly forward. It knocked the barrel from under him.

"Killer!" I cried. "*Blasphemy!*"

Knees bent, Jack fell. A hard jerk whip-snapped his spine. His knees drew tautly up to his chin, again and again, as if he were doing some very difficult calisthenic. Finally, wearily, his knees sank. His arched bare feet strained for the ground.

Staggering backward in the empty air I bumped against the crowd. They held me up, like loose posts stacked cunningly.

Then, with a shiver, his body loosely hung.

The barrel lay fat and still behind Jack.

The dumb, abstracted mind saw Jack as a pendulum, ticking off eternal time. Impossible that in one moment, falling, he teemed with life, his nose tickled by the gravel's limy smell, his ears humming with whispers, his fingers chafed by the ropes, the gravel looming up gigantically into his stinging eyes. *Impossible* that in the next sudden second, the life in his mind in a bright flash was blown away. I could not consider the nature of the nothing that now occupied his head. It was flopped lopsided. Its cheek was turned. It was as if with intense pity he had turned from an intensely pitiful sight. I had seen enough vanity in him to think that he might have adjusted his cheek just before the fall.

I had hoped the act would spark the true belief in me. But it was as if I had walked onto a stage, played the role well, and then walked off and became, in spite of myself, myself again.

In terror I thought that he would not make an ordinary death. But then his eyes began to bulge. White sightless balls protruded under the extended lids. His tongue twisted in a stiff purplish curl from the corner of his mouth. All noticed that his pants, at the fly, stuck out. It was an ordinary, disgusting death.

Unlike his body his clean denim workshirt was unmarked.

Senseless! It *still* impressed the eye. I backed my way blindly out of the crowd. A corrosive nausea foamed in me. I hobbled. I reached a close collection of mucky tracks. The place where I stood before! The small, deep center of my mind thought of the hope with which I had begun. The earth that soaked and chilled my shoes seemed to suck away my strength. The horizon wheeled around me. I braced my hands on my knees. I breathed deeply, mechanically. I intended the clammy air to clean away my nausea.

I am not sure how long I stayed alone on wobbly knees under the sky that moved as an ocean upside down.

The next thing I knew the deaconesses from the hospital arrived in processional, in full flowing black, with white hoods, humming mournfully. Spreading an enormous white sheet, they knelt in two opposite rows that funnelled into the hanging house door. Those nearest the door struggled to pull the coffin out.

I knew one young deaconess fairly well. In workaday wear Marie's soft and singing curves would stand out.

Not two days ago I had slipped through the back gate into the hospital garden. Nervously silent we sat within an inch of each other on the bumpy stone benches, hidden by the hedge from view of her superiors. Yet we never touched, not until she slyly handed me her hair brush. I felt it must fly from my clumsy fingers. Her head moved in a smooth and sleepy rhythm against my brushing. When I finished, she turned, snatched the brush, and kissed my cheek. She fled. She left behind *me* more warm than the sun.

The covered coffin between their rows bulged in the shape

of a boat. It beamed as white as surf and snow. Our neighbors would not see the sardonic correctness of this flippancy of taste. They would see the honor of bigness and brilliance and striking design. Jack had murdered. I could not agree with my father. To Jack, who had dressed to suit himself and the circumstances of weather, it was an insult. They would laugh at my father.

In the empty hanging house, the gleaming rope curled, like the last sunset twistings of a dying snake.

The deaconesses folded their hands at their chins. They sang a prayer for forgiveness, though Jack's hidden head remained cold to their song. The coffin would soon be carted to the cemetery. There, no doubt, my father had arranged another garishly solemn display, possibly burying Jack and the stranger side by side, brothers.

He marched toward me, arms swinging precisely, conscious, if nothing else, of the eye of the sky upon him. My throat was sore. A force in me held back on a hardening harness.

At that moment, about noon, the sky impossibly opened, a tiny rent in the whole wide overcast. Rays of the sun shot out and focused on the crucial hill with a unique accuracy. All the rest of the countryside stayed dismal, untouched. But on the hill every rainy surface glowed. Grass, mud, the hanging house roof, people, the unbelievable white of the coffin, the black deaconesses, each hovered in a quivering glow. Neighbors stood at the end of each ray as if they could lift a foot and walk up. It was a grand trick of sun and air, a spectacle of chance. It stopped them in their tracks. They stared up with as much pure wonder as fear. Mine was mostly fear. As the others looked up the rays of the sun, I looked into the future, appraising a failure greater than all the calamitous weather in the world.

I had once seen my father as at least different from them. That was my last fantasy. Now he stood trapped at the foot of a ray, staring up, mouth open, blobs of light poised like coins on his glasses. He was not even aware that *I* was there, just as each one of them was not aware that another was an arm's length away. I surveyed a glowing waxworks, a monument to our stupendous lack of common sense. It was pretty to see. Nature had always done Jack's bidding.

I shivered. Senseless to maintain the constriction in my throat! It resembled too much the force that magnetized their eyes.

Be it to father's credit, he was the first to step free. Again he marched toward me. My clammy hands gripped together as if in prayer. He clutched them violently.

"My son! It is a magnificent coffin! The best I could find!"

I echoed. "The best, Father!"

Nothing but professional expressions were available to him. He took my response for what he wished it to mean, the way *I* wished him to take it. Tears obscured the lenses of his glasses.

"No one is left now but us," he said, in a bereft but eager cadence, again of benediction. "We must be strong. We must stick hard together. Together we will be strong."

"Yes, Father."

I committed myself to cunning forever. My hands flushed hotly damp, clutched in his. We looked up.

A deaconess was running down the hill. Her skirt was plucked above her knees, exposing black-stockinged calves like two milling brats surprised in a secret place. She was swathed in light. At the end of one row, her superior sprang up. But the superior was restrained from open disapproval by the same force in her that disapproved, as she would sturdily ignore a bodily error at table. If only because there were certain circumstances, and only one deaconess who would violate them, I knew by the natural diabolical order of things that the running girl could be no other than Marie.

She cried wildly to the neighbors she passed, to the deaconesses she had left behind, to the shining air,

"So terrible, it is so terrible!"

She flung herself in the mud at my father's feet. "Forgive us, Father! Oh, touch me and forgive me!"

I wondered if a kiss of mine could make her that radiant. For her now there were no others, only herself in the center of a uniquely radiant world, and the uniqueness was simply seeing what she wanted to see, misinterpreting the very sun and air to serve her own selfish ends. She believed her transport. Thus she acquired in her mind the privilege to presume on whomever she wished, the way the mad are indulged, and the querulous old.

Father's reaction was consternation, as if someone cursed in church. He bombarded her with questions.

"WHAT is going ON?"

"Forgive us, Father! Touch me! Forgive me!"

"Marie!"

The look springing from her face stopped my hand in mid-air. A consummate actress! With tones of tender childish pleading, her eyes hurling hot hard hate, she walked on her knees to me, and she said to the strange me,

"Forgive me for what we have done! Touch me! *Give* me that much!"

I felt my expression change, my lips curl. I started to push her away as I would shove away food that revolted me. She grabbed my right hand, kissed it. I cringed. It had not been given, she had *taken,* just as she might kiss my cheek and run. Neatly she rose. The skirt fell over her muddied knees.

Her hand dived into the flowing black folds. It came up with something wrapped tightly in brown paper sacking. She slapped it into my hand.

"Your name is on it! He wanted you to have it!"

When my surprised hand hardened on the object, I knew it was Jack's knife. She had pilfered the dead. I could no longer cherish her lack of propriety. True enough, my name was scratched on the paper. But she could not understand that I had rid myself of the knife's mystique. Her attempt at humiliation honored me.

She curtsied, then dashed up the hill, where she regained her uniform place in the two rows of black and white figures. The coffin was poised between them, as if a gentle push would launch it down the slope.

I heard my father's secret whisper, "Be strong, my son."
"Yes. Yes."

I was crying. And if he knew why it would hurt him.
Neighbors, who knew not why either, gathered around at a
respectful distance, islanding us. They came offering death,
sheathed in talk of condolence and forgiveness. They
closed in.

My blood drummed. I shucked the sack off the knife. I
pressed the button. The blade sprang, dazzling. Chance had
buried the singletree at my feet. With my other hand I tore
it loose from the ground. Swinging it high, one last illusion
was granted me, that I towered above them all. Dirt and
crusted rust showered, streaking red on the ground.

"Stand back! Leave us alone! Don't one man step near!"

I lunged. I grunted loud animal-like warnings. I scared the
screaming daylights out of the nearest. I spat. I harried them.
They fell back and back. They left us alone.

They would talk for days. They would think grief had
driven me mad. Triumphantly, from now on, the shame
would go unnoticed by us and by them. I could manage for
father. I had proved myself. It was accomplished. I could not
yet feel its magnificence, and would not for a long time take
pride in it, because some things, even the best things, are
difficult to learn. Their indulgence would serve our end.
The energetic directness of madness they must hold in awe.

Again my father took my sobbing, my victorious
expression, to mean something else.

"We will be all right. We will be fine together."

The crowd retreated, growing smaller in the sunny air.
Pallbearers bore the white coffin away, followed by mourning
deaconesses. All receded to the cemetery.

"My son!"

Clutching mine, his cunning truth, what I must learn, were
his hands of pleading need. My heart cried out.

The name it cried has echoed long in an empty, icy place.

CUSTOM

No sooner had I walked from the highway to this *Best Hotel In Town* than I dropped my bags and sample cases in the only available room, with a window that opened smack against a wall and barely room enough to sneak sideways around the bed, and headed into the hall to take a shit. No sooner would I finish the shit and I'd pretty myself up and go looking for a whore. But there I was, my gut going crazy, pacing outside a bathroom that permitted *no* distinction between guests and employees since the hotel clerk was locked in it that very moment.

You should have seen me driving in a figure-eight up and down that hall. I dodged the ceiling light every time. Evidently a man with a head on his shoulders was something new in town. Action-precision hardened the feeling of bodily control. Every time I passed the bathroom door, I kicked it —just to show the clerk my needs were as democratic as his.

A long time it took him to consider my needs.

At last the toilet flushed.

I jumped to the door. An eager turd, just waiting the chance, elbowed out of my ass. Enormously straining internally upward, as if praying myself bodily into heaven, I drew the turd back into place, no thanks to the clerk. I heard him washing his hands with care. I wept.

He dried his hands with care. Now he was trying the lock. He took his time. There was no lock on my asshole.

I stood jittering. Passing beyond the human! A rubbery radio wave, a great stuttering tuning fork, a six-foot-six-inch hellbent hard-on!

He dawdled in the door *in my way*, the top of his bald head beaming, his brown eyes looking doggily over his glasses.

"Yes, sir? Can I help you, sir? Would you like a towel, soap, anything, sir?"

And the only command I could not give him was—*to evaporate.*

"Excuse me, no thank you," I said, ducking past him into the bathroom.

You could have shoveled that air into sacks and sold it as fertilizer. I firmed my lips, held my breath. I closed and locked the door with one hand, jerking my belt loose with the other. At the stool, shoving down my shorts and pants, I stopped, seeing a brown streak on the bowl at the water's edge. And though all seemed otherwise in sterile order, I knew the seat would be *crawling* warm.

It was explode, shit, or smother.

My buttocks grimaced against the warm seat.

First came a spattering explosion. And then I unloaded a long, an unbelievably long, a miraculously lengthy turd. A lengthy sigh escaped me too. The turd broke off, and slapped into the water, and went on breaking and slapping until, after awhile, the sound changed, shit hitting softly on shit. A long-oppressed exaltation rose in me, a cool clean transfiguring peacefulness, as if I were actually ridding myself of darkness and turmoil.

And higher grew the pile.

I eat big. I live big. I shit big. I am a big man.

Now my own smell attacked and dissipated the alien stench, and the bathroom air stood transfigured too. Almost spring air. Oh, I breathed deeply. Isn't there just one person in this world whose shit smells as good as mine?

I was almost melting with pleasure into the pile myself.

I winked at a dirty drawing on the wall.

A new town. Virgin territory. Never say never to me, that's just exactly when I'll *do* what *never* can be done. I peddle medicine, Bibles, cosmetics, photographic equipment, caskets, and I always have a new line that I'm trying. This time it was toilet equipment. Now to be able to sell a new line, you have to use it, get into it, *like* it, the way you learn new customs, meet new friends. Now I liked shitting. No, don't misunderstand me, I *really* LIKED shitting. And I was certain selling toilets would be second nature. Caskets are the hardest, my feet start shuffling, my eyes get shy and jumpy, and I'm like a kid out with his first nice girl. Am I supposed to say—"Why, Ma'am, I use them myself!"? I did lie in a casket all night once, to get the feel of it, believe it, *like* it, and it isn't so bad, just that every now and then you wake up and wonder why the room got so small. But caskets are profitable, almost as profitable as I'm sure selling toilets will be. I meant to get into this town, this virgin territory. I meant to leave the people hardly able to move without bumping into something they bought from me. And the quickest way to get into a new town is to get into some cunt there. Let me tell you I pump my whores more ways than one.

And there he was, the little booger, rising out of the bush between my legs.

"Just couldn't keep your nose out of all this talk about whores and virgin territory, could you, boy?"

I gave him a sly pat on the head.

The piling-up pile mushily tickled my buttocks. The smell of your own shit is good. The feel of your own shit is just shit.

I stood up.

And the moment I looked for the roll of toilet paper I knew there would be none. And I knew I shouldn't have felt the way I did, as if I could never endure walking with my pants up again. But I wouldn't be in this predicament if I hadn't improvised myself out of other predicaments.

And there it was, *firewood*—with thick, loose bark stacked under the hot-water heater. If God had to use clay to make man, I could use bark to wipe my ass.

I scrubbed my ass raw. I flushed the soiled bark strips down the toilet and serve right the best hotel in town if the damn thing plugged up and overflowed mossy shit clear out into the hall. What the hell did the clerk use? I suppose he walked around with an asshole caked shut that he had to knock open every time he wanted to let something out. A salesman is really a missionary, a civilizing force.

I pulled up my underwear, hefted my pants, zipper, buttoned, started buckling my belt, but didn't finish, because I could feel now that it just wasn't right. I walked aimlessly seeking around the bathroom, keeping my buttocks clinched to avoid discoloring my underwear.

I parted the shower curtains and peered into the enclosure. Like one of my coffins set on end. I don't know why it suddenly occurred to me that there might be someone hidden there. It *could* only have been that tapping noise, a leaky shower. But with all my experience on the road, I wasn't going to attribute a *reasonable* cause to every sound or movement. I looked up into the shower. The fucking thing didn't know any better than to drip right in my eye! *Best Hotel In Town,* my ass! If they ever went to a really good hotel, they'd think they were dead and in heaven, and I was just the salesman to show them the way.

I checked the door. It was locked.

There was soap in the dish on the sink. I let down my pants, satisfied with seeing my underwear still clean. I set my buttocks backwards into the sink. I lathered up suds with my hands.

Thoroughly I scrubbed and rinsed my ass. Thoroughly I dried my hands and my ass with my handkerchief. A most useful thing the handkerchief—tourniquet, bandage, gag, substitute towel, signal, and I don't know how many other uses I've found for it. I flushed it down the toilet too.

WELL!!!

You look the way you feel, you feel the the way you look. And I felt clean. And I felt good.

I stooped and there, in the mirror above the sink, *there* the old bastard was, with his hawky high cheekbones and his cunning close-set eyes. I motioned to chuck his chin with my fist. "We'll give 'em hell tonight, won't we, boy? Hot goddamn!" I smoothed my shirt, a blue shirt, long-sleeved, hanging loose around the thighs, just the thing for a whore. I combed my hair, patting it into shape. The triangle of chest-fur that I saw in the mirror reminded me of cunt, and that reminded me I should get going. I curled my chest-fur with my comb. Whores like that. When I turned my back, I had the feeling that the fellow in the mirror was still watching me, as if the person I combed and put together was the one in the mirror, not me. I touched my hair to make sure it was me I combed.

I went back to my room, got another handkerchief. Never without one, and if I started selling them, no one I met would be without one either. I leaned out the window to get a view of the town. My gaze banged against four close walls. I could have touched each of those walls with my hand, but they'd have dirtied my fingertips.

I felt so good I forgave the clerk, tossing my key right between his nose and his bookwork. I winked at his jerked-up face. I went into the street with him watching my

back and appreciating the joke of where I was going. I know
my hotel clerks. He said,
  "Have a good time, sir."
  I didn't ask him where the whorehouse was. I wanted to
worm into the workings of the town the hard way. Get to
know it, you know.
  Hours later I was still wandering lucklessly. No street signs
in that town, and the so-called streets were really alleys,
striking helter-skelter over a group of sharply rising hills. No
sooner did I finish climbing the stone steps of one alley-street
than I immediately descended another series of decrepit
broken overgrown steps. There's no mistake that I saw plenty
of women. Well-dressed women too. In ankle-length
velvety-rich skirts, they paced with slow grace in gardens, on
balconies, in private courts. I saw them bend from the waist,
examine flowers, and the flowers lie with fat beauty in their
hands. Or they reclined in sloping chairs, great flowers
themselves, sipping tea or coffee. It seemed they couldn't
arouse themselves, not even to talk to each other. And I
never saw a man among them. They lazed in a state
luxuriously satiated with waiting. I tried to think they were
courtesans idling away the hours, storing up lush feelings for
the evening. I ogled them over square-clipped hedges. But
even my ogling head wasn't recognized by the women's eyes.
  I thought they might vanish any moment. And then I began
to doubt my own substance, as if I'd already vanished. My
chest prickled hotly against my shirt. My eyes watered. I
sighed after the bougainvillaea that ascended in rampant

ruffled masses from the gardens into the balconies. I imagined them as carpets set for the descent of a fairy-tale princess and myself ready and waiting at the bottom *on my knees* if that would bring her. But I might as well have expected the flowers themselves to heed my longing. Every rose nodded yes and no. I forced my eyes politely higher.

Blue lantern-like clusters filled the acacia trees. And those jacaranda trees glowed, dozens of sunsets, throughout the late afternoon. Flowers in cataract abundance, up and down the hills, interrupted each other in beds everywhere—poinsettias, red and orange cactus flowers, petunias, geraniums, pansies, gladiolas, beds of myrtle. And always the women were somewhere near the flowers or the flowering trees. There was no sense violating my own urgency by violating them with my eyes. I watched my feet gripping each step, carrying me up, bearing me down.

Shaking myself erect, I came briskly onto a main market street. Vendors squatted on the sidewalk beside mats piled with their wares. They made a hell of a noise hawking to passers-by.

I shoved my face down toward a screeching black-shawled girl mothering a mat full of pots and pans. I said, just like this,

"Where's the whorehouse?"

And she said,

"A hundred feet that way, and then to the left just a few doors down."

The most unabashedly open market in the world! She

straightened the handle of a pan, making it conform in the rank of pans on the mat.

But another girl, standing pressed from heels to shoulders with her cheek turned against the building, said the information was only partly right. Why'd they both stand and hunch so strangely?—as if, from somewhere behind my back, a gun was pointed at everyone before me.

The second girl said,

"That's not just exactly right, sir. You go to the next corner and then go two hundred feet to the left. You can't miss it."

Such wonderfully exact directions!

Now both girls insisted the other misled me. They differed only a few feet! Indeed, it flattered my own feelings about doing things exactly, and I thought I'd get along well in this town.

I thanked them just the moment they burst at each other, shouting, spitting, shaking fists. Certainly unreasonable as their former gun-point postures of fear. Neither noticed me hurrying along the general course of their directions.

At the corner I couldn't get it out of my head that I must turn *right*. Yet *left* was said by both girls. My fear of making a mistake and the urgency of my desire pushed and pulled, intensified. I threw myself into the street to the left. All deep holes and crumbling cobblestone. Going up out of one hole and down into the next, a two-legged jeep six and a half feet tall, that was me, working my way past one-story bright-colored jammed-together stucco houses. *No* windows. Just big shut oaken doors. And then the street upended sharply ascending a hill again. Could I just knock on any door and ask anyone if this was the whorehouse? But it wasn't the open market place. It was a very private little side street, very empty, collecting evening light. I doubled my fists. I wiped my eyes. I raged. I snatched a stone and hurled it up the hill. A second after the stone hit, rattling, there came a quick, poignant cry.

I scrambled up the steps. But it was the *same* thing, women walking and lazing on balconies, in gardens. Now my throat went bitter. Now I suspected that these were the town's true whores and customs were different here. But *no* part of the world asks you to climb over fences into private gardens *with your money in your hand*. Really those women seemed in the preserve of some Important Man, where they prepared themselves for maybe one day's extraordinary activity each year.

I hopped, stumbling, down a rocky slope, intending to short cut to the girls in the market place. At the foot of the hill I rolled off balance over a retaining wall.

Picking myself up I faced a window as large as the wall itself, divided by blue frames into small squares all frilled with ivy. A roomful of bustling continued inside it. Very private-minded with their windows in the walls behind the streets. It drew me forward entranced without shame. I cupped my hands at my temples and pushed my nose through the ivy against the glass. The living room became deeply clear. Several children and a woman were playing with ships, building blocks, every sort of toy. A lavishly decorated Christmas tree stood in the corner like a tall hero waiting for another medal to be pinned on. So it was that time of year? And I thought sadly I don't even remember my best holidays anymore.

Suddenly the woman leaped up from the knee-deep turmoil, in a yellow blouse and brown skirt, and ran smack toward me. She threatened crashing through the window. I threw up my arms. A section of the window jumped open beside me, a door.

Breathlessly tossing her shoulder-length brown hair, she said, with rich casual hospitality,

"It's Christmas and I know you are a stranger here. Won't you come in and share Christmas with us awhile? I'm Mrs. Tarrington."

How could she have known me so surely? Her hands flew quivering about her body, never quite lighting. Willowy, but maternally full where it counted, she was skittish and squirmy as a young mare on spring pasture, chic as a first-night royal bride, with always the air of the nursery.

Her hand darted into my hand. I feared crushing its fluttering life.

"You don't even know me," I said.

"Nonsense, do please come in."

Her quick white and winning smile leashed and drew me with her hand. That woman must have been a foot shorter than me, but I always seemed to be looking gratefully *up* at her. And then I jolted with the thought that *this* was the whorehouse, the strangest, the most enticing in the world. Why else be so eager for my company?

Inside she hooked a bawling boy under his arms, swung

him upright. She helped him straighten his train on the track.

"Now this is no place to be shy," she said, "please play with us."

Might as well shit or piss as grin the way I did.

My fingers throbbed digging into the carpet. I strove to keep my head low so the kids wouldn't treat me as a foreigner. Mrs. Tarrington traipsed from child to child, giving praise, guidance, caution. I played with an erector set. She was pleased discovering that I was building a ship.

I said, brazenly jerking up my head,

"Where is your husband?"

"Oh, he left on some business. And what difference does it make? He won't come back for quite awhile."

"A shame he can't enjoy himself with us," I said.

I noticed that we were all boys. I had the feeling a little girl sneaked among us, but I could never turn quick enough to see her.

And then we only wanted to play with the ships.

Everyone was pushing ships. She saw our irritation with the way the carpet roughened the ships' movements. She said, with a dreamy abruptness that intrigued the whole room,

"Now here's a game we play when we tire of everything else."

Her hips moved with easy grace avoiding collisions with furniture. She approached a huge faucet that protruded from a wall across the room. Kids were rushing around my legs, picking up toy trains and trucks. The only inside door stood at the wall-end of a landing that jutted about five feet high into the room. Steps led down the front of the landing to floor level. Arms jamfull of toys, the kids dashed up these steps and through that door.

With a sailor's lanky leg-bending sureness Mrs. Tarrington worked the faucet's wheel-shaped handle.

An inundation poured out, spreading through the living room, already flowing over my uppers and creeping up my ankles. Toy ships were jogged afloat, rocking on the waves, the building blocks among them. How could I protest? I've been in many strange places and seen many strange customs, and it's my business to accept and figure their reasons. But, with water steadily rising up each leg like a tickling ring, I sure needed clothespins to keep that polite expectant grin clipped on my face.

The kids came running back through the door, no toys with them. They leaped screaming into the water. I was up to my thighs, and the kids were up to their necks, walking on tiptoe or swimming for dear life.

Her brown skirt drifted ballooning on the thundering turbulence around her waist, her slip floating out from under it. She was like a flower coming apart. Breathless, I tell you, with the water ever rising.

She spun the wheel and the flow ceased.

Ah, there were limits, there were rules! Now I understood why the door opened onto the landing, and why the entire room was waist-deep below ground level, a system built into the building and into the mind!

Buoyantly Mrs. Tarrington smiled over bobbing children's heads and toy ships. She waded hard through the melee. She cheered herself with her hands above her head. Clap, clap.

"That's that. Now we play with the ships. And it's almost real, isn't it?"

With a grin supported by all my teeth and gums, I said, "Remarkable. How on earth do you manage it, Mrs. Tarrington?"

"Traditions that have been in the family for years and generations aren't at all difficult to do. You know that."

"One could travel to the ends of the earth," I said, "and never cease seeing how clever people are."

Shouting children hopped straight up and down in the water. Scooting, paddling, darting, they played motorboat with their mouths and pushed and turned the toy ships before their heads, as if the ships were only slightly disengaged parts of themselves. Lovingly and skillfully they were well acquainted with this custom. Any moment I might discover its purpose too. Mrs. Tarrington wrapped her hands delicately water level at her waist. With bright hummingbird quickness her eyes went from child to child. Heartily I knew I could learn this custom conducted in secret by mother and children. Energetically I could learn it, until it became second nature, the way I sell things.

I desired less and less height.

I sank on bending knees up to my neck. Soft and warm, that water, with the special feel of a juicing-up cunt. Little waves tickled under my chin.

My prick swelled and would give me no comfort trying to nudge out. I unzipped. It stiffened up with long eager ease. I feared it would reach my chin.

A ship loomed by each boy's head. I don't know how I
got attached to a *totally unarmed* merchant vessel. Islands
and promontories jutted everywhere. Behind them warships
hid and sprang ambushes. A terribly complex sea. But I was
grimly conscious that I must pilot my bulky lovable
merchantman, wallowing from harbor to harbor, carrying
great important cargoes, the very guts and goings of
civilization. My spraddled legs duck-walked, my submarine
prick rode between them, an underwater guard. Destroyers,
cruisers, battleships slid from the most unlikely places, with
me as their target. You have no idea how unnerving it is to
peer into a five-year-old's face and then to watch, helplessly,
a battleship, come from behind his grinning head, bear down
on you. I aimed toward the nearest green harbor. Yes, I
know now the harbor was only an armchair with a white
doily dressing its top, but so inviting to rest in the green
harbor under the snowy mountains after the dangerous
journey. More than once I wished to transfer my ship's cargo
to my submarine prick, but there seemed no getting the one
into the other, while incredible noises ruined the air, blasting
cheers and salvos of splashing. I banished the terrors by
ducking my head underwater. I guided my submarine gripped
in one hand and pushed my merchantman blindly on the
surface with the other. Then I became uncertain where was
water and where was air. Violently I coughed. All around me
voices were shouting that I was *sunk,* a simple merchantman
wending his way with honorable cargo.

Vehemently I denounced their barbaric interruptions of

free neutral commerce. And with revivalist vigor and sincerity I proclaimed the natural rights of merchantmen as granted by God when He first created ships.

A hand patted my head. Far above me Mrs. Tarrington sang,

"Really now, it's not as if you don't have another chance."

I groveled down into the water and wrapped my arms around her legs. I looked up. I sighed.

I choked. I shot up fast but stopped with my chin against the water, coughing horribly, not wishing to rise above this height. My hard-on prick hovered between my legs.

"How absolutely silly you are," she said.

"Yes, silly, silly, silly," I said.

"Shame on you. Don't you know children get tired of adults playing with them."

"I do get tired," I said.

"Are you ever going to listen to me?"

I whispered with intimate fear, "Don't do anything but say what you mean."

Her hands hooked under my arms and pulled.

"Now we don't want to remind the children of their father, do we?"

I couldn't help but notice myself becoming coldly father-big. I looked over the inundated furniture, over the playing children, through the window, where the sunset fretted the slope. A fair-weather friend, my submarine prick, if I ever saw one.

"You don't want to do that, she said.

I zipped up with secret ease.

"I mustn't do that," I said.

I understood that I must rise. My water-logged clothes dragged me down. I strove. She pulled. The water surface shaped itself with great elastic strength over my entire straining back and held me down. A back-breaking ball-busting effort burst me up to full dripping height, shaking beside her.

"How absolutely *silly* you were! And how the children did enjoy you! I *do* wish my second husband would play with them like that."

"Such fun," I said. "A man should play with his kids."

And the light went dark in her features and manner, or maybe it was the sun going down outside. "You are so right," she said. "But do you know that he always leaves the room when I turn the water on? And I can't stand him that way. And I can't stand not turning the water on either. And I know it's because he doesn't want to be reminded of my first husband. And I don't want to remind him. I don't do it out of spite. Just this time I turned the water on because that was the way to welcome you."

I was too proudly embarrassed and knew it wasn't the moment to try fucking her to comfort her.

I slipped my arm around her and rested my hand on her thigh underwater. I twitched my fingertips on her thigh, only to accustom her to the idea that my hands would *move* when touching her.

Gigantic side by side, we surveyed the ocean's activity.

"And the children love it so," she said. And I thought she'd weep right there.

"Such a truly unusual custom. Such a *fine,* satisfying thing," I said, "for kids."

She swayed on my arm, looking beautifully distracted up at me. "Are you really interested?"

My pants were soaked, but not down. My trusty smile was ready. "Mrs. Tarrington, such original, such gracious traditions can't miss getting my interest and care."

"I can see you are really, you are actually very fine. You are worthy. Wait here."

As if against tides she waded all forward-fighting purpose to the landing. She climbed up on all fours, her head hanging between her arms, gasping.

She stepped toward the door, her wet skirt wrinkling like a second skin against her thighs. She said across her shoulder,

"You will see, see everything, I promise."

She disappeared.

And there I was deserted among those that sank my ship. *Unprincipled warfare,* they were ganging up on another innocent merchantman in a corner across the ocean. It touched me poignantly using him to keep their attention while I side-stepped with surging legs through the difficult water into the corner behind the Christmas tree. I solidified with fright when a tinsel ball tinkled against my nose. But the full-scale persecution made so much noise they missed important little sounds.

Ever tighter my arms pressed against my sides until I was

certain I resembled the shape of the tree itself. And there is no more perfect concealment than looking exactly like what you're hiding behind. But I couldn't be sure that I was really hidden so long as I could see through the cedar branches. I saw the merchantman sinking. I closed my eyes. I grieved, marvelously hidden behind the tree with my eyes shut tight, while those rabid children went victory-crying after other game.

Only when Mrs. Tarrington returned could I afford to become more exposed by opening my eyes.

On the edge of the landing, clutching some things against her breasts, she peered around, disbelieving hurt in her face and the hunch of her shoulders. My smile prickled against the cedar needles. A warm and absolute sense of safety went pungently deep into me, soothing every muscle, secure in every way, even into my spleen. Yes, a perfect hiding place is miraculously relaxing, better than a hot bath.

She called to the kids. They didn't obey or even listen. Her head was turned away from me. Legs breaking against the resilient water, I waded fast from behind the tree. Now she wouldn't know where I'd been hiding and that would be like hiding behind the tree, always my own, the tree, in my mind.

"Oh, *there* you are. Where *have* you *been*?"

I shrugged grandly. "I've been here all the time."

"You have not," she said. More and more she mocked a little girl's enticements.

"If you don't look directly at me I'm hard to see," I said.

"Don't speak so strangely."

"Nothing strange when you look directly at me."

"Don't make fun. It's all because of you I went out to get these things. Now *hurry.*"

I understood that her husband might return any minute. Only a second husband to be sure, but nevertheless a husband.

My legs piston-drove toward her. It wasn't water. I know now it couldn't have been water. Powered only by the thought that I mightn't reach her before her husband's arrival, I became certain that time is properly measured only by the size of the effort, the amount of spent energy. And if that's true, it took me a solid year to get to her.

By the time I gained the landing, my thigh muscles were knotted, aching together. Agonizing, with my thumbs and fingertips clamped on the upper edge of the landing, I pulled myself up an inch at a time toward her, struggling up the steps on my knees underwater.

"What in heaven's name is the matter with you? Hurry, can't you?"

Sweat oiled the water over my body. The mixture flowed off my brow, burned in my eyes, and tears joined sweat and water. My blood vessels would burst and rushing blood would join sweat, water, tears too. I mustn't resist dissolving. I must ease into solution. I more than suspected that total dissolution was the real end to this curious custom. And I was tempted to get it over with right now.

She coaxed with disparaging sympathy.

"It is tiring if you're not used to it and not in shape."

I am never too tired to grin suggestively. "Yes, my exercise is limited."

Hugely dripping I hauled my mass up beside her on the landing. It was just too thoughtful of her to sit on her heels and save me the major shame of failure in rising to my feet.

With the back of my hand I wiped the bitter solution out of my eyes and my hand wiped it burning in again. I was terrifically concerned that I might be near to expending the last of my life energy before it could be renewed in me. *How did the kids have it so porpoise-easy?* Simple. If you immersed yourself, you had it easy. If you stood up against it, you had it rough. I rested my gaze with extreme care on the things in her hand. A photograph and a naval officers cap.

She said,

"This is his hat."

I nodded. "That is his hat."

She said,

"You know nothing about the sea and sailing."

I spent no precious energy saying I'd no desire to learn more. And I knew I was on the point of giving up the ghost when I said, "You could teach me, couldn't you?"

"You'll just have to imagine for yourself. See this?"

The photograph vibrated between her thumb and finger.

"You have to look closely," she said.

Getting larger, no, coming closer, the photograph loomed blotting out the kids raising a terrific rumpus. A sickness stuck like a dart into the bottom of my belly.

"May I?" I took the photograph. I lowered it to knee level.
I know when to be polite.

I looked up away from the water and out the window,
remembering myself happy among the flowering trees and
looking for a whore. *Why wasn't Mrs. Tarrington wearing a
velvety ankle-length dress?*

She jabbed the photograph. My face and feelings shook
offended.

"Do you know what that is?" She answered herself, "That
is his ship."

I said,

"That is his ship."

Now my eyes cleared, and I saw toss-tipped waves in the
foreground, a ship on the horizon in the background, all
marred with scratches and blurs. A bad developing job. But
I didn't sense in myself the least anticipation for making a
mint selling photographic equipment. Salesmen are necessary
only among the higher orders of civilization. This town
needed doctors.

She prodded the photograph, calling my attention to a
naval officer's cap floating in the craw of a yawning wave.

"It is *his* hat," she said. "It is *this* hat."

And the hat jumped on her finger, a clever movement,
imprinted terribly forever in my mind. I knew now I couldn't
elude the story in the pinkish-gray stain across the white on
top the hat.

She began,

"His name was SHIPLEY," an unforgettable emphasis as

clever as jumping the cap on her finger. "It was in the Antarctic and Shipley fell, yes, *fell,* or perhaps, *only* perhaps, he slipped off the deck. *Or* he jumped. Did you know a man can freeze solid in that water in two minutes?"

"Two minutes," I said.

"You don't believe that?"

"I believe."

"I tell you," she said, "Shipley could swim twenty miles and only that cold, cold water stopped him."

"Only that," I echoed.

"A strong man, a brave man, and sure on his feet."

"And froze solid in two minutes," I said, "a *remarkable* man."

Her voice changed.

"So remarkable on his feet I can't believe he slipped."

My feet and shoes embarrassed me with sucking noises. "Yes?"

Contemptuously she said.

"I am *certain* he did not slip. He did not fall. He did it *deliberately.*"

She paused, working every way to truss up my attention so she could drive her point home. How could I tell her I was as ready now as I'd ever be?

"No-o-o-o," she said, "it was something Shipley saw in the water. He was leaning there on the rail and he saw *something* in the water." I peered into her eyes to show her I truly saw the something she meant just as clearly as he'd seen something in the water. "A man," she breathed, "he saw a *man* in the water." Her eyes got shiny, blinking, and now it was time and I put my arm around her shoulders. "A man in the water, yes, Shipley saw *himself* in the water. I *know* that's how it happened. All bundled up for that cold, cold weather he didn't recognize his *own* reflection. So strong and so brave and so sure on his feet he jumped *in*—to save the man, to save *himself*, without a second *thought!*"

"And froze solid in two minutes," I said.

"Yes, yes, *yes*," she cried, beating her fists on her lap one two *three*, herself into silence, telling the story and no reverence from me. I'd gone in over my head once. Not again. I cuddled my arm closer around her shoulder.

"*Look*," she said, pointing one finger at the photograph and then shaking it at me, "the only reason why we have the photograph is they sent out a boat as soon as he went over, or as soon as they could stop the ship and lower a boat, and that was too late. Oh, yes," as if I mustn't believe all that other gossip, "many men were jealous of his strong goodness and that may explain why he was never rescued."

She fished a handkerchief out of her bosom, blew her nose, and stuffed the handkerchief back hastily, as if she'd sneezed gold and didn't want anyone to find out that this was the way she lived so well, afforded all these shenanigans.

"A seaman," her voice got stentorian, "a man of the ranks who loved Shipley's firm goodness, that was the man who took this picture from the boat before they picked the hat out of the water. And that's all I have to remember him by. Oh, there should have been more, *much* more, so much that I can hardly endure having so little of him, only the hat, this photograph and—the custom!" She spread both arms to embrace the flood.

I said.

"That's enough, isn't it?"

"Everything was made just so before we moved into this place. Everything according to *his* family's tradition. The walls. The floor. The furniture. The windows. All watertight and waterproof. All made of material that can't be damaged or discolored by water. And the faucet was installed, with special plumbing. And Shipley swung me up and carried me across the threshold. You should have seen him, the way he turned on the faucet, twirling it grandly with his little finger, and we splashed around stark naked playing ship on our wedding night. So long ago," she sighed. She shrieked, "*Stark* NAKED," as if I mightn't believe that either.

Maybe that's why the kids were so wild. A little of that peculiar water dashed into the semen.

She didn't notice my hand sneaking up her thigh, past the casing of stockings, suddenly lost in a twanging maze of garters. Crazy with wargames, nothing turned those kids' heads either, not even their mother's screeching sing-song or their mother's legs spread for their eyes to see with a stranger's hand between them. If I'd pulled up her dress and rammed in my prick, she'd just wrapped her arms and legs around me, praising Shipley, who probably didn't have the sense to hold his nose jumping into the Antarctic Sea. And the kids would go on BANG-POW-SPLASH-WHAMMING.

Incisively rude, I said,

"I just can't see why a naval officer would build a home in a town so far from the sea."

"Oh, that was part of his sea-going family's tradition too. He didn't want us to live where we might hear rumors, most likely *exaggerated* rumors, you understand, about the sea, but how would we know if they were *exaggerated*? Worry us too much, Shipley thought. And he didn't want us running out onto a hilltop to look for ships on the horizon. Best, he thought, if we just saw him leave and walk away one morning on dry land and no sea in sight, and then months later saw him come walking back on dry land. So kind, so considerate."

My hand was snared in the garters under her dress. I gave it up as caught and lost forever. I prepared myself to bite, oh gently bite her neck.

She untangled herself without a thought, the way she'd push back the covers and crawl out of bed. My hand came undone, falling out of her dress. It lay in my lap. I looked at it. An absurd, useless hand. Couldn't even bring a blush to the face of another man's wife.

And nothing could stop her giddy steady voice, sweeping sex as dust away.

"We used to have coffee and cookies on this landing, and watch the children play ship, celebrating when Shipley came home. You know, you remind me of Shipley; something about your *manner*." She squeezed the absurd hand in my lap. "Would you like coffee and cookies? Of course you would, just for me? Oh, BETTT-EEEE!"

My helpless body jumped, as if touched by a free-floating

electrical charge. Clucking and cooing and purring and patting my shoulder, that jumped under her hand too, she said,

"Some people are so affected by the story, it gets at them so much, they become *physically* miserable. And then it is so-o-o soothing to have coffee and cookies and watch the children play. BETTT-EEEE!"

I always turn when a door opens, always expecting something new. This time I wasn't disappointed. I saw that I'd been spending my time in the wrong room in that house.

Tall, with black hair, blue eyes, crisp green uniform and a white apron, the maid leaned through the door, as if also leaning backward against the weight of her bosoms. She moved with care too. And it did seem highly likely that one sudden movement might throw her off balance. So widely and deeply she looked at me that I thought if she blinked I'd be cut in two.

There must be no mistake in our communication. I intensified the hot expression in my own eyes. If she wouldn't do it, she'd know where it was done. I know my maids.

"Yes'm?" she said.

Mrs. Tarrington answered with a matron's curt jealousy. Anyway, her tone nearly made me forget that Mrs. Shipley-Tarrington was young and desirable herself, at least at first glance.

"Isn't it beautiful, Betty? It's been months and months, years maybe, since we turned the water on. How long *has* it been, Betty?"

"Months and months, mum. Years maybe."

With my eyes I tried hard to inform Betty that such a long time of going without would soon end.

"Yes, Betty, dear, but that's only calendar time, mere *clock* time. Heart time's been centuries." And Mrs. Tarrington's face lit up on the play of the children, teamed into two grim navies that closed toward each other over the water, heads behind boats, one navy green, the other brown.

Hand on her hip, Betty cocked her inconsiderate body through the door. A heat trembled in my belly, lungs, and groin. My jaws worked as if against some strong elastic substance.

Outrightly condescending, Betty said,

"Mum, do you want coffee and cookies?"

"You remember so well, dear." Mrs. Spectator-Tarrington didn't turn to see Betty looking snottily down on her, and didn't notice me looking at Betty either.

Betty firmed her lips with spite. "In a moment, mum." She jammed the door shut.

A moment, a moment, only *one* moment, I instructed my surging balls and prick.

Mrs. Shipley-Tarrington brooded rapturously in the part of the wargames-observer, with flushed face, full slack lips, half-lidded eyes. "Look," she said, "at the cruisers flanking wide and the battleships lying back for the opening and the kill. I tell you Shipley taught them everything. How to do it right. How doing it right was better than making the kill."

I listened with the same thrill as hiding behind the Christmas tree.

64

"Both sides so equal," I said, "it must be difficult for one or the other to win."

"*Very* difficult. Sometimes, even with the most skillful maneuvering, it goes on for hours and hours and that's what counts, the *art,* even in your own living room."

I was jarred again. I hadn't thought of this place as a "living room" for some time.

The door jerked behind us. Almost my fly sprang open with it.

Betty's white-shoed foot nudged the door wide enough to permit passage sideways of the tray with the silver service. A man could say, if he wished, that her high young huge breasts were also borne on that tray. I wished to say it, and I wished to shout victoriously to the kids in the water to quit that vicious silliness and come and learn that *here* was the *real* game.

Betty lowered herself between Mrs. Tarrington and me. And I could see that the silver tray was also contrived to suit the family custom, resting on a real-sized life buoy. I suppose that it served to send aid and sustenance to the shipwrecked in the living room.

"Oh, *look* at the cookies," Mrs. Tarrington said, "oh, Betty, dear, you are *so* considerate, you remember *so* well."

The cookies were shaped like ships—cruisers, battleships, destroyers, aircraft carriers. Yes, it was true that I had the only submarine.

Betty worked with her arms bowed out avoiding her breasts, as if they were sore with their beauty.

"Cream this time, mum?"

"Straight black. And two cruisers, please."

When Betty turned to me, her lush smile clutched on her lips, her eyes widened. My whole body tipped, ready to dive into her.

I grinned. "With cream."

"Cream," Betty assented, liquidly prim. "Say when, sir." And she poured cream into my coffee until it almost overflowed and I said, "*When?*" meaning *no* coffee and cream could mix as well as me and her.

"And two battleships," I said.

Over the cookie tray my absurd hand unmistakably sparked against Betty's hand. Her startled lips and eyes jumped at me. My smile threatened to split my face as my prick was splitting my fly as Betty rose and departed with silky flurries and rustlings that raved in my groin.

Behind Mrs. Tarrington's back my eyes screwed into Betty's eyes. Betty back-kicked the door shut.

"Oh, *oh,*" Mrs. Shipley-Tarrington moaned, "an opening *already.*"

Near the big armchair's back protruding above the water, two green crusiers had straddled one brown battleship. I clucked my tongue tch-tch. "Now that's art," I said.

"It's *terrible,*" she said.

"Yes, I've heard wars are like that."

"*Terrible* that they've forgotten so much. I must take the chance on whatever Mr. Tarrington thinks and turn the water on more often, much more often, lest they forget."

"Speaking of forgetting," I said, "it seems your girl forgot the sugar. Excuse me, will you, Mrs. Tarrington, a moment?" And there I was, devil that I am, being *so* polite again. But Mrs. Shipley-Tarrington, black-coffee-drinking-wargames-observer, didn't notice me rising and exiting. Her shining eyes were ravishing the two cruisers circling the ambushed battleship, while she held her coffee cup trembling at her lip.

My damp pants thrummed against my legs. I wished to kick the kitchen door open, enter triumphantly. But I knew when to control myself, and closed the door softly, click, behind me.

I was *in* the kitchen, and I was almost ready to get *into* the town too, remembering my progress from outside among flowers and distant women, to the laborious scene in the living room, to the kitchen now, to the inside of Betty in a minute, and I'd come out just dripping with a working feeling for this town.

Across the kitchen Betty stood at a table, using a rolling pin, thumping and rolling a round of dough on a board. A window black with night framed her head and shoulders. She hadn't heard me come in. I tiptoed. Great pleasure it gave me to stand an arm's length behind her, with her well-shaped back peacefully toward me and her hair fanning down it. Now she stamped out the ships with cookie-cutters and placed them in a buttered pan. Let me tell you, when I get with a tall hot woman and we both start coming, our thrashing threatens to bring the house down around us.

I whispered with insidious glee,

"There was no sugar, Betty."

Her hand stopped in mid-air with the cookie cutter. A
pause. And then stamped down. She didn't turn, but her back
registered my presence frankly. That's what I loved in her
body, its *frankness*.

"Well, sir, do you want sugar?"

My hot wrinkly hands grasped her elbows, smooth as cool
sunlight, just below the cuffed sleeves. An apt beginning, a
variation on the firm handshake.

"Betty, *oh*, Betty, you can't think you'll find the sugar all
by yourself."

I drew her backwards until her butt pressed against my
hard-on prick. YES-S-S, I wanted her to feel the same dirty
driving lust that a dog feels rubbing its side against a post. I
tickled her neck with my tongue. I probed the inner workings
of her ear. She shook her head hard.

"Sugar's in the *pantry*, sir."

"Sugar's where you find it, baby."

Now, not just her words, her body became a liar too. I
grappled her around the waist, locking my hands together on
her belly. She writhed upward against and pushed down hard
on my arms, pushing my hands below her belly. My hands
went delving through her dress. Sad the way she used
seeming accident to guide me.

She whispered run-on with a pretense of warning,

"Mrs. Tarrington. Mrs. Tarrington. Mrs. Tarrington."

"She's getting hers in her own way," I said.

My prick jammed against the cleft of her ass. Terribly she

thrashed. Maybe she was only trying to make the game as exciting as possible with struggle short of actual escape. But she made me seem to myself like some fool at a circus, jacking myself off with one hand and holding onto seven fighting cats with the other.

My chin was hooked over her shoulder. My fingers worked in her crotch, pulling up her dress until it was wadded under my wrists. My hands crawled downward against her rough panties, already *wet* and *warm*. Anything I can't stand, it's a *liar*. My God, how many times had I sighed in that house?

I tried inserting my hand under the bellyband of her panties. It wouldn't go. I tried again. That elastic was strong. I tried getting under the leg bands.

Strong, that elastic, unbelievably, intractably tight and strong.

Panicky, but I couldn't dally. If I wasn't the man to make her good and ready to take her panties off, I don't know who that man would be. I rubbed on the down-curve between her legs. My fingers got slick as pickles and the groove formed, yielding. That panting itch began in my belly and lungs. I rubbed rapidly. I rubbed deeply. I rubbed gently. I used all the attributes of good rubbing. I increased my speed and it was her whole thrashing body, not just her voice, that *gasped.*

She whirled in my arms. She kissed me, her tongue digging in my mouth. That woman was *hungry.* She jerked my belt open. She unzipped me. My pants slipped down my legs onto the floor. My shorts were more difficult and hung at last between my knees. It was time to put on my rubbers, but she

wouldn't give me a moment, and for the first time in my life
I decided to risk it without them.

She cuddled prick and balls with both hands, kissing
prick's tight little mouth. She wasn't speaking to me, she was
speaking to *him* with those heated reverent gasps,

"Sh! Sh! Sh!"

She was right to talk to him and not to me.

They rubbed cheek to cheek. They looked at each other.

And then she popped his head into her mouth and slid it
up and down and sucked and licked slowly. An incredibly
high-pitched shriek sailed past the hearing of humans, out of
the kitchen, and into the range of dogs perhaps, but I still
don't know whether it came from me or my prick. Ecstatically
I beat her back with my fists. She hungered with groans and
hmm-mmms. And then she forgot that she had teeth in her
mouth.

I shoved her backwards onto the round of dough on top
the table, and the panful of cookies jumped, clattering cookie
tins.

I grabbed her panties at the hips with both hands and
yanked.

Strong, that elastic, *very* strong.

She wrestled herself up into a sitting position on the edge
of the table.

"Sh. Sh."

Spreading her legs wide, she took hold of prick and pulled.
She pressed him into the sopping warm groove. Absurdly she
joggled her butt up and down.

So this was the way she meant for us to fuck? No sense fighting her panties. She seemed as helpless as me. How in God's name did she pee? For all I knew Mrs. Tarrington might have been responsible and Betty couldn't get out anymore than I could get in. I moved in accordance with her wishes. Happy fellow, my prick, sliding up and down in the groove. My excitement dug deep and climbed high, wrecking me from top to bottom.

"Oh please don't stop. Oh please don't stop."

She couldn't possibly so underestimate me.

And then I wanted to get into the raving gripping real screw. I tried forcing prick to flatten and slip under the elastic and seek his own as water seeks its own. "Why are you so fucking *round,* you fucking prick?" But prick was totally unsuited to present needs. That elastic was as watertight as everything else in this house. And then I knew past doubt Mrs. Tarrington was responsible for Betty's imprisonment. I shouted,

"GODDAMN MRS. TARRINGTON!"

And it inspired us. In our strange way, we fucked harder.

A crisp click. A bracing white light sprang and exposed the edged shapes of everything in the kitchen. Words poured into my ears, craze-gripping as ice water.

"Is this what you call getting sugar?"

Like a load of wood Betty dropped from my arms onto the table. Over her head I saw a face in the window drift immediately away. That's about all I have to do sometimes, look at people and they know where they should go.

A vision of how I appeared from behind came to me. My blue sports shirt hung over my lard-colored buttocks, with my shorts strung like a clothesline between my hairy knees, my pants heaped around my feet on the floor. Yes, I had more sense than to turn and add another decoration to Mrs. Spectator's sight.

Some women of her class and kind would shriek and stamp their feet and be just a bustling bundle of indignation, as if stamping out a fire that threatened their entire home. Others might be cold and haughty and clear the situation with a few cutting orders. Others might just run away in violently pleased embarrassment.

But Mrs. Shipley-Tarrington stayed a spectator.

"My husband is coming home soon."

I said,

"*Which* husband?"

She answered plaintively,

"Maids are hard enough to get."

"This one isn't." And I laughed heartily in the infectious way necessary to get a conversation started with a so-so joke. Nine times out of ten it works. But from the silence I judged we were probably outside the sphere of ordinary laws.

Surprisingly Betty didn't object to my remark. Heartwarming, that girl's trust.

I tried another sure thing. I tried changing the subject.

"Which navy won? Green?"

"Brown." Mrs. Spectator's word fell with the bounce of one round hard turd.

"But that's not the way it looked when I left," I said.
She said,

"That's the way it is now."

"Well," I said, "you never can tell what's going to happen, you have to keep in touch all the time. So Brown won? Well, what do you know about that?"

"You unspeakable person, if you knew anything about a mother's feelings, you would leave right now."

"Then why are you so hot on talking to me?"

"My husband has much influence in this town. *Quit* talking yourself."

"I wonder what he's going to say when he sees the water on in the living room?"

"I don't think he will bother to go as far as the living room."

"Think he'll die before he gets there, hunh?"

It was obvious she wasn't going to dirty her hands cleaning up any shit. And the whole business was so botched I knew I might as well get my private kicks.

"My husband is past mayor. My husband is so respected that whoever he wants is elected to any office and will do anything he says."

And I said,

"Leave it to you to marry another remarkable man."

Bang, the kitchen door struck on the edge of mine and Betty's table. A man almost exactly my height stood in the doorway, a red tie slashing down the front of his dark business suit. Astonishing how quickly you *saw* his icy gray eyes and the slicked-back blond hair that seemed carved on his head.

He folded his arms, elegant creases filling out from the elbows, so immaculately still, correct in every respect, his pants sharp, his lips and manner creased and certain too. The most distinguished mannequin in a men's store! It was hard to believe he'd ever committed such violence as banging open the door.

I remembered when I'd folded my arms like that on the occasions when I was acknowledged master. Now, myself a salesman in a strange town, I was in professional need of clothing my image in other people's minds with this most important man's approval. And here I was hardly clothed for meeting him.

Admirable presence of mind, he loosened his arms and said with a brisk paternal sigh,

"I might have known."

Mrs. Shipley-Tarrington pressed against a cabinet giving way to him as he marched through the kitchen. I saw her face and neck taut, the drained-out color of dirty chalk.

Betty hugged me, as if trying to hide in me.

All attention, from myself and Mrs. Spectator, went out of the kitchen, zeroed on Tarrington. He paused on the landing and surveyed the living room. He gave a most royal sigh and stepped with tall precision down into the water. Children splashed to meet him, shouting, "Daddy, daddy, daddy, come and play," dancing and batting their hands on the water.

Betty shoved me away. I couldn't believe my eyes when she started stamping out cookies again.

No, I *wasn't* surprised that the lordly Tarrington waded, shoes and pants, up to his elegant thighs. A clever gesture of restrained and noble suffering, that's what it was, placing everyone around him in the status of shamed children. But now he did surprise me. He plucked up each sleeve from the wrist. This senseless action shamed us more as he stooped and slipped his arms, sleeves and all anyway, into the water, struggled, and came up straight with a big drain plug in one hand.

A whirlpool swung suddenly out around his legs. In a moment only a few puddles glistened on the carpet. And Mrs. Tarrington was right, the furniture shed water, showing not a mark of soaking or discoloration. Ships were stranded on cushions, teetered on the arms of sofas, and lay on their sides on the carpet, such was the violence of the water's disappearance.

Now the children stayed several steps away from him. And they stayed still, with fingers hanging in their mouths.

Tarrington said to them,

"Put those toys away," and the group of children wavered as one, and then scattered as individuals, and began picking up the toys.

I shuffled, shorts around my knees, toward the kitchen door. And there was my prick, staying up all this time. I suppose he didn't want to miss the show.

I leaned against the door jamb. Betty hunched diligently, trying to disappear into making those goddamned cookies. Surely she knew that Tarrington abhorred this particular celebration. But maybe she wished to insult His Majesty by carrying out Mrs. Spectator's orders. Or she wished to get Mrs. Spectator in deeper trouble. Or Betty wanted to get herself in his disfavor. Or she wanted to cause an anger in him that would make havoc of everyone and everything. Only a jackass could believe she was just working off nervous energy. Maybe she wasn't really a liar. She just wasn't aware that she was lying.

"If you're really in bad trouble, Betty, I can get you lots of jobs, and better pay too."

I had one particular job in mind for her.

Clever girl, she spoke down to the rolling pin, so no one could suspect us. "Oh, don't worry, sir. You can see they have to pay very well to get any maid to stay in this house and despite Mr. Tarrington's so-called influence hardly no one will do it. Oh, I'm safe, sir, snug, sir."

There was something hunchbacked with spite in Betty. It fired up my balls for her.

"That's why you're going ahead and making the cookies, just to prove they can't fire you. You're smart, Betty. I like you."

I winked. I mentioned my hotel just in case she was really in trouble. Hope a hope a hope.

"Thank you, sir."

A comradely feeling warmed us together.

"Betty," I whispered, "where is the whorehouse?"

Her blue eyes looked up pitifully scooped out by fear.

"It's just down to the corner," she said. And I was heartened that she didn't say "sir."

But I knew about directions in this town.

"How far is that, Betty?"

"Going left out the door, it's at the first corner, sir. A blue-fronted house, you can't miss it."

"Right or left side?"

"Your left, sir, going that way. It's very expensive, sir."

"*Good,*" I said, with a laugh meant to loot her soul and body.

And she could go on "sirr-ing" me forever, if she kept on smiling that way. "Maybe I'll see you in the cafés," she said.

"Tonight?"

"I go there once or twice a week," she said.

Her eyes steamed with that deep exciting peace again.

I meant to ask which café, but my presence of mind went prostrate, seeing the Law himself striding across the living room, up the landing in two steps, scooping up the naval officer's cap and the photograph, and into the kitchen, where he thrust cap and photograph into his wife's hands.

"Burn these right now," he said.

Apparently it was only the cabinet that supported Mrs. Shipley-Tarrington.

"Please," she said.

"All right," he said, "*please* burn them right now."

She went down on her knees slowly.

"*Now,*" he ordered, and tossed a packet of matches onto the floor beside her.

She chose instantly to strike a match and put it to the photograph. The way her hands shook would have roared the balls of any man. The photograph flamed, her face hardening in the flare. And then her hands became as firm as her face. She struck several matches and dropped them on the hat. Amazing how quickly it became a fire. And *always* there would be that charred spot on the polished floor to remind her of her spitefully ecstatic humbling. She watched him proceed toward me. Tarrington spoke, that was all, and other people's bodies acted. It was lovely to see.

He said, as if he'd given me more than enough time to make an honorably unobtrusive exit,

"You still here?"

Could I leave at the behest of mere words? I thrust my face forward. I make it a point to stare down any man that so much as glances at me. Very nearly with equal intensity, his gray eyes darkened as the deepest ice.

"*Well*," he said.

Now wouldn't you think that was a compliment from a man who anticipated meeting his match? I was certain he only stepped closer to intensify the staring contest. But there he was beside me, and I discovered that sometimes he did do things with his own hands too. He wrapped one arm around my bare thighs and the other round my chest and back. I am a very tall man. But that man Tarrington hefted me bodily and hurled me headfirst through the door. I skidded on my back in the debris of the alley. A shock all right, but I wasted no time being shook up. I sat up.

Dark, it was dark out there.

A carbonated giggle raced in my blood at the sight of the

completely black silhouette in the door, Mrs. Shipley-Spectator, recently converted to Tarringtonism. I crossed my ankles under me. I placed my hands on my knees like fat gods I've seen.

"SUCK MY EGGY ASS, YOU BITCH!"

"Now you be quiet, now that's enough, quite enough," she said. "We were kind to you, a stranger, inviting you in from the streets, and just look how you repaid us."

She meant her little speech mainly for Tarrington.

"I could tell your husband sto-o-o-ries."

"He's not interested."

"Lady, you're talking to the man that diddled you for half an hour."

"He's not interested."

"No?"

"Definitely not."

Out of her black-silhouetted head protruded her husband's head in full human profile and human coloring using the phone on the kitchen wall.

"Mrs. Prissy-assed bitch, I could tell him why you turned the water on. I could tell him all the things you said about him."

"He's not interested."

His profile didn't turn once toward me. But I suspected my words weren't getting past her to him, that she caught my words and hid them somewhere. Only the back of his head on top her silhouette faced me, nodding, emphasizing on the phone, and now I was the one that couldn't get his words past her. Never trust a good-looking bitch with a lot of good-looking kids in a good-looking home, you never know how they got it.

I braced myself on straddled legs and steadied prick's aim. He cut loose a sparkling arch at her. That's his equivalent of a banshee wail.

Now *here's* the thing that made me *really* distrust her. She didn't do anything that human women do. She didn't shriek. She didn't slam the door. She stayed hidden in the silhouette. Such bitches are always afraid to come out in the open and show what they feel.

I lifted my shorts lazily and adjusted them. I lifted my pants, zipped them, buttoned the button and then, taking my time, buckled my belt. Mrs. Spectator stayed so silent, so watching, that when I finished I didn't know what to do with my hanging arms. I had the strangest feeling of standing at attention ready for her inspection. There was only one thing to do. I cocked my butt toward her, revved up pawing the ground, and fired a fine fart. Not a misfire in a gut-load.

She said,

"I can assure you that we will never meet again."

Tarrington's human head bobbed yes and he hung up the phone. He walked away behind her into the house without *once* looking past her at me.

"There," she said. She slammed the door.

In the kitchen window the light went out. Lord God, I couldn't even see my hands.

But I didn't move an inch until I'd checked my pockets to make sure I still had my money and my personal papers and things. You can never be too sure about these seemingly well-off sophisticated people. Maybe the whole watery business was only a cleverly rigged way of pickpocketing my every last penny. But the only worthwhile possessions of mine left in the house were Betty, maybe a few bits of pride and my sweat and tears gone down the drain in the living room. Just because they weren't able to filch a single thing, was I supposed to be satisfied? If I traveled among thieves, and only my wits brought me out with my shirt on my back, weren't they still thieves?

Well, I wasn't going to just stand there thinking bitterly.

Idling people just barely keep warm.

I fished out my comb.

And even when working by touch in the dark, it was a good first-aid feeling combing my hair, adjusting my clothes, putting myself into the shape that was me. I did wish for a mirror, and soap and hot water and clean clothes too. Those would heal me completely.

Then I strode down the alley whistling a march that summoned my strongest happiest feelings, my heels crushing the remaining bad feelings.

I was following Betty's directions letter-perfect.

Then a horrible unaccountable thing happened.

My foot stumbled on something yielding. My body jerked with fear of hurting it. That terrible internal jerk almost flung me sprawling.

Two yellow eyes danced before me. An agonized soprano growling and shrieking paralyzed me.

"Shut up," I said.

It didn't know any better than to stay out from under my feet and I knew very well it could see in the dark. Apparently it didn't know enough to shut up when I told it to shut up either.

I kicked it.

"Now you'll shut up."

If you've heard live steam blasting through a rusty organ pipe, you may've heard the noise that came out when I kicked it. My stomach cringed more than my ears, and my ears crawled inside my head, while those two bodiless yellow eyes streamed comet-like ahead of me and went suddenly straight up. About ten feet above the ground the eyes stopped. They hovered without moving. That doesn't mean the noise stopped. The damn dumb thing was denouncing me and every salesman in the world, and the sorrier my feeling the angrier I sounded.

"Shut up, shut up, you sonofabitch, shut up."

What a night, no stars, no moon, only a darkness so thick you could cut it into chunks and serve it on a plate, and two yellow eyes that did not shut up.

I knew a man should face a raging animal, stare it down, make it peacefully place its tail between its legs and creep away. How could I stare it down? My only human eyes had no power in that darkness. But *it* could see me. I was naked and unnerved. The shrieking jittered me uncontrollably. It was run or shake to pieces.

Yes, it followed me along roof tops, fence tops, or whatever. Always above me and always directly behind me.

CUSTOM

You have no idea what it's like to have nothing but two yellow eyes following you.

Something drastic had to be done.

I sank onto my knees. I extended and lost my arms in the darkness. But those eyes could see my supplication.

I pleaded with the profound sincerity that even dumb beasts can feel and forgive.

"Please, I'm sorry, shut up, kitty cat. Please be quiet, I'm sorry, shut up, nice kitty cat, please shut up, you sonofabitching kitty cat."

It didn't shut up. It couldn't have hurt me more. And its eyes were getting bigger. No, not bigger, and it wasn't me seeing double, it was the screaming that doubled. Now there were two pairs of eyes.

No sense and no use, I knew, but I ran.

And then more and more pairs of eyes came trooping after me on both sides of the alley, only you couldn't see the sides of the alley, you could only see two columns of yellow eyes moving across the night toward me. Surely Tarrington had exercised his famous influence to improve cat breeding until they saw things with light manufactured in their own bodies.

My breathing came and went in frenetic marching rhythms that generated more and more morale.

Get me they might, but they'd get only my sweated-out skin and bones, with no strength or will power left for their teeth to chew, no sustenance for their stomachs to grind, no energy for their blood to absorb. Only then could they carry

away my remains, because by then I would have lived my
life, as much in that long desperate run as in a long three
score and ten.

I couldn't see the turns in the alley. I crashed body-long
against a wall.

I am not made out of rubber. I am not fitted for running at
top speed into walls. I do not bounce and dissipate the shock
soaring through the air.

I don't know how I got up running on my feet. My body
jangled uncoordinated.

I went sprawling one two three four five six times. My
frantic breathing counted each time with the certainty I must
never fall nine times. Next time, what would have been the
seventh time, my right hand struck down to prevent a real
fall, and smacked a melon rind. *Germs* in billions swarmed up
my hand from the clinging mush. It takes billions, but billions
of germs you can *feel*. I kept the hand away from me. I
didn't slacken. If it wasn't the cats, it'd be the germs. If not
the germs, it'd be falling nine times, or running crash into a
wall. All that remained intact in me was the urgent sense that
I must not yet give up, only when the spiritual dynamo went
fttttt, spitting sparks and then the dead dark short-circuited
stink.

At last, ahead, an opening, daylight coming out of a cave.
I revved harder. I lunged through the alley-intersection and
collapsed directly under the blessed street light.

I just lay there discarded and sobbing. I knew the cats
were afraid of honest light.

My lungs thrashed in my chest. An aching bitter dryness throbbed in my throat and eyes, as if I'd grieved and cried for days.

From the length of time it took me to recover a certain pace in breathing, a good twenty years of my precious life energy steamed toward heaven in that long and terrible alley.

On my right the street zoomed out of the darkness in a downhill curve, slowed on the grade turning past me, and then swooped away to my left. Buildings seemed made from slabs of the moon, stark doorways and curbs. There wasn't a single human being up and down that street. My stomach practiced tying knots.

I called myself to attention. I stood up.

I had not forgotten my right hand dangling slimy with melon mush. I noted the itching progress reaching now to the middle of my forearm. I became the strategist. I kept the arm away from my body so the germs must go the long way, but also rigidly straight down so they must ascend almost vertically too. I figured it gained me a half-hour. And then I'd be fighting them to the death inside myself.

I scavenged past dark store fronts for soap and water. I found only water, a bucket deserted by some sloppy wage-working window-cleaner. A dirty sponge floated half-sunk, reminding me of those maniacal children sinking my defenseless merchantman.

I rolled my right sleeve up to the middle of my bicep, carefully using only the fingertips of my left hand. Now *you* have to listen carefully or you're going to miss something, and who knows, it might help you someday too. Yes, my left hand became slightly contaminated when it touched the right cuff, but only slightly, a manageable amount. I seized the sponge in the bucket with my left hand, making certain my contaminated fingertips stayed on top the sponge, while only the underside touched my skin, washing from my bicep to my fingertips. I laid the contaminated sponge on the sidewalk. I was using my left hand all the while. I took out my trusty handkerchief. Some men feel naked without a pistol. Myself, it's a handkerchief. I started to dry my arm but jerked the handkerchief away before it touched—*because* I remembered the contaminated rolled-up sleeve. I permitted myself no panic. I laid the handkerchief clean-side up on the sidewalk. I took out my pocketknife, always honed to an edge that would shave hair. On its handle in silver were the words CENTURY'S FIRST SALESMAN. Century was the name of the company, but I siphoned much mileage out of people who thought it was an award to the hottest salesman in a hundred years. With the pocketknife, left-handed, I nipped the stitches on the seam of my right sleeve where it joined the shoulder. Getting to the back of the sleeve I had to work by feel with an unbelievably detailed attentiveness, about as soothing as hopping on one foot along the edge of a cliff. You can imagine my relief when the sleeve just quietly slid down my arm and onto the sidewalk. But now I saw the water in the bucket contaminated by the first washing. It swam with trillions of germs becoming visible as they multiplied. If I'd sat down ten feet away, and stayed put, they would have multiplied out of that bucket and swamped me by sheer numbers, so bent were they on my destruction. But I wasn't licked yet. I threw the contaminated pocketknife away. A gift for a job well done, it had served me well in making another job well done. I said it then, and I say it again,

"Farewell, faithful pocketknife."

I reasoned that most of the contamination in the bucket was near the surface. Again with my left hand I picked up the sponge from the sidewalk and squeezed it into a tight ball in my fist. I plunged it, arm and all, to the very bottom of the bucket. I let the sponge fill out under my hand. I snatched it out. I reasoned that I passed both times with such bewildering rapidity through the upper contaminated area that the germs couldn't take advantage of this chance to get a free ride. *If you have followed very closely,* however, you've noticed that I did *something very wrong.* But again I scrubbed my arm inch by inch. I dried with the clean side of the handkerchief inch by inch. The closer I came to pushing the germs off my fingertips into empty space, the more I suppressed my rising glee, since the germs might have rallied to a disastrous effort if they'd sensed my coming triumph. I mopped them off each finger in quick succession. My victory cries rioted echoing in the street. And then, yes, *then* I remembered my left arm, plunged into the bucket, the wrong thing you should have noticed too. Remember?—while the sponge filled out under my hand, my left forearm was ringed by the upper contaminated water, with plenty of time for the germs to sneak into a new position of attack. Right there blubbering, sitting down, I gave up. But giving myself up to a good cry released my most basic common sense. In the bucket I saw the light of my salvation, the reflection of the street light itself, bobbling by the dark reflection of my own head.

I dashed across the street and shinnied up the pole. Don't assume my haste meant sloppiness. I did not use my left hand and thus did not contaminate the pole, and myself in less washable places. I hitched up with my heels and right hand. I have learned to be polite. I can, if necessary, learn from cats too. At the top I crouched on the overhanging steel bar, balanced most delicately.

I gripped the bar with my right hand. That steadied me. I wrapped my left hand around the naked bulb. Now I wasn't just washing the germs away. Now I was killing them! Searing pain grew out of my arm and blossomed with thunderous proof in me. It concentrated my attention, rousing my voice into single-minded bloodthirsty battle hymns. They didn't stand a chance.

I sterilized all contaminated skin on my left hand and the outside of my sleeve. Burnt-out dots appeared on my sleeve.

I teetered on my knees on the bar unbuttoning the cuff. Every inch a true man's job. One mistake and good-by me.

I sterilized my left forearm and the inside of the sleeve past the point where the surface of the bucket's water ringed my arm and the sneaky germs climbed right into my trap.

For my right hand the first washing may have been good enough. But good enough isn't good enough for me. It was my right hand's turn. An easy job with no sleeve to complicate it. A craftsman's final flourish. Grasping the bulb, I howled hymns.

It was certainly a good thing I'm not afraid of heights. An ugly orange-striped cat stalked under the street light, its eyes flashing up, giving me a deep sense of height. I feared the flash was recognition. But the cat continued ambling down the street alone, its head turning to keep its eyes on me. Inconsiderate beast.

Blisters swelled up on my hands and arms. It was an incendiary attack beyond the germs' ability to cope! No further proof needed, I chaffed my hands climbing down the pole, receiving an intense sense that I was safely alive.

My legs tottered.

It's best not to sit down at such times since the soul knots up the way muscles do. I managed to loose a soppy little fart. Nothing to be proud of, but it got me going.

Yes, like most men achieving a narrow escape by sheer wit and energy, I suppose I was a silly sight, marching lustily down the street, singing, swinging my burned clean arms, my right arm sleeveless, my left sleeve iron-crisped by heat and dotted with burnt spots. Night air flowed over my hot arms. Not much worse than sunburned. A new feeling. A wholesome spicy feeling! My searching gaze whistled into doorways. All empty. But I don't give up so easily. I was heading back to the alley where Betty said the blue-fronted whorehouse was. Never say never to me. It would be on the right, and it would be about ten blocks from the bucket and street light.

Two alleys, after ten blocks, sported blue-fronted houses

on the right. I had a fifty-fifty chance the first time, hundred percent the second.

I knocked on the fifty-fifty chance. No windows in the walls, just a big wooden door studded with iron plates, a lock and a knocker. It wasn't easy knocking with my burned hands. I started kicking. At last a scuffling stirred up inside and then a noisy playing with the lock. A cautious woman's voice said,

"Who is it?"

I kicked the door hard. "A customer. Come on, open up, it's urgent."

"Can't it wait till morning?"

"I'm a busy man. Open up."

"Who are you, busy man?"

"It's me that's got money and you that's got work."

"But I can't work now. There's bad light."

"Sure you can. I'll show you how."

Just a crack the door opened, and I jammed my foot in it. The first time I ever used the fabled professional trick! It was wise. Only a section of her face, as wide as my wedged foot, peeped through the crack, a big nose, one eye, stringy black hair, ugly ragged grayish nightgown, with lamplight glowing deep in back of her head. "Oh, it's *you!*" she said.

And I recognized the pots and pans girl, one of the two who gave me impossible directions to the whorehouse. "It's mostly me," I said.

"Surely you don't want any pots and pans fixed at this hour?"

I thought of a clever remark, but didn't say it.

"You didn't find the whorehouse, did you?"

"I've found it," I said.

"You should have followed *my* directions. It's only because she talks louder and faster that people think she knows more than me. You'll know better next time."

Placidly, from full height, I appraised her stringiness, her fat pimply nose. I concluded the best of her wasn't immediately visible. I stated in a plain business like manner,

"I have thirty dollars. I'll show it to you."

"From all I hear you better use it to buy a ticket out of town *fast.*"

"Such strange things you hear."

"Hardly strange as the things I hear about *you.* Now you get out of town, and I'll get back to bed."

"Thirty dollars," I said.

She shoved the door. It only wedged my foot more comfortably.

"So you *are* the kind they say you are?" she said.

"You're even getting friendly, personal," I said.

"You should be glad that's all I'm not friendly!" she screeched, spitting with stupendous accuracy into my face.

Contemptuously I licked her sprinkle of spit from the corners of my mouth. "If I understood you I'm sure I wouldn't understand."

"Did you hear those phones ringing all over town, up and down every street? *Did* you?"

"A phone's always long-distance, baby. I don't like talking long-distance."

I laid both hands and all my weight against the door and readied myself to shove and break into her house and into her. My grin was deadly.

"If *that's* the way you *are!*" She jabbed her heel hard on the toes of my jammed foot, *hard,* again and again. "There, there, *there,* if that's the way you are!"

And I groaned, "Oh, oh, *oh,*" somehow keeping time with her.

My foot slipped out, and I thought with terror it slipped out because it had become a bag of mashed flesh and bones. She slammed the door and worked the lock.

I leaned my shoulder against the door, holding my screaming foot in both hands, and cried,

"Your directions are the worst in town!"

I meant to taunt her into telling me the way to the whorehouse. She laughed uproariously on the other side. It was a forced laugh. I yelled.

"You couldn't tell a man which hole's your cunt."

She sang,

"I'd tell a man it's in the looking place!"

I roared,

"Where's the whorehouse?"

She twittered,

"In the looking place!"

She stamped in echoes away inside the house. I screamed inspired,

"Go on to bed and be cold and lonely, you bitch! With your stringy hair, your pimply nose, your knothole cunt!"

She sang again,

"It's easier to get through a knothole than to get where you want to go!" Another door slammed deeper inside. I shouted in a way that could be heard through walls twelve-foot thick.

"*Baby, I'll get where I want to go without any fucking body's help!*"

Electric twinges leaped up my leg from my foot. But they hadn't tested the limits of my first-aid know-how yet. I forced my weight onto the bad foot. I exercised it walking down one block to the other blue-fronted house, *the one-hundred-percent chance.*

A plain lit bulb swarmed with bugs above the door. The light was a good sign. They wanted to be seen.

I braced one hand on the door and lifted my throbbing left foot. A fucking stork would have mistook me for its nearest kin. I knocked twice, then three times more rapidly. The coded sequence pleased me. *Musical instruments,* something I hadn't noticed in this town, something to SELL. Now I *knew* my faculties were intact! Best to start out selling drums and cymbals, though, since these people obviously weren't elevated enough to tell a wind instrument from a skinflute.

Exhilarated I reached up and swatted around the bulb, crushing a handful of moths and knocking others sailing cuckoo into the darkness.

Ecstatically swinging my arms I beat the door. Making a symphony! And the more climactic my symphony the more certain I was the hundred-percent door would stay one-hundred-percent dumb. But if not me, my symphony would enter! My symphony would rape their sleep, if not their bodies!

Noises roused up on the other side. Maybe I'd hit on their code! I stopped knocking. I pressed my hands and one ear against the door. A lot of women were arguing intensely. They agreed again and again not to open the door, no matter what, it might be *him*! I was famous! I picked up a stone in each hand. How that big solid door resounded! I listened flat against it again. One of their number, so-and-so, they said, was still out in the streets and that terrible urgent pounding might be *her* trying to escape *him*!

I attempted a feminine whine. "Yes, it's me. Oh, please let me in."

"*Yes?*"

I battered the door.

My symphony grew in its variations, invading every cranny of their rooms and beds and bodies. It woke my prick. Naturally he tried to get out into the thick of it.

I unzipped. I couldn't let prick think I hadn't done my damnedest. I laid to against the door with the stones in both hands. And he was standing up, my cheering section!

Thunderously tumultous, all my feelings, yet the clearest sensation reaching me became a slight, mystifying, heated pressure on the small of my back. It had to be *eyes*. Pained flesh, such as mine, is sensitive even to the minute temperature changes caused by burning hating eyes. If I turned around, I would see, I was certain, a spectacle bent on my ultimate persecution, rank upon rank of pairs of yellow eyes across roof tops and fences and on the street. It was my back against their eyes, but, as everyone knows, the human back has only limited staring power. I stared at the grain of the wood in the door with my nose against it, developing intensity. Now I was ready. Prick and me spun, thrusting forward to meet them eye to eye.

I was wrong about the ranks of yellow eyes. I wasn't wrong about the eyes.

Across the street a hippy, tall, busty woman leaned against the lamppost, with her arms folded in a black shawl that wrapped her head and shoulders. Her eyes glowed as diamonds melting.

A mistrustful familiarity made me hop and limp toward her. She slanted her shawl covering her cheek and mouth.

It was *Betty!* I whooped, threw out my arms, staggered on my bad foot.

For one moment I admitted enthusiastically that I was mistaken and it was only the street light, reflected in her eyes, that caused the pressure focused on my back, the way a magnifying glass concentrates the sun.

Shy and jittery, just like when selling my caskets, I said, hobbling up to her,

"Thank God, it's a small world!"

"Small enough," she said.

For one bitter second I wanted to fold up and cry.

"So you're against me too, Betty."

"Listen, Mister, you'd save everyone a lot of trouble, including yourself especially, if you just packed up and left town."

"You know, Betty, it took two to bake those cookies."

And then I noticed her cheek lumpy with a dark bruise split in the middle by an oozing cut. Bruised too was the spirited sexy look in her eyes. I'd like to have seen that sonofabitch try that shit when I was around. I reached to touch her cheek.

Shuddering, she turned her face away from my hand. "How awful you look!"

"Yes," I said, "my capacity for survival amazes even me." I took her by both shoulders, shaking her just a little to make her know how serious I was. "Betty, dearest, you must *believe* me when I tell you I think you and me are the *only* human people from here to the mountains and all the way back to the sea! Betty, you must *listen* when I tell you I have thirty dollars! *Listen* and suggest a nice little café, with nice food, nice music, nice people, nice drinks, nice soft light and dancing!"

"Mister, button up your pants, you're on a public street, and button up your mouth!"

"Only thing public in this town is everybody's privacy. Betty, let's go where we can be very, very private."

"Go where?"

"Go *away*! I know a town *faraway* on the sea, the real living killing sunny sea, where even the sharks are nicer than the kids in that living room. Betty, if you're the only one that's managed to stay human here you'll be past all believing in towns away from here."

Raving with surprise at myself, so help me I don't know why I started sneezing. Everywhere I turned I sneezed, and no choice but to cry out, "Betty, let's get *married!*"

"You're *hideous!*"

I lowered my crippled left foot onto the ground.

"So it's hideous to take you away from Tarrington? Hideous to take you to another town where you'd live as people here only dream of living?"

She hissed, "This is my home. I love my home."

"You real whore!"

She sobbed with a hard body-jerk. Cheeks working she spat a big gob right into the fur showing through my shirt-neck. Germs, for sure.

"You're not going inside that whorehouse without me following you. You know that, Betty."

She spat again. "I've slept on sidewalks before."

"I've got thirty dollars, Betty."

"Anything I would do with you, mister, is just as awful as your thirty filthy dollars!"

"Now, baby, I'd heard dollars were democrats."

"Your money won't pass around here and you neither. Button up your *pants,* mister, button up your *lip,* and get out of my *way!*"

Snootily she headed past me toward the whorehouse. I grappled her ass-backwards against me. There was no sweet nostalgia in my grip.

"Let me go! If you'll just please let me go!"

"I'll let you go when I've let you have it. And if you don't shut up and stop kicking, I'll shout, and we'll see what the town and the Tarringtons think seeing you and me together again." And it gagged her all right.

I bore my weight down on her back. She doubled onto her knees. I jerked her dress up over her back. And there was her ass, with no panties whatsoever, a cold exciting surprise! Maybe those special panties were part of her uniform at the Tarringtons! Maybe at the end of the day they blindfolded her and used their secret method to take them off!

I discovered prick hardly knew what was going on! An absurd situation, holding the cramped violence of the woman around the waist with one arm, coaxing prick awake with the other hand and then reaching into my rear pocket for the rubbers. Her struggling chafed my burning hands and arms. She would soon learn that I was past pain. I rolled on one rubber. Prick swelled against it unreasonably. I rolled on the second rubber. I have heard of one breaking and there is a certain probability of two breaking. And some say that using a rubber dulls the sensation, lessens satisfaction, drastically, they say. I say using two prolongs it, double your money and safety too.

She tried to keep prick out by keeping her thighs together. I pushed on the back of her head, grinding her face on the pavement. Prick went butting under her ass. He entered suddenly. And don't tell me she wasn't ready to enjoy it, that cunt was primed as juicy as a hubful of grease, holding onto prick for dear life.

"Don't lie, you bitch, you feel it, I know you feel it!!'

So dog-fashion under the street light we did it, just what this town deserved. And no matter how hard she tried to hold it in, her excitement escaped between her teeth. And then prick probed the limit of the heavenly pipe and started shooting her up inside, *so he thought,* but he forgets the rubbers.

A dangerous moment! I had to keep my wits about me while he was coming! I shouted,

"Spit on me, will you?" I jumped back. I raised my arm "You're not going to get the chance to fuck with me, poor Miss Betty!"

Like an ax I swung the side of my hand against her neck. She rolled. She huddled with jerking curled-up knees against another windowless wall, whimpering, whimpering, whimpering. At least now she had reason to whimper.

WELL!!! A good calisthenic, that's just about what it amounted to. Never say never to me.

How wonderful to stretch and feel as tall as I was! And how easy to breathe, and no pain could come from my arms and foot into the great clean gladdening!

I hobbled away. I felt so good I was singing hymns.

But you can't forget some things, and I couldn't forget how sweetly passionate Betty was in the kitchen.

I went back to her. I stuffed a ten-dollar bill into a pocket of her skirt. Ten was enough. After all, I'd done most of the work. And she'd be glad of the money in the morning. Maybe she'd think it was only a bad dream and she'd really been working because there was the money to prove it! She must need the money too, working two jobs. Besides it was only because I'd hit her that she was feeling bad. Too bad I couldn't have trusted the excitement she was feeling and then it would have been really fine and all thirty dollars to go with it. A warm tenderness swelled my belly. My eyes got sweetly wet. I couldn't love her whimpering against the wall, but I could love the Betty I remembered in the kitchen. I pulled her skirt down over her legs. I kissed her cheek. "Sweet dreams, Betty, maybe you'll learn someday."

It was all better than great stretching in the morning after a good night's sleep. Yes, a little tenderness is almost as bracing as a good fuck, now and then.

Hiking away down the street, my whistling rode the roof tops, her whimpering its undertone.

And then the whimpering stopped behind me.

It stopped so quickly. I took a few steps, slowed, listened. I saw her getting onto her feet. She screamed. Light creviced the whorehouse front. A head poked out.

Blubbering Betty staggered, holding her head, to the door. She accused me of *attempted* rape! So she proved herself a a liar in more ways than one!

I bellowed down the street,

"I assure you I always finish what I start out to do!"

And Betty pointed at me and shrieked without conscience again and again that I was a *liar*!

The whorehouse doors swung wide, and whores disheveled in nightgowns stampeded into the street howling after me.

It wasn't easy to run on my bad foot. Only when the

whores came too damn close did I start running adequately. Twice they hit my back with stones, and once with a rotten vegetable that sopped my shirt against my skin. YES, but I had good reason to believe the germs in this town were less virulent than the people. The blows on my back merely loosened my muscles. I kept on running.

Then I realized something strange.

Their shouting and cursing sounded mechanical, and they didn't chase me with their hearts in it either, only making a good show of a try at getting me. I didn't have much energy to apply to this puzzle, but I wasn't about to give them a chance to make a good show of trying to kill me.

Onto the town square I came running under a long arcade. Echoes cheered my slapping feet. A block away, light projected onto the sidewalk below the hotel's sign.

Jammed up behind me, where the street opened onto the square, the whores taunted me, going no further. Like the cats, they were afraid of honest, civilized light.

No need to go on running, but by now I believed my body was made for no other purpose. I was pleased with it, and pleased with the precision of my breathing too.

I loped easily under the hotel's marquee.

Up at the head of the steps a man leaned against the side of the entrance, his hand in his pocket hitching up his suit coat. Light poured over his shoulders from inside the hotel. I raised my hand against it. But only one man in this town possessed the total wherewithal to express himself with sureness and ease.

Beside Tarrington my bags and sample cases were ranked

in a neat stair-step row, children rigid for a family portrait. I recognized them instantly by number, size, and shape.

He must have started talking as soon as I ran up. But I needed rest and the light hurt my eyes. I stayed on the lower step, entrenching my head snugly in my arm against the wall. And it was easy to breathe, hearing my heartbeat, alone and man to man, his voice without body filling the darkness.

"Yes, I managed to come here before the clerk tore your bags to pieces. Do you know that when I took the knife away from him he fell on your things raging to tear them apart with just his bare hands and teeth? That's amazing, you think?"

A big wobbly roach crept from under the wall and scuttled toward my foot. If I couldn't trust the cats, much less the whores in this town, I'd every reason to suspect the roaches were organized on Tarrington's side too. And he might just be distracting me with talk to facilitate the roach's sneak attack. It scuttled under the warp of my sole. I rocked the shoe down firmly.

I chuckled hearing Tarrington,

"You do find it strange, don't you? Oh, you mustn't think his rage was honest, spontaneous, true, whatever those words mean. It was mainly his simple desire to please me. And how you distinguish between his own desires and his desires to please me becomes almost impossible. If he appeared beyond restraint, it was only to show how beautifully helpless he was before the strength of his own passionate fidelity to me. And I'm afraid the whole town has treated you with the same honest sort of dishonesty. And I think you know why I tell you these things."

An asylum, this town, and I didn't have the qualifications for admittance, that's what he meant. But maybe he was jealous of the spiritual time I made with his wife too. And maybe Betty was his whore.

Now he got folksy, confiding.

"Remember old Shipley? You couldn't have stayed thirty minutes in that house without me there and not heard of old Shipley. When I came to this town, Shipley was just gone. And these people had never seen my kind before. Just as they've never seen your kind. But soon you'll be gone too." His laugh was cool and easy. "I think you really don't understand me."

He *was* damned hard to understand. I dropped my arm. I faced him. I shriveled with the awfulness of my appearance. You only see yourself when others look at you. He didn't change his leaning position.

I started up the steps. I couldn't trust that my words, going through the air of this town, would arrive in his ears still believing and saying what they'd believed and said when formed on my tongue. You have to watch a tongue closer than a woman anyway, treacherous the way it changes its mind.

I stopped a couple steps below Tarrington. Past him I gazed into the vaulted hotel lobby, at the cream-painted walls with walnut trim and the mint-green deeply cushioned furniture. Doggily the bastard clerk bent writing over his desk.

Behind him the pigeonholes stacked up honeycombed. His glasses flashed at me.

While I talked to Tarrington I stared ferociously at the clerk, daring the clerk to meet me *any* night, *any*where alone.

"I could use a night's sleep," I said.

"I would have to stay up all night guarding your life and limb."

"Well," I said, "I don't suppose you can be blamed for the customs in your own town."

"Not mine," he said. His smile aggravated me with the sense that he thought it was amusing that I couldn't perceive some simple mystery.

"Yes, I forgot everyone was only trying to please you."

I moved up another step. I looked level into his eyes so porcelain cold and gray coming to meet mine. So I was really taller than him. I stooped to pick up my bags. True, in one there were long-edged knife cuts and three sets of teeth marks so deep you could have taken a plaster cast and made that fucking clerk a set of dentures, though it was obvious he didn't need them.

"You should never have said never to me, Tarrington. And never fear. I didn't get any of your doors open, but I got into one of your holes. Besides your town, I mean."

"Have you seen Betty?"

"*Who's* Betty?"

For once Tarrington's eyes changed about uneasily and he shifted the position of his feet. "She's an impetuous girl," he said. "I'm just afraid I treated her a little roughly."

I clapped his shoulder. "You know, Tarrington, it makes me glad to think you and me might just be guilty of the same thing."

He yawned. He said,

"An hour should be time enough for you to get out of town."

A nerve, that bastard, telling me to get out of town. And he stayed in that sassily comfortable leaning position too. I don't know why I didn't give him a shove and beat the shit out of him right there.

But I was already going down the steps with my bags under my arms toward the big park in the middle of the town square.

Horse turds were strewn over the street. I set my bags down. I pretended brushing my pants. I sneaked one moist, firm turd into my hand. I turned suddenly, hurled it.

Tarrington sprang from his leaning position, into the middle of the hotel's entrance, legs apart. And then I must have hit him. He jumped, dashed into the lobby. My war cry glee rode out of my mouth. I fired the turds until the clerk ducked below his desk too. I shouted between my hands,

"Now you know not every man-jack will lick your ass!"

I picked up my bags, and went into the park, at a jittery but honorable pace.

All the park's cobbled paths led in darkness from the street. Through the branches and leaves I could see the center well lighted. But I just couldn't shake the tension out of the muscles in my back.

Again there were beds and beds of flowers along the walk. Lilies, the only distinguishable variety, stood together in groups, sticking out their big golden tongues, *goddamn them*. Swinging a suitcase, I knocked those lilies silly. Flowering branches, acacia and jacaranda and bougainvillaea, hung over the walk, drooped in my face. Putting my bags under one arm, I gave them the back of my hand.

Many benches were set in alcoves. They resembled lovers' benches, but it didn't surprise me that they were empty, a custom that hadn't yet reached this town.

A statue poked up into the trees in one alcove. Weeds reared up from between the stones in the walk leading to it. Obviously this statue wasn't visited except by a few oddballs who maybe wanted to fuck in private. I paid a visit. I crowded with weeds and branches around the statue standing on a pedestal. That's about all I could tell about it. I struck a match, and there was the name on the base. SHIPLEY. Yes, that was the remarkable man, strong and brave and sure on his feet and froze solid in two minutes. Or maybe it was his grandfather. Anyway, if the weeds were as viciously determined as everything else in this town, the name wasn't due to be remembered.

I hurried away, not liking it that my body thought it was necessary to crouch.

In the park center, in the middle of a concrete circle, was a roofed pavilion, illuminated by lights hanging in the trees. Great brass frogs, rearing goats and monkeys faced inward, water spewing from their mouths into the moat that surrounded the circle. *Yes*, the damned pavilion was named

CUSTOM

TARRINGTON, in mosaic for the dancing men and women of centuries to see. A real coup, treble for his sonofabitching money, a zoo, a fountain, and a dance floor all together in his name. Wouldn't have been any sense anyway in my pursuing a livelihood in a town that couldn't afford them separately. I crossed the bridge and deposited my bags under the roof. How still, with the water spattering ceaselessly, and the good water smell easing down into me.

I went out to the moat again. I opened my pants. Hanging there in a goopy mess were the two rubbers, and poor prick almost smothered. I dropped the rubbers into the moat.

My gut quaked polluting the water that smelled so good.

So I pissed in the water.

Beside me a huge brass frog raised his mouth agape as high as my chest. I patted his head.

"Tarrington sort of put you in place too," I said.

I moved along the edge of the moat away from where I pissed and washed my hands.

A branch, bejeweled with thumb-sized red fruit, extended over the water. That the tree stood untouched in the middle of the town square meant that Tarrington didn't want them picked. I ate everything on that tree. I mean I stripped it *ragged*. Sweet, very sweet, the lean yellow flesh loosening and soothing my throat.

My back hardened, facing what it could never see.

Under the pavilion roof, I arranged my bags as pillows and rests for my head and my aching foot, my blistered hands and arms.

Settling down for a night on the road, I get philosophical.

I see that things come and go and nothing makes much difference. I feel small, cuddly small, under the far, faraway stars. A good night's rest cures all, and I can't remember a morning when I didn't wake hungry and ready for all comers. Tomorrow I would head south into the world beyond these pint-sized city limits, into other towns, other territories, other women. No doors would open in this town. I'd plugged the last hole. I jostled about among my bags. I slapped a few mosquitos and cleaned my fingers scraping them on the concrete. I listened to the brass zoo steadily pissing and spitting streams of water, the buzzing of insects, and the air buttery with the scent of flowers.

Then, in the dark bushes beyond the moat, a small and stupid noise announced itself. A man who hadn't slept much alone in many strange places mightn't have noticed it.

Noises flurried through the bushes.

They were almost clever enough to let me go to sleep right under the lights.

I tried to control myself. I sat up. I was trapped, shivering with sweat.

Right there I hunched my head between my knees and started crying. I would let them do what they wanted. I just didn't want to watch. I sobbed, gulping the good water smell.

But I didn't let myself go on that way for long.

I took charge of myself with a jerk.

They were in perfect darkness beyond the light. I didn't know what I was going to do, but I wasn't going to let them get me lying down. I cracked a suitcase. I pulled out my pistol, concealing it against my thigh. Who was in the darkness? The cats? The whores? The whole fucking town, roaches, rats, and all?

Let me tell you I was lonely, a perfect target in the center of those white lights.

I unzipped my pants.

Now I wasn't alone. My friend muscled out, standing up to keep the watch with me.

We knew our only chance, and not a very good one.

We must lull them. And then take them by surprise.

I bowed my head. I pretended to pray, out loud, for someone to watch over us. Not many people will shoot a man while he's praying. And most get sleepy waiting for him to stop. I became absolutely musical, lulling them. At the moment when I was rolling my head and raving LORD, WATCH OVER US, we leaped up, banshee screaming, in one terrific jump over the moat.

I cleared the way firing into the bushes. My friend, admirable foolhardiness, entered the darkness first. He is a little younger than me. Chilling gusts whoomed up and down the street, bumping us. *Empty.* Everyone was in the park. Dodging into an alley, we surprised their rear guard. A pair of eyes. I am an excellent shot. That was the only noise.

We reached the highway.

We crouched in the ditch, keeping shoulders down in the weeds. My friend was tired. A job nobly done. I complimented him and tucked him in.

A sudden wind shotgunned me with sleety rain. "Fucking shit!" I yelled, trying to dodge and slap the rain away.

I waited until, icily drenched, at last I saw headlights

moving through the shattering fall of rain. Certainly wasn't the moment to twiddle my thumb politely. Standing square in the middle of the pavement, waving both arms, I flagged down the big semi.

I put the pistol in my back pocket. I didn't want to scare the driver. A bull-chested, big-headed man, with a red beret, and his chin burrowed into the sweat shirt seamed around his neck.

I was so furious and sad we didn't talk much, just where you going, fine, how are you, could do with a little less rain, me too.

He drove with his eyes gripping the road, and very fast, careening through the endless rain.

Was I supposed to feel good? My bags and sample cases were deserted among barbarians who knew no better than to use the medicines as spices, and would decorate themselves hanging the toilet equipment around their necks.

MORGAN

Sfc Lewis Morgan, who had a rep as the best mess
sergeant in the KComZ, always played a game in the streets
of Pusan to see just how close he could nip the foot-traffic
with the fender of his jeep. He managed at last to kill a
gook, a baby boy slung on the small of its mother's back.
"Shit, boysan," one of Morgan's buddies said, late the next
day, after all hell broke loose around the headquarters
compound of the 68th Engineers, "she'd a froze to death
long before this if the American Army wasn't here. Why, you
better mother-fuckin' believe it, sarge." Morgan himself never
said so much. His glasses flashed as he looked up at his
buddy and his smile was meant to please and threaten. His
smile was straight as the side of his hand. He went back
to planning menus, sitting alone at a table in the middle of
the empty messhall, while his buddy shuffled uncomfortably
away. Morgan had a black belt in judo, and it put a stamp
of license on anything he did. GIs went out of their way to
visit friends in the 68th so they could eat in Morgan's messhall,
where the food was good and everything was clean.

In the streets, people tumbled to get out of his way, and heavy bundles rolled and spilled apart. Morgan particularly enjoyed two things, the steep, narrow streets where he could make a man jump for his life, spread out flat and quivering against a wall as the jeep whipped by. And the other was the spider-men. These were men with no legs, amputees at the hip, who walked by swinging their torsos between their arms. They used thick gloves on their hands and their torsos were padded at the bottom. They were always black with filth, and you could not tell their skin from their clothing. With incredible agility they darted in front of vehicles, among people's legs, everywhere. Morgan swerved his jeep and tried to tick the spider-men so they would lose their remarkable control and fall over in the street. More than once, in his rearview mirror, he saw people helping one of the spider-men get his arms and torso into position again, though usually they were quite able to do it themselves. "Jee-e-e-e-sus, *Christ*," buddies riding with Morgan would hiss and holler, scared and glad he'd done it. "Whooo-eeeee, look at old mama-san go." If it were a couple of whores in Western dress he would send them scurrying off the road, stop the jeep abruptly, back up, smile at them, and the jo-sans might tell him off in the finest pidgin cussing and even then end up climbing into his jeep. He loved to drive with a whore sucking him off, and grin at the people in the streets who couldn't help but see it.

He was alone in the jeep jouncing off the bridge between Yong Do island and the mainland city when he bumped the woman. He had just done the business that he did every week selling extra meat in the black market. It was in the first traffic circle on the mainland side of the bridge that he veered toward the woman with the baby slung in the small of her back. Morgan was zeroed into his game staring through the windshield at the baby's head nodding out of the shawl, its wide dark eyes looking back at the jeep's fender as the woman plunged to get away. When he saw the catch of her body, her foot slip on some filth, his split-second timing was destroyed. And yet it was as if it consummated something, as if to make a mistake was to know that he was playing the game as closely as possible. The jeep's right fender hit the baby on her back. She rolled on the street in baggy, ballooning pants that were made out of a dark green American OD blanket. She screamed and then screams came from everywhere. He saw the legs of people running up around her. Morgan, not even knowing if she or the baby were hurt, shifted down to second and roared away in a jerk of speed, permitting himself only a tight grin and breathing between his teeth as he looked in the rearview mirror at a gook in dirty white clothing running as hard as he could after the jeep for nearly two blocks.

Morgan told the dispatcher at the Motor Pool that he had bumped someone with the right fender. They looked, the jeep wasn't marked, and they let it pass. Morgan spoke only to the dispatcher but by evening chowtime it was all over the compound that he had bumped a woman in the street. No one found it trivial. Morgan's buddies were

men who were loud, ate a lot, exploited every sexual
possibility that could be forced or paid for, and got great
kicks making gooks jump. They were slapping their knees,
throwing their heads back when they laughed, and
talking about Morgan, Morgan, Morgan.

2

Sgt. Berens, the medical clerk in the medical detachment
on the 68th's compound, hated and feared Morgan. But
Morgan didn't seem to know him even by name. Berens
pretended to clean his bifocals and squinted and squinched
whenever he saw Morgan walking across the parade ground
to the quonset hut shower in his white judo outfit with the
black belt. When Morgan's glasses caught the sun, Berens
felt the flash go right through him.

He was US, a draftee, who made his rank on waivers-of-
time-in-grade. He was the medical clerk, but he really
wanted to be an aidman and avoided it through a simple
fear of blood, pus and open flesh. He played a game
with Koreans too, doctoring and giving medicines to those
who couldn't get it any other way. He was teamed in this
enterprise with the young Korean queer who virtually ran the
PX. Pong Nam, who lately dressed more and more colorfully,
spoke fairly good English and acted as the go-between for
sick Koreans and Berens. Korean laborers would step away
from their work and bow with big smiles when Berens passed

near them. They also bowed to Pong Nam in a way that
pleased Berens but irritated most of the soldiers because
it made them know that the "PX boysan" was definitely upper
class. It was easy for Berens and rewarding, until, just
recently, he found himself guilty of letting two children
of one of Morgan's dishwashers die.

He had masked his good-will doctoring by writing fake
prescriptions in the way that medics treated friends and
others useful to them off the record for VD. It was easy with
the common antibiotics and sulfas. But when the young
Korean queer leaned richly with both elbows on the
PX counter and told him about the dishwasher's kids and
Berens got the symtoms straight, he knew the kids had
typhoid. There was only one medicine that affected typhoid,
Chloromycetin. The bottle of Chloromycetin in the dispensary
security cabinet was there by accident, the seal was
unbroken, and it was unlikely that it would ever be broken.
Berens could not fake this prescription without question
coming up about it. He tried to enlist the dispensary doctor.
It ended with the doctor, who had signed all of Berens'
waivers-of-time-in-grade, telling him in sudden anger that
all indigenous personnel employed by the army and their
families could go to the General Dispensary and get any help
that Berens could give them and probably more. He, the
doctor, was not going to be put into the position of
explaining to the IG why the seal was broken on the bottle
of Chloromycetin. Berens went back to Pong Nam and told
him the dishwasher could go to the General Dispensary,

but Pong Nam said nó no no that the Korean personnel had found this not to be so. Berens was caught, in anger with the doctor and anger with Pong Nam's easy insinuation that it was his duty to break the rules, as if it were easy for him to do. He was also conscious of walking between the stripes and rocker with the big black centers on his two sleeves. He told Pong Nam to tell the dishwasher to take his children to the General Dispensary immediately.

The dishwasher stood at the end of the line of steaming tubs, where the soldiers came out of the messhall and handed over their dirty trays. The tubs were lined up on the side of the messhall toward the motor pool, rather than the side facing the outside fence where they had once been, so the soldiers would not have to look at the children hanging on the fence and staring at the GIs scraping away waste food. A big smile was always given to Berens by the dishwasher. Then he noticed that the ever present smile on the dishwasher's face over the boiling tub was straight and wide and trembling, as if the sun had stopped on the horizon. He went straight to Pong Nam in the PX. Pong Nam did not lean on the counter, and seemed to have taken a few cool steps back into his body. Yes, the two children had died of the fever. Berens put his fist on the glass counter and asked what kind of pills were given by the General Dispensary. "He show me pills," Pong Nam said. White pills, by a Korean nurse. APCs. Chloromycetin usually came in green capsules. There was a likelihood that the children would have died even if given Chloromycetin. But white pills. APCs. Berens stalked

to the dispensary, into the pharmacy, and ripped the seal off
the bottle of Chloromycetin just to show himself that he
could have given the capsules, without any personal
consequence. He waited and then dropped the death of the
two children like a dart into the doctor's face. The pharmacist
was angry about the broken seal, the doctor was angry, but
they would cover it for the IG with some explanation. That
was that.

There was no agency to name the crime a crime. So
Berens found himself guilty of letting the two children die.
Korean laborers no longer bowed to him. He saw something
else in their faces, he saw fright and ready trembling smiles.
He was a sergeant now but he kept on eating in the EM
messhall rather than the NCO mess because the only way he
could feel his guilt was to face three times a day the
dishwasher at the end of the line of tubs.

He came through the chow line the evening that the noise
was all over the compound about Morgan bumping a woman
in the streets. The uniform in Korea was fatigues and
everybody in the chow line was in fatigues. A man wore
khakis on his own time and his own money and Morgan
always wore khakis. While a cook ladled chili on top the rice
on Beren's tray, Berens ducked his chin and squinted behind
his bifocals at Morgan walking up and down behind his
white-jacketed cooks, in sharp khakis tight around his husky
chest, with three lines of ribbons above the left pocket, no
medals, just three areas of campaigns. But the ribbons gave
the impression of being worn the way a cock pheasant wears

his colors. No one in the chow line said anything about the bumping of the woman to Morgan. Berens did not say anything either but he stared. To his surprise, Morgan stared straight back, with his hands on his hips, long past the moment for shifting the eyes. Berens became one smooth jelly of fear but he could not let his eyes waver. Morgan flicked his gaze to the cook at the end of the line and told him he was fucking a-well going to burn the coffee if he didn't turn down the flame under the tub. Berens was quivering as he went into the messhall with his tray full of the messhall's good food.

"Still slumming, sarge?" Berens wasn't used to being called sarge, and he looked around to see who was being talked to as he sat down at the table. Every table within hearing mentioned Morgan bumping the woman in the street, usually with a scared laugh and a shake of the head. But, when Morgan came down the aisle, square and silent face with glasses, there was nothing to be heard of it from any table. He glanced at every table, he glanced at Berens, but he didn't seem to notice that Berens stared at him all the way down the aisle back into the cookhouse. "He's one fucking good mess sergeant," said a voice at Beren's table, a man he didn't know. Berens waited for the sharp simmer of fear in his belly to go away so he could taste Morgan's food.

When he handed over his dirty tray, he forced himself to look into the dishwasher's smile and eyes. He couldn't help himself from picturing suddenly the man's two dead kids boiled in the tub. It meant something about Morgan. He was trying not to let his breathing show when he met Pong Nam, by accident seemingly, several steps away on the cindered ground of the motor pool. The young Korean was dressed in blue silk pants, embroidered jacket, with a pink parasol over his shoulder. He had a lover somewhere now.

The compound was at the bottom of darkness, in the smell of the harbor, and the small lights of the city twinkled over the hills around them. Berens said, "Anyonghi hassimnika?" They greeted each other. It heartened Berens that Pong Nam lessened the distance that had been between them. Pong Nam twirled the parasol throughout their talk, and Berens had to look away from the constant invitation in the bright eyes and wide, slow lips. Berens put his hands on his hips and stood as straight as possible.

Pong Nam glanced at the lit-up messhall. "Sergeant hit woman today with jeep," he said.

"Yes, the fucker's going to kill somebody," Berens said.

"Sergeant Morgan," Pong Nam, said, caressing the parasol handle with his cheek.

"He ought to be put in jail," Berens said.

"Yes," Pong Nam said.

The lazy invitation never left his face, even when he said goodbye.

3

The next day Berens discovered that there *was* something for which Morgan ought to be held to account. It began in the middle of the morning.

Pfc Levin, who had just come on duty in the guard shack at the gate, hardly noticed a few Korean men craning around in the street. They were joined by more men and women, all looking at the 68th's compound with unusual energy and frankness, and then a mob was blocking traffic and pressing toward the compound gate itself, in a sudden chanting roar. Levin stammered between using his M-1 and the phone in the guard shack and then just yelled out for help and stacked himself behind the white bar of the gate swinging his M-1 back and forth at the avalanche of people that seemed mostly eyes and mouths and fists. He forgot the Korean word for halt, and was screaming in English, pointing his M-1 at a woman in the lead, with a masked look on her face, clean and pale about the eyes from weeping, and muddy on the cheeks. She was carrying a bundle in her arms and pressing one end of it to her breast. There was a fury in her face and voice. It was the righteousness of her fury that addled Levin, a righteousness that came out of her in a sort of shock wave, out of her rags and the baggy pants made from an OD blanket. Then there was the moment when he should have been overwhelmed and he was fighting to wake up as if from a nightmare. He realized that a Korean man, in a white shirt, a dirty white American shirt, was holding his arm in the air to signal the crowd to pause and was trying to get Levin's attention across the white bar in broken, but understandable English. The man said they didn't want the Pfc, they wanted the Mess Sergeant.

"Morgan," the mob was chanting, "Morgan."

Without even being shown what was in the bundle in the woman's arms, Pfc Levin understood what had happened the day before. "Morgan," he said, as if he were speaking to a stone in a dream. "Ne. Morgan," the man in the white shirt said. Then the man in the white shirt was looking past the Pfc into the compound with a wry sort of smile. There were rapid sounds of boots on cinders and then helmeted soldiers with bayonets fixed on their M-1s stretched in a crescent before the white bar of the gate, with First Lieutenant Weems on one end with Pong Nam to act as interpreter, and First Sergeant Cummings, a veteran of forty five years in the Army, a head taller than anyone else, on the other. The helmeted line leaned toward the mass of Koreans on the other side of the gate and the sun glittered on the bayonets, as upon water. Levin heard himself ordered to get a bayonet on his weapon and fall in line.

First Lieutenant Weems kept the .45 in his right hand pointing high over the mob, whose shouting was sledgehammering his ears. Tall, gangly, he rigidly took a breath and stepped up to the gate. Pong Nam was beside him, in blue silk pants and embroidered jacket, no parasol, but langorous even now, so deliberately and gallantly queer that he put himself beyond anybody's retribution. Pong Nam addressed the man in the white American shirt. With a heaving motion of her arms above the white bar, the woman pleaded with the Lieutenant to look into the bundle.

The Lieutenant asked, "What do they want?"

"They want Sergeant Morgan, sir," Pong Nam said.

"What for?"

Pong Nam shrugged and smiled, briefly. "They want to kill him."

"Tell them it was an accident."

"They say it no accident."

Lieutenant Weems listened to his interpreter translating the demands of the mob. They wanted an eye for an eye. They wanted Mess Sergeant Morgan. They wanted him delivered into their hands right now. They knew the 68th by reading the bumper markings on Morgan's jeep at the scene in the first traffic circle. They knew him by rank, by name, and by job. Later in the day Lieutenant Weems came to the sudden understanding that someone who worked on the compound had informed these people. "Well," the Lieutenant said, "you'll have to tell them that they just can't have him. If there is any justice to be done, it will be done by a military court. Now there are ways—"

Pong Nam was blandly delivering this reply to the man in the white shirt who already understood and was saying it in Korean over his shoulder, harshly, sarcastically, to the nearest faces. The woman screamed. The crowd tightened toward the gate. Sergeant Cummings, at the other end of the line, whispered sharp, fast commands. The soldiers stepped back tensely, stepped forward, stepped back, pulsed with the movement of the crowd, and with their bayonets almost tickled the pressure in the air. The weight of the people behind the man in the white shirt pushed him hard against the gate bar and nearly bent his chest upon the bayonets. He was looking behind the rifles into the eyes under the helmets and then tore his shirt apart with both hands, baring his brown chest. "Kill me. Also kill me."

Weems interjected himself between the bayonets and the man. "Are you the husband, the father? Who are you?"

"He is friend," Pong Nam said.

The last thing Weems wanted was trouble. He had been the executive officer of a cartography section in the Pentagon before he was transferred to Korea. Maps were his career and maps were his delight, and his main wish was to finish his tour of duty in Korea as simply as possible and get back among maps again. His wrist ached and was chill from holding the .45 pointed up. He let it down by his side. "Now, look here, wait a minute," he said. He tried to tell the man in the white shirt that there were ways, legal ways, that they could make their complaint and see justice done.

"No work-ee," the man said.

The foremost demonstrators were jammed against the gate. The woman's thighs were forced against the bar and the pain of it showed in her face as she stooped over and said, in demanding agony, "GI meeta meeta, meeta meeta," meaning look, look. She was trying to display the bundle to the soldiers who, out from under their helmets, stared past the tips of bayonets, at eyes and faces in the crowd. "They want sergeant," Pong Nam said.

"Sergeant hav-a-no," the Lieutenant said.

Then,

"She can get a indemnity, sir."

It was First Sergeant Cummings who spoke, a sixty four
year old man, tall, lean, his cheeks dry and grey as emery
cloth, with the slumpèd shoulders of a tall man shaped
forever by the trenches in France in WW I. He was the one
who kept the right taut distance swaying between the line of
bayonets and the pressing people, close enough to threaten,
not so faraway as to suggest license but enough away to
appease. Morgan played his game driving in the streets,
Berens played his game doctoring Koreans, and Cummings
was the virtual support of an orphanage. He had no love for
Morgan but he bided his time. He saw that Lieutenant Weems
wasn't hearing the chant of the crowd. The Koreans of the
street were roaring for Morgan. Cummings gave Morgan's
messhall a surprise sanitation inspection two or three times a
month and always managed to find behind the leg of a
refrigerator or somewhere, a small gob of mess. Rather than
be gigged for it, Morgan kept food going from his private
trade into Cummings' orphanage. Weekly Cummings took a
three-quarter truck and bought a huge bag of rice for his kids.
When his men came back with pheasant, duck and even deer
from hunting in the Korean countryside, he shamed them out
of some of the game, for his orphans. He won the hateful
respect of his men at every morning's calisthenics when he
did all that they did. If he punished a man with 75 pushups,
Cummings was stretched out on the ground, facing him,
doing them too.

He was always practical.

"She can get a indemnity," he said.

"Speak as the sergeant says," Lieutenant Weems said to

the resplendent Pong Nam. "Tell them that anybody killed or injured in an accident with an American vehicle can apply for an indemnity. They always get it. About six hundred dollars. Tell her we are very, very sorry." He said it firmly.

Pong Nam, with little shrugs, spoke to the man in the white shirt.

The woman screamed.

"Taksan hwan, mama-san," the Lieutenant said.

The man was more sarcastic than ever. "*Taksan*," he shouted at Weems. It was more money than the man in the white shirt could expect to make at a usual job in a long time.

The angry pressure of the crowd bent the woman almost double over the gate bar. The bundle tumbled out of her arms onto the cinders. Lieutenant Weems flinched. He actually expected the baby to cry out, and was nearly unmanned by rage when only the dirty little brown feet slipped out of the rags. "Oh, my God," somebody said. Cummings gave a quick whisper to his men and the line of bayonets stepped back.

The woman was weeping and reaching over the bar.

"She want pick up baby," Pong Nam said.

Nobody was going to touch the bundle and give it to her.

Cummings jumped lightly forward with his carbine pressed against his chest and urged people back so the woman could duck under the bar. Immediately an angry mass of dirty white clothing and brown faces and brown fists and the smell of street sweat and kim-chi swelled up in the woman's place, as if she'd somehow held it back before now.

Now she stood, a small woman, looking up at the colorful

Pong Nam and the Lieutenant with his .45. The man in the white American shirt was still jammed against the street side of the gate bar, keeping the pain in his thighs tight in his face. The woman cradled the bundle in the crook of her arm and separated the rags with her fingers as if she were about to nurse the baby, and wailed, with an upward heave of her body, at the Lieutenant. "Meeta *meeta*," she said. Lieutenant Weems barely glanced down at the small brown face, among the rags against the woman's breast, with its dead eyes wide open. When he saw the dirty white cloth bound about the woman's breasts, a suffocating fright invaded his gut, of drowning in all the dirt and dirty clothing and the dirty brown bodies. He was hearing for the first time what the crowd was chanting. Morgan. Morgan. He felt himself going faint and he moved slowly for a moment. With a deliberate lack of response, he shouted at the man in the white shirt, "Sergeant hav-a-no."

"Sergeant hav-a-yes," the man said.

He was pointing with outstretched arm.

There was Morgan, in his white judo outfit, with the black belt draped around his neck, just back from the showers, standing with two cooks in white at the corner of his messhall, as many other GIs were standing over the compound watching the action at the gate. Morgan and the cooks saw the man pointing their way and they looked back and forth at each other. Weems' anger went sharp at the man in the white shirt when he saw that he also knew Morgan by sight.

"Sergeant hav-a-yes," the man said.

He whipped his arm and fist in the air.

Koreans crawled and piled under the bar. Cummings was quick with his commands. The line of men with fixed bayonets leaned forward but shifted back a step, then back another step, and another. There were several furious people inside the gate now. Weems backstepped rapidly threatening with his .45, while Cummings levelled his carbine with his left hand grasping the top of the barrel. The space between the two groups stretched in and out violently. Weems fired his .45 over the heads of the crowd.

Counted to three.

Fired again.

Counted to three.

Fired again. Every man and woman, in the streets and in the compound, was standing still when he finished.

The man in the white American shirt bared his chest again. "Kill me. Also kill me." Weems was breathing hard and deep, watching the man. Cummings turned his back to the crowd and made a sharp motion of his hand for Morgan to disappear. Morgan was brisk, as if going back to work, but there was a sort of shrinking among the cooks as they went with him inside the messhall. The Koreans and the soldiers closed to talking distance again, with several Koreans now just inside the gate. "Eye for eye," Pong Nam explained to the Lieutenant, with a bland shrug, "they want sergeant."

"That is not justice," Weems said. "They can't have him."

Near the gate was the residence of the Colonel who

commanded the Engineer Group, a little cottage made of concrete blocks, with a few square yards of imported bluegrass sod, the only grass anywhere on this side of the City of Pusan. The Colonel was behind the screened window of his living room peering at the gate. On the edge of the little lawn stood the whitewashed flagpole, with the Stars and Stripes finding a breeze in the blue sky, more than three stories up, just above the Headquarters building. Koreans out in the street were lofting rocks over the Colonel's cottage at the flag. They misunderstood American vanity, and the GIs merely waited to see if the rocks would be thrown at them.

The energy at the gate milled and pulsed. Lieutenant Weems was saying again to the man in the white shirt, "You people must go through appropriate channels. Your plea will be heard." Then, to Pong Nam, "You have to make them understand that."

4

No one else on the compound was sweating.

"Eye for an eye," Berens exclaimed, clapping his knee, "they want Morgan." The men around him on the steps of the dispensary were excited too, watching the gate, not because of any grudge against Morgan but just because the jump of adrenaline was welcome. "Whoooo-eeeeee," they whistled.

"Let's get closer," Berens said. He was grinning, and then

working his eyes and cheeks to make his glasses comfortable
on his nose. They moved down the asphalt ramp between
the Headquarters building and the flagpole. When the first
rocks thrown by Koreans at the flag clattered down the side
of the Headquarters building, they skipped and whoooo-
eeeeeed back to the dispensary steps. They were all asking
and looking around, "Where's Morgan?"

Morgan heard the chant of the crowd and kept his face
square and restrained but he was nearly jubilant because
now he didn't know what to expect. When Cummings
gestured for him to disappear, he recognized the woman's
baggy pants and understood the bundle in her arms. He was
leading the cooks down the aisle between the empty tables
in the messhall with a smile blazing on his face and
snapping his black belt at a chair.

It was the first and second cooks who made sure how the
other messhall personnel would act. They whistled, stamped
their feet, snapped their fingers, slapped their thighs, crowed,
and the other GIs and Koreans either tried to hide in
absorption in their work or smiled a little timidly. Then a
messenger from the Orderly Room came into the cookhouse
and told Morgan he was to go to the third floor, that is, the
top floor, of the Headquarters building and stay there. A
deuce-and-a-half, with canvas covering, backed up to the
cookhouse door and Morgan, in khakis now, ribbons and all,
climbed over the tailgate into the rear of the truck. The
deuce-and-a-half drove right through the middle of the small
compound, where the Korean rioters could have seen

Morgan if he had walked. Behind the Headquarters building, it backed up to the back door. Morgan was hustled up the stairwell to the third floor into the big sunny drafting room. He was told to stay there until further orders.

The men who worked there were leaning out the windows watching the action. Two men edged apart at one window to let Morgan lean on the sill too. He was keeping his lips tight. Somebody said, guardedly, a couple of windows to his right, "You ought to be impressed, sarge." Morgan's smile was quick and straight as he looked around for the voice but no one was looking at him. He looked back at the street without saying anything.

It was a soft mild May day, blue as the eyes of most of these soldiers when they were babies. The crowd choked the street half the length of the compound. In places, groups of Koreans were hanging onto the fence and shaking it. On the far side of the street, signs and placards and banners were raised above the heads, and a new chant began to rap away, "GI go home." Korean police and their jeeps were nosing into the outskirts of the crowd, not yet trying to clear the street.

"I hope them mother-fucking gooks don't find out you're up here, sarge." The excited conviviality in the drafting room was the same that was straightening every back on the compound. Morgan kept watching and listening to the street.

"Mamasan just wants to make sure she gets her fucking indemnity," a voice said to his left.

"Six hundred dollars is a lot of hwan, boysan."

"That's about—let's see—that's three hundred shortimes."

"She must have stood out in the middle of the street just to make sure. Right, sarge?"

Morgan didn't say anything.

"Oh, shut up," somebody said.

Morgan looked around for the soldier who said shut up. Again no one was looking at him.

5

Everybody at the gate was dark around the collar and under the arms and shiny-faced with sweat. With the bundle crooked in her arm, the woman kept spreading the rags to show the dead child's face to Weems, to Pong Nam, to Cummings, to the man in the white American shirt. Then she walked up sideways between the bayonets and tried to show it to the soldiers who, at Cummings' whispered command, stared straight past her into the mob. She pointed at the little body to show where it had been hit, in the back. "You could smell it," Pfc Levin said later, and it made his gut grind. She wept, sharply, when she saw the soldiers wouldn't look. Pong Nam said to the Lieutenant, "She say sergeant make her run off street. She say sergeant do this all time." Lieutenant Weems wanted badly to shift, from his cold right hand to his left, the .45 that he kept pointed in the air.

"You're accusing the man of manslaughter. This has to be done in court," the Lieutenant said.

"Court no good," the man said.

"Goddamnit," Weems said, "the court *is* good."

"No good."

Lieutenant Weems looked, beseechingly, at Pong Nam. "Why won't he believe me?" Pong Nam shrugged, and gave a big, slow smile. With a drawl, "These people," he said.

"GI court no good," the man said. "Korea court no good."

"We just convicted a soldier for beating up a prostitute a month ago."

"Ahh, prostitute, yes," the man said. "She no prostitute."

"I didn't say she was a prostitute. I said that our courts do render judgments in favor of Koreans too."

Suddenly, out in the middle of the cindered motor pool, the very ground broke open in one place, and a Korean heaved himself up on his elbows, climbing out of the old sewer hole. "Now *that's* exciting," Berens said, on the asphalt ramp by the flagpole. The men around him whistled with the rigid recognition that they might really be carried into this event. Cummings shouted something on the double and four men dashed away with him into the motor pool, while the riot formation spread out leaning toward the gate more tensely. The unarmed Koreans climbed out of the hole one by one and stood up, brushing off cinders and even flashing big smiles, inside the circle of bayonets that closed, stepped back, pulsed, threatened. When no more came out of the old sewer, just now revealed to the Americans, Cummings gestured with his thumb and the smiling invaders from under the ground were herded to the gate, chanting,

"Morgan, Morgan." Cummings posted two men at the hole. Berens was disappointed that it was over so quickly.

"You little ol' mother you," a soldier said, to the woman at the gate. Every GI in the line grinned, and Cummings told them to button their lips, for fear the man in the white American shirt might understand. A GI photographer, taking pictures of the entire crowd, walked the length of the compound fence and then climbed onto the roof of the Colonel's cottage. The pictures would be given to the Korean police. The Colonel, with other officers, was still watching the event through his screened living room window. "There have to be organizers," he had said, and detailed the photographer to take the pictures.

Then, just opposite the messhall, men in the crowd threw blankets and mats onto the fence and across the trough of barbwire at the top, so they could plunge and pile against it, clamber over, and maybe break it down. The Korean police moved fast and in force from all sides into the crowd, threatening with a speaker truck and a jeep mounted with a .50 caliber machinegun, plus other jeeps and trucks for hauling away demonstrators. Rapidly the crowd shrank into a mere huddle around the compound gate. Lieutenant Weems successfully advised the Korean police not to arrest the woman and the man in the white American shirt. The woman saw that they were defeated. She loosed a prolonged scream and stripped away the rags of the bundle and lifted the naked brown dead little boy high in both hands, turning round and round.

There was no one there who did not see it.

Berens was socked coldly in the gut. The dishwasher's smile came to him.

By midafternoon there was the usual jogging traffic of people drawing carts and carrying loads in the street. The woman stayed, sitting outside the compound near the gate against the barbwire, with the bundle wrapped up again in her lap, rocking it and whimpering a little. The man in the white shirt sat with her and kept a hand on her shoulder. Cummings went out the gate and talked with them, but they didn't go away. The woman looked through the doubled barbwire into the compound with the plea in her face that somehow one of the soldiers would do something. Then the Korean police came and took the woman and the man away in a jeep because the Colonel thought that her presence would affect morale.

Berens stammered at the gate wanting to say something to them too, but Cummings came up out of nowhere and took hold of his arm. "It's all took care of, sarge. Now go on to chow." It made Berens feel childish. He stammered with a different indecision, then went to the NCO mess rather than face the dishwasher at the end of the line of tubs.

6

Berens believed that Morgan would be punished in some way. But Morgan was only restricted to the compound

for one week, for his own good, among talk that he would
be transferred, up north, to Inchon, for his own good and
for the good of the company, so everybody could start clean.
Berens felt betrayed to find that even First Sergeant
Cummings did not support the transfer. Morgan was staying
with nothing changed. It was said that the woman did not
even get her indemnity because that would have been an
admission of guilt. When the restriction was lifted, Morgan
was driving back and forth across the city in his jeep again.
Berens hoped that Koreans would ambush him in the streets.
But they didn't. Then Berens thought that Morgan would at
least count himself lucky and not make such a game of
driving again.

It was three weeks later when Berens, on dispensary
errands, found himself jammed with buddies of Morgan and
two cooks in a jeep going to the Station Hospital. It was the
only ride available. The cooks had packages in their laps.
Morgan was driving. Berens sat in the rear and said nothing.
He didn't even know why Morgan was going to the Hospital.
Then, in quick succession, Morgan ran an old man off the
road and stopped abruptly within inches of running over a
spider-man. The old man jumped and just barely reached
the ditch in time staring back into the jeep, as if into the
mouth of a gun, as it went by. He was dressed traditionally
in white, with the black horsehair stovepipe hat and grey
oriental beard. All in the jeep, except Berens and Morgan,
thrashed and laughed and whoooooeeeed through their
teeth. A second later Morgan caught the spider-man in the

middle of the street, and stamped on the brakes just in time. The spider-man stared over the hood at the GIs. "Well, chogi out of the way, mother-fucker," the tall first cook yelled. The spider-man walked on his arms swinging his torso, to the side of the road. Anyone could see that he was shaking. The GIs glanced at Berens' silence, and it gave emphasis to their scare and their bursts of laughter.

It was hard for Berens to do it alone.

When he finished his errands at the Hospital and came up to the jeep for the ride back to the 68th, he said, "Got any little kids in your oven, sarge?" Morgan's smile stayed straight. The others, with different packages in their laps— some exchange had taken place at the hospital—hid their mouths until on the way back Morgan made a gesture of the steering wheel toward a Korean woman with a baby slung in the small of her back—just a gesture, but Morgan's buddies laughed and stamped their feet on the floorboards and looked at Berens. Berens' mouth was stiff, dry. "How does it feel to put the notch of a baby boy in your black belt, sergeant?" Morgan glanced to the side at the rearview mirror. "He's the best fucking mess sergeant in the whole KComZ," said one of Morgan's buddies.

That night Berens was on CQ duty at the dispensary with an ambulance driver. It came time to get some coffee and he was afraid to go to the messhall but he couldn't give into his fear and couldn't let himself not go and couldn't let the ambulance driver go in his place.

Only the first and second cooks and Morgan were in the

cookhouse. No one said anything about all of them having been together in the jeep that afternoon. The tall first cook was chopping onions and didn't look up when Berens asked for some coffee, but instead said that he'd heard a lot about Berens' talk around the compound. Morgan was sitting on a pile of sacks of potatoes, in khakis, with his elbows on his knees. Berens leaned on the edge of the counter with both hands and asked again for coffee. The tall cook, after a moment, nodded at the tub of coffee and Berens lifted the flap of the counter and went into the kitchen area to fill the two canteen cups.

Morgan stood up with his hands on his hips in front of Berens. The second cook was stirring a tub of tomato soup and Berens felt the heat from the field burner on his boots. The second cook asked loudly if Berens had heard the first cook, *what was all that talk Berens had been doing?* Morgan was looking with his smile and his glasses up at him. Berens felt dirtily weak and incompetent, but he couldn't let himself not speak. "You've learned nothing from what you did, sarge," he said to Morgan, nearly dizzy with the dryness of his mouth, "and you ought to be court-martialled. That's my talk." Morgan bumped his chest against Berens. Berens was pushed bump bump stammering backwards. His canteen cups fell and the cooks kicked them bang across the kitchen. He couldn't let himself fight back and he couldn't let himself run or yell. He was pushed by Morgan and the cooks into the storeroom back of the kitchen.

They shut the door. One small bulb hung in the center.

Morgan tripped him backwards, and jumped on top of him
on the concrete floor slapping him back and forth. The cooks
were holding his arms. His glasses were dashed against a stack
of C-ration cans. "Hold it, hold it," Morgan said. He was
testing the blade of a short kitchen knife by shaving the hair
on the back of his wrist. Berens was blindly saying no no and
then he was saying something he himself didn't recognize
about his face.

The first cook mimiced, "Not his face, not his face."

"Listen to the pretty boysan," the second cook said.

"Pull off his clothes," Morgan said.

"Yeah," the cooks said.

Morgan cut the laces and the buckles and jerked off
Berens' boots, pants and briefs. Berens was so cold and slick
with sweat it was hard for them to hang onto him. The cooks
stuffed a towel in his mouth. Morgan flipped the knife so
that it stuck in the door. Then they flipped him over onto his
belly and the cooks held him down each with a knee on a
shoulder and bending an arm up and back. Morgan dipped
lard out of an open can and screwed him in the ass. Berens'
humiliation was complete, he got a hardon and came all over
his belly and shirt and the concrete. "Looky there," said the
second cook.

Then the cooks took turns.

"Not his face," they said, laughing, "not his face."

They turned out the light and closed the door.

He stayed there pressing his cheek on the cool concrete,
whimpering and jerking with small sobs. It was some time

before he got up and found the light and dressed. The cooks
were busy at the counter in the kitchen serving coffee to men
on guard duty when Berens staggered out of the storeroom,
as if trying to stay upright on a heaving surface, his boots
flapping the broken glasses on his face. The cooks smiled
over their shoulders at him. "Why, hello, sarge," they said,
and the men on guard duty laughed because Berens looked
funny and because the cooks were laughing. Morgan was not
there. Then something happened that was always happening
a couple of times every night. The light shrank to a red glow
in the bulbs, the power failed, and everything was dipped in
darkness and outcries. "Catch-ee shortime," the guard duty
men yelled, "catch-ee shortime." The emergency generator
started up by the motor pool. When the lights came on again,
Sergeant Berens was not in the messhall. Four jeeps were
discovered in the motor pool in the morning with their
windshields smashed and their tires flattened.

It was Berens who was transferred, to Inchon, a week later.
First Sergeant Cummings handed him the orders and there
was a lack of expression in Cummings' face. Berens read the
mimeographed orders through his second pair of glasses and
nodded at Cummings. He smiled a lot when Morgan was
nearby, but he talked with only one man. He asked the young
Korean in the PX if he had told the people in the streets
about Morgan. Pong Nam brightened eagerly, silently, the
invitation constant in his face for a long moment. He looked
around and then touched Berens' arm. "Take easy," he said.
"Take easy, sergeant." One evening that week Berens stood

on the edge of the motor pool and watched the line of
dishwashers outside the messhall for a long time.

No one on the compound said goodbye, not even those in
the dispensary whose records he had kept for six months. A
few men near the flagpole took the time to look at him
hunched over on the bench in the back of the three quarter
truck going out the gate. He was hugging his duffel bag
between his knees and squinting back at the compound, as if
everything there were unobtrusive. The last thing he saw was
Pong Nam with his face hidden by the pink parasol in front of
the PX talking to Lieutenant Weems.

7

The faces in the NCO club were sweating. It was a night
in August and First Sergeant Cummings managed to find
himself insulted by Morgan. There was quick laughter and
stamping of feet when Morgan made a comment, that no one
could remember afterward, about food going out of the 68th
to Cummings' orphanage. It had burned down a week before
and most of the kids disappeared into the swarm in the
streets. Cummings rapped his glass on the table and picked
up his coke and asked Morgan to come outside. Morgan said
that it was his pleasure.

They agreed to go to the far side of the motor pool, into
the darkness behind the garage, where, through the big open
doors, torchlights blazed and mechanics worked on two

deuce-and-a-halfs. Cummings sauntered in that direction
with Morgan behind him. Cummings was taking deep slugs
from the coke bottle as he walked, as if he meant to finish the
coke before the fight. "He's trying to psyche Morgan,"
somebody said back at the door of the NCO club, where
most of the sergeants were outside watching. "Morgan will
kill that old bastard, hot goddamn," somebody else said.

Halfway across the grounds of the motor pool, Cummings
belched a big one. He hiked the empty coke bottle in his
hand so that the butt end was out—done just as naturally as
if he were going to palm the bottle into the trash barrel at
the corner of the garage. They were nowhere near the
agreed upon place. He swung around in a haymaker and
the butt of the bottle caught Morgan on the side of the
face and broke his jaw. Morgan screamed. He managed to
give Cummings a hip-toss and Cummings came down on a
tire rim breaking two ribs in his left side. But the pain of the
shattered jaw maddened Morgan so much that Cummings
was able to get on top of him and stay there bashing at his
face with the bottle. Morgan was grabbing at Cummings'
balls and, at the same time, in awful confusion, trying to
protect his face. The other sergeants pulled Cummings off
of him.

Cummings came back from the Station Hospital the next
day with his left side taped up rigidly, while Morgan lay in a
hospital bed with his face in a cast and his jaw wired shut
and tubes in his mouth, for a month. The compound waited
for the meeting between Cummings and Morgan. There was

curiosity about seeing Morgan's face too. But the scars did for Morgan's face what the ribbons did for his chest. "That's a *ba-a-ad* mother-fucker." If they had company business to talk about, Cummings and Morgan stood about six feet apart, not threatening, but always six feet apart. That was all the meeting there was. Morgan kept on driving in the streets of Pusan.

It was winter before Cummings was once again seen stretched out on the ground doing push-ups with a man he'd punished.

THE HICKORY STICK RIDER

The postulate is that I can forgive myself.

As a monk awaiting a vision I had been staying in bed. But with no word from her faraway in New York there was just no more sense staying in bed. I got out of bed. I am not one to depend on grace. The vision would not proffer itself to me, I would take myself to it. I would mount and ride. I walked down the long hall and up the stairs with a grim, determined look. I would do the role by playing the role. The door opened. I stepped out.

At sight of me my faithful hickory stick leaped from long lassitude, wildly prancing over the lawn. This thoughtless eagerness was sadly characteristic. I did not indulge it. I gave him no promising looks. If I indulged him, I *served* him. I yawned. I stretched. I breathed. I whistled. I tapped tunes with my foot. *Thus* I implied to him that *I* would decide when the journey began, *not* he. With doting, slavish antics he tried to win me to his will. So I never, in *no* case, mounted until he, exhausted, wholly accepted that nothing he could express would hasten or change my decision, that nothing but quiescence was for him until *my* moment of decision charged him with purpose, life. Often, however, he went quiet much too fast. This rudimentary cunning played on my pity. But I could not give an inch. I would kill time until the primitive spark of his witless will went out in him.

The night glowed like a cauldron on the clouds above Chicago. For a long while cries of distress had reached me from the Loop. I could *help*. I even permitted myself pride in my talent for giving aid. And a talent wasted is like a woman scorned, a fury inside myself that I could not endure if I passed up a chance to render aid. The cries were such that we must delay our journey at once. First things must be put first, the horse before the cart, with a driver efficiently aiming for kingdom come. I folded my arms to suppress my rising impatience with my inefficiently rebellious hickory stick. I could not let him become aware of my impatience. It would fan that fire of selfish hope in his heart. That *I* knew better than he what *must* be done only burdened me more. He did not want to win, to spill out the driver. Without reins there was no joy of achievement for him. I sensed on the instant when his heart had gone as quiet as a lovely, sleeping slave.

Then, for the first time that fateful night, he received from me an amused, negligent look. Its prospect aroused him. Shed of his shabby, rebellious role, he leaped up. He butted excitedly again and again against the walls of the house, actually trying to kill himself with this incomparable joy that I could give to him, when he wholly knew his place, a joy I

146

could never give myself. I could have wasted my life simply satisfying his whims for satisfying me. Whims! I slight him, I cannot praise him enough! It was not whim, it was a passionately single-minded mission! Whole-hearted loyalty and service! Incommensurable! Paid off only by continuous complicity! The accounts, red and black, his and mine, were in constant flux! If I had let them get out of hand, it could indeed have created in me a crippling guilt, a feverish emotional scramble, this flux of payment and debt! And that was *exactly* how he must labor to master me. Master me by serving me! Thus his service could not be other than subtly and completely selfish. Thus I must maintain ceaseless vigilance. But I must also trust and live and risk my chance!

I leaped from the stoop onto the lawn. I caught the reins and clapped a hand upon his back. It triggered in him a · paroxysm of eager anticipation. We spun wildly round and round, vied freedom and service, tore up petunias and phlox, but there was no getting away for either without the two of us welded together! And *that* was when he expended himself for anything I wished to do. He lunged down the street in purest joy as perfectly aimed as a rifle-shot. Ah, his faithfulness!

We entertained and thereby strengthened ourselves by passing through five fine gaits into a smooth headlong gallop. Not a second wasted we rose above first, second, third, fourth, fifth floor windows, into the zooming stillness of the starry sky. Gigantic yellow and black diagrams of Chicago loomed below. I patted his knotty head. His hard pace leaned out even swifter! There was nothing, *nothing,* he would not do for me! How beautiful, life and its web of reward!

Rendering aid, for instance. Open gratification of this natural ethical urge lacks simplicity. But I, in my maturity, had figured it carefully. One, it is a kind of spiritual bank account building up for a stormy day. Two, it *is* natural, making it misery to ignore. Three, the practice of it furnishes an example that ensures the general welfare. Thus it is, I may say, altogether, *creative security.* We are not among the living unless we further it.

We circled, searching, over the Loop. Cries of distress beat from closeby. We peered down into the canyons of streets that harbored a veritable forest of neon twigs and limbs. But the distress was not down. My steed by instinct rose.

Lightning-like flashes winked on and off the Tribune Tower.

"Oh, horrid man! Oh, help me! *Horrid* man! *Help* me!"

I never imagined or remembered such urgency. I coldly prepared my demeanor.

We reconnoitered wide around the Tower, drawing our circles ever tighter. In each lightning flash the Tower, with a young woman leaning sharply out of its window, leaped out of the darkness. Her mouth was fixed each time in a scream. In each utter darkness she was still screaming. She was lovely beyond belief, radiantly dressed in white, with a cone-shaped peppermint-striped hat based in her blond curls, her eyes big beneath. I must remain objective if I wished to properly render aid. I observed that there was no visible object for her

fear. It was so remarkably mysterious that it started me
jerking nervous looks here and there. I am not easy prey for
fearing phantoms. But the simple physical strength of her
screaming fear, vibrating the very air, had walked into me
like a radio wave. *Courage!* I commanded my heart. My
steed and I rode up magnificently before her window. I
cried,

"I can help you!"

And into a sudden stillness my words fell like cannon
shells. Appalling audacity! I must immediately retrieve myself.
Kindness is the better part of any solution. I said, kindly,

"Won't you let me help you?"

The flash of darkness fell. I cried,

"You *must* let me help!"

In answer, in the next lightning flash, she jumped up into
my very eyes, her round mouth rifling out the endless scream.
I took solid stock of myself. Quite coldly I observed that her
eyes still stared up, but not at me. And her words pierced
clearly into my ears, if not mine into hers.

"He came without anything! He mustn't have me!"

Such a lot of breath she had. So I recognized again that
some are born, shall we say, *constitutionally incapable,* just
as others come into this life with bad heads or bad hearts,
and those so incapable need help, *our* help, *my* help,
whoever or even *whatever* or *wherever* her mysterious
intruder or assailant might be.

"Who?" I cried.

She cried, "Him!"

"Where?"

"Oh, *there*."

It eased me to know that she was well enough to speak a little. Her delicate hand lifted and pointed forward and up at the angle of her trembling hat projecting back. My steed and I with quiet assurance made ready. I said,

"You will soon see. Soon it will all be over, and there will be nothing more for you to worry about."

For the first time her eyes levelled and she at last *saw* her natural benefactors. I straightened. I smiled. I looked kindly upon her. The oncoming darkness fell, full of screaming, intense and pure. I flinched. My hickory stick shied. In the next flash of lightning-like light the window was closed and the blind was being rapidly pulled down past the waist of her dress. Furniture rumbled across the floor. She piled it up against the blinded window, darkening it. Her hoarse cries barely reached me.

"No! No! No!"

I sorrowed. There was no understanding for her except *fear*. Nevertheless, we dutifully humped along up the slope of air indicated by her finger, toward a spire atop a building taller than any other. On the very tip a dark uncanny something was poised against the fiery glow of the city on the clouds. I eased our circles ever closer, closing in. Onto the unknown you impose yourself with the better part of valor. Genially I shouted,

"Hello, there! Hello! May we talk?"

No answer. Soon enough, though, I knew it had human shape, a man, hugging his knees tightly, as near to becoming a ball as the vertebrate spine will allow. I surveyed and summed up his circumstance, to enhance my strategy. His eyes looked out, or *in,* cross-eyed. The pupils were grounded against either side of his nose, with the whites beaming like beacons. His cheeks were sucked inward. The sense of it all must have been an honorable fast made possible by his peculiar position.

On the other hand I could see how a *really* cunning man, after whatever crime he wreaked upon that woman, would choose just such a place to hide. It was apparent that he needed help. And *there* was the secret already. Allay her misery by allaying his! My steed delicately footed flank-wise toward this inexplicably balanced fellow. At a little less than arm's length, I leaned, I peered into his beaming, crossed eyes, so close I could have taken him by the shoulder. I *could,* I thought, have knocked him into a long, bad fall. It is best that we know we think such things. The natural is all we have to work with. Genially again, I spoke to him.

"Are you after the woman down there? Really, now, you love her, don't you?"

With no perceptible movement in the face, "No," he said. I saw that he was reserved. I must deftly draw him out.

"I have loved too," I said. "We can talk."

"Talk," he intoned.

I decided then that I should use the statesman's way of getting things done. Let him feel sainted for helping me!

"It is so easy," I said. "Won't you let me know? Won't you help *me* by telling me?"

"I would not. I could not."

Man of principles! As if I had asked him to betray country or friend!

I proceeded then on the strategy that no secret is satisfying unless another is awed by it. My smile was ingratiating.

"That must really be *some*thing that you are not telling me."

"Perhaps."

Was there the faintest twitch of giving way in his face? I properly bugged out my eyes and let my mouth sag.

"What could it be?"

"Nothing," he said.

"It *could* be nothing."

"Yes," he said.

Nothing! Speech was too common for him. Then I must approach him directly and suddenly! Business-like!

"I am available," I said. "Do you want help?"

"No."

Not need help? Ridiculous! His absurd disdaining thought would make man no more dignified than a lone and prowling beast. I shouted.

"Then what are you doing up here?"

"I'm fucking myself."

He meant it metaphysically, I am sure. Indeed, metaphysically, I could believe what he said.

My teeth bent against my words.

"What have you done to that poor woman?"

"What I wished to do."

Strike him! Bring him to his senses! Uncross his stupid crossed eyes!

"*I have come out of my way and this is all you can say to me?*"

"My business is your business? Listen. I am fucking myself."

The beast was right! Plain flat statement. *My business is your business.* Otherwise there would be no business at all. A matter of point of view, and point of view is always a matter of being somewhere off base. I was closer to base than he. Beast! I had lost the day by losing control of myself. But if *my* self-control could not avail against him, then no one's could.

Down the slope of air, the Tower sprang up in the lightning-like flashes and fell back into darkness again and again. Again the window was open. Again the woman leaned out. Again her hand pointed up, and her red-striped hat projected back. Again,

"Oh, horrid man! Oh, help me!"

It was an old joke, treadmilling forever. And to sum it up the balanced fellow said,

"Fuck you. Fuck her. Fuck all."

Sadly I gazed down. There were many-colored trees of neon light in the canyons below. My glance lit on the ragged clothesline reins in my hand, the reins that held my hickory stick's lowering head, as if they were unrelated to me, as if on a stage. So poorly equipped were we. I could only help those who wished to help themselves, and there was no helping them. I readied the slack in the reins. A lump entered my throat. I did not allow it to master me. I spoke quietly,

"I am sorry for you. I came far out of my way. We could have at least talked. I am sorry. I could have helped."

No words from him. With his view of life there would never be much that he could say.

My steed and I turned suddenly and cantered down the plunging air, resuming our true mission, *to get word from her in New York*. Within hailing distance of the woman in the Tower, we turned toward the Lake. Her eyes drilled like bullets at us! She even stopped screaming. Anger alone could stop it. Selfish and self-defeating! Beasts! She shouted down into the street as if barking an order. Her cry was taken up, relayed from street to street, going south. She gave us one last pert vengeful nod. Then the panic, *true* panic, pierced her face again. We were no longer close enough for her anger at us to allay her fear. Oh, how it wearied me!

But you must not let these hitches that happen in life's plan get the best of you! Joyfully we kept up a headlong pace along the shore of Lake Michigan. I leaned low. My steadfast hickory stick would do and had always done anything for me! I could do that much for him, lessen wind resistance. When I noted that we barely kept pace with the relay of invisible cries far to the right, I sensed urgency. My steed's resources were admirable. We pulled ahead. At Jackson Point we veered over the Lake, over the deep and dangerously open water, to save time. Taking necessary risk proves personal capacity. New York was our unwavering destination.

Sometimes we dipped so low that my feet and the tip of my hickory stick's tail nipped the tops of the waves. Ah, that thrill! Other times we rode expansive heights in the still, starry sky. No night could have been so suited for the journey.

Such air! Such exactly cool, brisk air! Such clear spaces of lake and night to see! And silently together we experienced a high, clear ecstasy.

Then all at once I *knew* that the relay cries had specifically culminated behind us. Aim was levelled on us! *Radar!* Our ecstasy was vulnerable to radar! My steed responded by instinct and flattened into his strongest gallop. *It was because we had tried to help that they aimed on us.* Whistling Nikes rocketed up behind us. I shut my eyes. I steeled myself. We would meet it bravely together. In headlong level flight the Nikes hurtled alongside.

And nothing happened.

I opened one eye. No one could have been more surprised to find that the Nikes had green heads, with large, laughing duck eyes. Oh, the friendship offered by those laughing eyes! I gladdened. I understood. Their eyes winked at us! Ah, that wink! A far flung formation to right and left of winking eyes. Together in perfect drill, we played, we banked, we climbed, we swooped, we raced with deep intent at equal pace down the sky. Without speaking one word, what communication we had! But a purposeful life allows little time. Our play was soon done. The Nikes, squinting grimly humorous in the eyes, banked sharply in a full one hundred and eighty degree turn.

I could not dissuade them. I knew terribly what they were going to do. I hugged the neck of my steed. And at the moment I braced myself, Chicago, all of it, blew up far behind. A great hot wind, roaring with scattered debris, struck perilously, shuddering our flight, and passed. I did not look back. I did not have the malice. I do not enjoy such things. Solemnly black against the stars we rode. And all of a dark continent went by below us, or we went by above it, for it was as if neither were really moving.

It was daylight in New York when we lit on the street that we intended to light on. She sat on the stoop of her apartment house, her lips baby-like open. Her laced-together hands sinuously extended in a yawn and stretch, pushing her skirt down between her spread knees. She patted her chignon. Her cleverly distracted brown eyes welcomed the physical attentions of any man. It was necessary in loving her to keep my understanding, my objectivity. I understood that she did not consciously know what she was doing.

Rearing, prancing, kicking up a beautiful clatter, we reined up before her stoop, while children, filling the street, danced in circles and sang,

> "He's got posies in his hair,
>   What do *we* care?
>   He's got apples up the ass,
>   *That's* his ass,
>   *We* pass."

Every year, less respect.

The love in my look softened upon her. Yet I stayed solemn. She pretended not to notice us yet. She liked me solemn, reserved. I had to maneuver my hickory stick outlandishly back and forth before she cried,

"Oh!"—clasping her hands at her breast, *pretending* it was

not until then that she noticed us—"Oh! Can't I pet him?"

Indeed, she might mean it. She was prone to energetic improprieties.

"Oh, *him*," she cried.

She *intuited* my misunderstanding. She knew, what I had instructed her, that love's deepest communication was attained without words, and communication without words was attained only through arduous practice. She had practiced. She wanted to pet my steed. It seemed correct to use this natural nonsense to get acquainted again. But my hickory stick is not always receptive. I must be on my guard.

Dismounted, I walked toward her in a strange spraddle of my legs. She pressed her cheek on the back of her prayer-wise hands and gazed dotingly upon him. He shyly hung his craning head. Incorrigible cunning!

"I want so to pet him! He is so handsome!"

She often overflowed with this furry, childish sentimentality. She cuddled his faithful head, cooed at him, caressed him, and he flagrantly clacked his tail with awful pleasure on the walk. She was as unpredictable as he. Proof, I had had *no word from her.* And suddenly, seeing behind their eager expressions, a fearful insight unfolded for me. I prepared myself.

"He is so fine!" she exclaimed. "Can't I get on him for just a minute, just one minute?"

Head to toe I trembled. I spoke my first word to her. I said, "Certainly."

I hooked her foot in my hands and helped her mount. She hauled back hard on the reins.

"Whoooooooo-peeeeeeeeee!"

He reared, violently, almost perpendicular. She looked like the child surprised the stove was so mean as to burn its hand. Sharply I chastised him. He settled. I *had* been prepared.

She held the reins too tight. It cut my heart as much as it must have cut him. I would not embarrass him by calling her attention to it. Soon enough I could have words with her. She let go with the cries of a vicious little girl.

"Whee! Whee! Whee!"

Then in his faithful ear she hoarsely imitated the voice of a man. "Go! Go!" As if he were some common martial steed! But go they did, right up the stoop and through the open door and humping hard and fast up the stairs inside. It dawned, with neutral amusement, that she thought she had duped me. I would permit her to enjoy it for awhile. The singing children crowded around the stoop. Alone I surveyed their loud faces.

I whistled.

No answer. Nothing except the sounds of banging back and forth on the stairs, that came not closer, *but were going away*. He *must* come when I whistled. She was strong, very strong for a woman, but not strong enough to hold him back forever. I whistled a blast through my fingers that could *not* be ignored. How could I tell the silent, staring children to go home? What if *she* would not let him return? What if *he* did not want to? Oh, that faithless, frightening thought! He needed ceaseless guidance. I ran headlong into the house. High up the stairs I heard her yelling,

"Go! Go!"

And my own ears heard him clambering up as hard and fast as he could go. Betrayed! And it was bitter, bitter, so bitter it puckered the heart, so bitter that only silence could encompass it!

She could not elude me. I leaped up the stairs. The door on her landing was closed, but not locked. I pulled with both hands. Something strong and elastic held it. Around the edge I saw *her*, heels dug in, head down between her outstretched arms, hanging on. The door came to a stand-still. I could not apply all my strength. I let go. The door crashed closed. Something shrieked inside. I shucked off my clothes. Now I could apply *all* my strength. I let loose a yell and leaped. I grabbed the knob and planted my feet on the wall next to it. As barbells are lifted I pulled the door open steadily. Around the edge I saw *her* again, her lips hard set, an absolutely righteously angry look on me. She let go. I was smashed by the door against the wall. I could not forgive her. But it did show presence of mind, *if* you sympathize with her desire. Nevertheless, the door was successfully opened. Bruised, benumbed, I walked in.

All rooms dark. All silent. I whistled. Faithless! Betrayed! I listened for hidden breathing at closets and under beds. No breathing. Not even my own, until I realized that I was of course purposely holding my breath, *purposely* so not the slightest sound could slip by. Rooms. Many more rooms than I remembered. My bare feet dragged in clothes on the floor. Just like her to vex me by keeping an ill house. Her way of

telling the world that she was herself and not to be confused
with the desires however decent, of anyone else. What some
won't do to retain their vengeful identity! Yet all the rooms
were familiar. How could they be so dark, so still? Singing!
Soft and lovely! I made my way around furniture and
through rooms and halls with *caution* and *patience* and
courage. At times I waded in clothing up to my knees.
Stepping on a button with your big toe in the dark is
unspeakable! An incredible mess! Down a long hall at last I
saw a door, diagrammed in streaming yellow light.

> "O, he comes to me,
> He's a king to me,
> Brings a rose for me,
> *So* big to me . . ."

My hands felt absurdly bare of stems, petals, and thorns.
The busied mind is hard to put to remember roses.

The kitchen blazed with white light when I peeked in. She
was washing dishes. She was singing. The door jammed
against a chair, a difficult opening. Her smile welcomed me,
footing sideways in. Not once did she stop singing. Singing to
me as lovers do in the musical shows. Such staginess is
squirmy. I maneuvered to sit in my place at the kitchen table.
I composed myself. I could wait.

My faithless hickory stick cowered in the corner near the
garbage can. One sharp disdainful look from me and he
fainted to the floor. I did not look at him again. I rested my
arm calmly on the table. I confronted her singing. My muscles

squirmed against the chair. My hickory stick violently
knocked his head back and forth, punishing himself, pleading
forgiveness. But it could not be that easy. He was disgraced.
I was betrayed. Public display only made it more bitter. I did
not look at him.

She was not going to stop singing, or washing dishes either,
even if she had to put the dishes back in the sink and start
all over again! I tried to think of an adequate interruption.
Something I meant from the heart. Those are the only things
to say. I scratched my head. I struggled for the words. I
adjusted myself in the chair. I said,

"Forgive me!"

I farted. That is fate, a fart that happens in a man's most
holy moment, a reminder of his low-born mortality. She
pretended not to notice. She went on singing and washing
those everlasting dishes. Horribly I farted again.

"Forgive me!"

Arms immersed to the elbows, she stopped with astonished,
open lips and stared at me.

In the stillness I said more loudly than I wished,

"Why has there been no word from you?"

So slowly, so coyly, so sadly, her eyes directed me to the
kitchen table. Urgently I said,

"What? What?"

With a sly look she avoided me, and began that infernal
singing again. On the table a letter lay at my fingertips,
sealed, white with bright red ordinary stamps. I had to bend
very close, my nose against it. It was addressed to me. That

was *just* the kind of thing that she would do, write a letter to a man standing right before her. Displaying no unseemly haste, I opened it.

"Dearest,
"It has been so very long and we
are so very faraway ——"

I loved her! I could read no more! I cried out, "You must speak to me! You must forgive me!"

I sprang. My sole intention was to take her in my arms, hug her, kiss her, love her, my *sole* intention. And I *would* have taken her in my arms too if my hickory stick had not intervened. He dashed. He got between my legs. He thoroughly tripped me up. He sent me sprawling against the garbage can. Doubly betrayed! Nothing, *nothing*, could assuage this pain!

The light was out. That terrible noise was her screaming, I realized. Feet went swiftly pattering down the hall. A window heaved open. Sounds of the street invaded the house. Unmistakably it was her voice that yelled, *"Help!"* I would not fail myself, I ran to render aid. My hickory stick clattered in close pursuit.

It was bright in the furthest room. She was not there. The window to the fire escape was open. The shade bellied on the breeze. She had jumped! She lay dead in the street! That accounted for the mounting clamor. The grief I felt could not face walking to the window. My steed lunged past me. He leaped through that fateful window onto the fire escape. He went clapping down the steel steps. No time for grief! I had to go after him! From faraway down the hall in the kitchen her song came to me,

> "Brings a rose for me,
>   So big to me . . ."

How was she still in the kitchen? In emergencies, suspicion is a waste of time. So I must go to her! I must see if she was unharmed! Plead with her! But no time, no time! I must first catch my reckless, runaway hickory stick!

I vaulted through the window and onto the fire escape. I stood up in brightest day. The steel grill coldly marked the bottoms of my feet. I shaded my eyes and peered around. Some of the rollicking children below looked up. And *there* he was, my unregenerate hickory stick, halfway down, sneaking in and out of the mazed fire escape steps. My feet skipped one step after another down in fast pursuit. Above me someone screamed, *"Help!"*

It stopped me as if a shepherd's crook hooked my neck. It flung me against the rail. I had to go back and give aid! I *had* to go on and catch my dangerous steed! Oh, fear! Oh, terrible doubt, dilemma, and fear! But it was *her,* leaning from the window, shamelessly showing the cleft in her bosom, shouting, but enunciating clearly,

"Officer! Officer! He came here with nothing on! Without anything on at all!"

"That's not quite true, Officer."

My essential consciousness had detached itself and drifted

far above into the sky, looking down on the city and us. It heard her and me proposing contrary cases.

"He *lies*, Officer."

"Not exactly, sir."

"Lies! Lies! *Lies!*"

I had exactly in mind what was her complicity and what was mine. If we got heated up, in all reverence, we could never detail the crucial Truth.

"You see, Officer," I endeavored.

"Don't you listen to him, Officer! Don't you dare!"

"Officer!" I cried.

"*Lies!*"

"Not exactly."

"*Lies!* A horrible man! Nothing on at all! *That* is exactly the way it was. Officer!"

"But don't you see, sir. It was this way. We both."

"Lies! Lies! Lies! Lies! Lies! Lies!"

To the drumbeat cadence of her shouting Truth was marched to death. My drifted away self rejoined. No longer would I try to outshout her. I could not forgive her. I could not expect forgiveness from her. I was even convinced that she shouted *help* simply to distract me, for she delighted in frustrating the decent, responsible, objective act. But I could not reflect! No time, no time to reflect! I cried to the policeman standing fat and relaxed at the foot of the fire escape,

"Catch him!"

The cop was very kind. He collared my hickory stick the

second he cleared the bottom step. My steed at once launched into a vicious struggle to break free. Breathless I reached the sidewalk and took the reins. He became sullenly docile.

At last I had found cooperation! "Thank you!" I said to the cop.

My shame, my faithlessness, writhed and tangled himself between my legs, dumbly pleading with me. I kicked him off without glancing down.

"Officer! Everyone knows he's a liar! Take him away! I'll press the charges!"

Looking up through the fire escape, through the bright bars of sun on the latticed steel, I saw her angry face and her shaking fist. So many words she used in accusing me; hardly one had she said in loving me.

The policeman's face, I noticed, was rigid, red. Fat, he fitted into his uniform as the stretched rubber fits round the pressure in a balloon. His lips did not move when he talked. *That* was how calm and self-possessed he was. "Be quiet, now," he said to her. Her lips clamped shut, biting a word in two. Her eyes sparked hate. It saddened me.

The officer took my arms. "You will have to come with me."

"Of course. It is your duty."

We were in strict, true agreement! It seldom happens! I felt warmth and life flowing into me.

It was not possible to bring off a good farewell with her. Her face only responded red and resentfully righteous.

The cop held me by the bicep at arm's length. As if I were something you had to hold at arm's length! But I did not question him. I wished to maintain our true agreement. My hickory stick rambled along on my right side. And the street with prayer-wise children dividing into an aisle before us stretched out endlessly, endlessly narrowing.

"You blew up Chicago," the Officer said.

"No. *I* did not. *You* know I did not."

"There's no getting around it. We know the relation."

There was a form to keep up, look them straight in the eyes and say no. I said.

"*No.*"

"No? At the end of this street, when we get there, is the jail, the court, the electric chair."

"I don't think you would lie to me."

He said, "You can count on that."

Firm agreement! And when I remembered them, I did feel sorry for the young woman in the Tower and the balanced man. No agreement there!

My hickory stick dolefully knocked his head against my thigh. He pleaded. He needed help. *I* could help. So I patted his head, and it did ease him, my forgiveness, and he capered a little. I felt an increasing, tender sorrow, we had gone through so much together.

"We are afraid you will blow up New York."

"*No,*" I said.

He fairly sighed with relief. I was glad to ease him too. But whistling, high up, came fast from behind. A few of the duck-headed Nikes alone escaped to save us. I did not turn my head. I would not betray them. We held the same lovely, wordless communication.

I gave my steed another affectionate pat. Forgiven, he followed in peaceable joy at heel. But it did not ease *me*. If he had had the intelligence, first requisite, I would have asked him to forgive me. It was then that I considered *that I could forgive myself*. *I* needed help. *I* could help.

I recounted rapidly. The whistling overhead gained closer and closer. We would never get to the end of that endless street, never get to the jail, the court, the electric chair. No need. *I* supplanted them. I had helped all I could. I had offered more than most. I *could* forgive myself.

The calm and blissful light came into me, filling me. I *am* forgiven.

My shoulders are straight. A strong smile is on my face.

EENIE MEENIE MINIE MO

The old black was just about the first thing I saw when I woke up every morning that fall. I'd snuggle on my side and look over the foot of my brother's bed—dew shimmered rosily in the corners of the windowpane—across three fields to where the negro moved along the dirt lane fence, like something shuffled along on wires, until our woodpile hid him. I first saw him in town a couple of years before when he was talking, easily enough, in front of the bank with Sheriff Walt Jeffries. I never even wondered until that fall why the black's two kids didn't go to school with us. They were the only colored family in town. They didn't go to school anywhere.

Every night now I made up a story about me and the quick country girl, Patty, who sat across the aisle from me in the sixth grade. The story drove right through me and ended with me rescuing Patty from a burning house. When I woke up, I was watching the black move along the lane fence.

"Michael, rise and shine! Timmy, up with you!"

"Don't step on my plane, mom!"

"Don't leave your plane on the floor to be stepped on!"

She smacked Timmy's bottom under the covers. My brother was hard to get up.

I beat him into the kitchen. The sunny blue burst of morning glories waved around outside the white windowsill of the breakfast nook. A bowl of oatmeal, a half of grapefruit, a couple of slices of bacon, cinnamon toast, a glass of milk, and a Wheaties box. "Eat your oatmeal, Michael."

Every morning.

"Aww-w, mom."

Dad cleared his throat in the living room. "Eat your oatmeal, Michael."

"You eat your oatmeal," Mom said, "and then you can eat your Wheaties." Oatmeal slowed me down getting boxtops and another balsa plane that Jack Armstrong was giving me the chance to get on the back of the Wheaties box.

"Put raisins on it," Mom said.

Every morning.

But when I shook the raisins onto the oatmeal, it was good.

Timmy came sulking into the kitchen and turned with his back to Mom. "Aww-w, I cain't get it," he said, and she flipped the overall gallus over his shoulder and hooked it. I ate fast because I wanted to ask Dad something while Timmy was still eating.

I braced myself with my elbows on the arm of Dad's chair getting up my nerve and pretending to read the war news in the St. Louis Globe-Democrat on top of his students' history papers in his lap. I liked the way he smelled of cigars. My dominoes were still messed over the cold concrete apron of the fireplace. He had read the story of Little Black Sambo to Timmy after we'd played dominoes the night before, and I pretended that I was too old for the story but I kept wondering about the black's two kids. I did, before I rescued Patty from the burning house that night, make a tiger go so fast round and round a tree that he turned into pancake batter.

"Dad, how come there're niggers?"

He looked at me with a sort of pleading look behind his glasses. "There just are," he said, "Negroes."

"They come from Africa, they were slaves, and Lincoln set them free. Dad, can I have a nickel?"

He went hunh with that hesitation that meant he wanted to give it to me but suspected it wasn't the right thing to do. "It's not Saturday, Michael."

My allowance came on Saturday. My allowance was a nickel.

"It's Thursday," I said. "It's almost Saturday."

"What do you want the nickel for?"

"I want it, dad. All the kids got nickels," I said.

I wanted the nickel to buy a few more torpedoes. I had a cardboard box full of firecrackers, rockets, roman candles, and sparklers hoarded from 10 cents an hour I made digging potatoes for Perkinses. I had a gallon bucket of kerosene with cattails soaking in it too on the back porch. I thought of it as my arsenal.

"You have your homework done?"

"It don't take no time, dad."

Mom was in the doorway with her arms folded. She was a nuisance whenever it came to money. "It's not Saturday. *Jerry*, what are you doing?" I could tell Dad was just starting to reach into his pocket.

"I want a nickel too!" Timmy cried.

"See there!" Mom said.

"I'm older! I ought to get a dime every Saturday!" I cried. We both got nickels.

"Jerry, for heavens sake," Mom said. Then, "Michael Dannhauser," her voice rose, "when are you going to clean up those dominoes?"

2

My brother and I headed across town for school with our dinner buckets, picking up friends along the way. It was just the beginning of October, with a hazy golden roar high in the trees. At the downtown corner the black was sweeping off the sidewalk in front of Kinder's grocery. He was soft and loose and dusty.

Junior Charles was chewing tar and he pulled off some for me. Junior was barefoot, and had a cigar box with a garter snake in it. Billy Petersen had a letter in the bib pocket of his overalls from his dad who was a sergeant in the mountain troops in Italy. We saw with our own eyes the secret APO number on the envelope and asked Billy if his dad told him anything about the war. "Naw," Billy said. He was tearing apart a grasshopper a leg and a wing at a time and the brown juice was working out of the grasshopper's mouth and smearing over his hands. "That's poison," Larry Dickinson said, trying to scare Billy. Then Larry started kidding me about Patty.

"She's a girl," I said, in my flattest voice.

"You bet your bottom dollar she's a girl," Larry said. "Ask Russell." Patty was a year and a half older than me. She was my comrade inside the school in the sixth grade, but outside, the eighth grade boys traipsed after and frisked around her, with Russell Sutherland always right beside her.

"Bet you cain't tell me where niggers come from," I said.

"Niggers come outa little black holes," Larry said.

"They come here on slave ships from Africa," I said. "Lincoln set them free with the Emancipation Proclamation in 1863."

I was called Michael and never called by a nickname except when someone wanted to get under my skin and then they called me Big Words. Now Larry called me Big Words.

I shot it right at him.

"The Emancipatoriness of Lincoln's reconstructional attitude of statesmanship," I said. "It's too bad that he died." Larry even thought that I knew what I was talking about.

He got uncomfortable and moved ahead throwing a softball in the air and catching it. He farted, loud. "Shitfire and save matches!" he yelled.

I farted. "Remember Pearl Harbor!" I yelled.

"Join the Navy and see the world!" Billy said.

Then Junior Charles farted. He yelled, "Buy War Bonds! Save Scrap Iron!"

I yelled, "Uncle Sam needs you!"

Timmy and Al Suter got the silly grins of little kids that want to make you think they know what you're talking about. We all laughed.

We passed the bank, the pool hall, the Ford Garage, the newspaper office, and then the clapboard Congregational Church. Reverend Harkness smelled with a smell that grownups couldn't smell. I smelled it. My brother smelled it. But Mom and Dad got angry if we complained about the smell that drove us crazy and whimpering if we had to stay near him. I thought the smell came out of the mole on his right cheek.

He was closing the church doors, with hymnals bunched under his arm. I crossed to the other side of the street and walked along the curb keeping my balance.

"How are you today, Michael?"

"O.k.," I said. "We're going to school." I said it loudly, with the piece of tar I was chewing jammed in my cheek.

"Oh, I see." He was smiling.

The black swept the church every Monday morning. I'd seen Reverend Harkness give him a dollar. I thought maybe the black could smell him since my parents couldn't. I wondered if the black went to any church.

I had asked once, "Why don't he want to be with his own people?"

"They say he killed somebody in Jeff City," Larry said. "He couldn't stay around there 'less he get killed hisself."

"Why didn't they put him in jail?"

"They couldn't prove nothing, dumbbell."

"There lots of niggers in Jeff City," I said. "Who says he killed somebody?"

"Curiosity killed the cat, Big Words. The Sheriff says it, dumbbell."

My dad said the Sheriff thought maybe the nigger killed somebody. If you ever saw them together you'd swear that the Sheriff was the nigger's only friend in town.

3

It was good to come into the large, loud room of the sixth, seventh and eighth grades, lighted by tall, clean windows all around. I was excited expecting the story of the exploding sun in science that day. "Let me see it, Michael." Patty wanted to see my new slingshot that I'd made yesterday out of the fork of an oak, and inner tube rubber strips, with a shoe tongue for a pocket. "I kilt a sparrow yesterday. With a marble," I said. "A English sparrow, not a song sparrow."

Science in the sixth grade came just before recess that morning.

Mr. Herman read through the lesson about the sun exploding and all the whirling hot masses cooling down and becoming Mercury, and Venus, and Earth, and Mars, and all the other planets. It was as good as Captain Blood. Then he

put his finger in the book and looked out over the class with
the sort of silence that meant something was wrong.

"I hope none of you children believe that."

I didn't know what he meant.

"I hope none of you children believe that," he said.

His solemnity became terrible.

"I believe the Bible," Judy Moss said.

"What does the Bible tell us?" Mr. Herman said.

Judy told him what the Bible told us about the Creation.

"That's right," Mr. Herman said.

Then Mr. Herman came up to Junior Charles in the front seat
of my row. Junior had his garter snake in the cigar box inside
his desk. "Do you believe the story in this book, Junior? Or
do you believe the Bible?" Junior Charles was let to run loose
and barefoot by his family, and sometimes came to school
with no shirt on, only overalls, and big staring freckles on his
shoulders. Junior had to sneak and steal the things he
wanted. He even crawled down a ventilator shaft to get into
the picture show above Kinder's grocery every Saturday night.
Junior Charles got mostly Ds and Fs. Junior Charles was
astonished that his answer could be important to Mr.
Herman. "I don't disbelieve in the Bible, Mr. Herman." Junior
giggled. I stared at Mr. Herman as if he'd become the column
of a tornado to wipe out this story. One after another they
all said the Bible was right and the exploding sun
was wrong. Now Mr. Herman's finger and big smile
pointed at me.

"I think the story of the exploding sun is right, Mr.

Herman." Mr. Herman waited as if for a little skid in time to straighten out. "I didn't hear you, son."

"I said I think the story of the exploding sun is right, Mr. Herman." Now the seventh and eighth grades were watching the sixth grade, and Patty was watching me. They all waited because Mr. Herman used the razor strop, the hickory switch, the yardstick, and the slap of his hand in a way that was still remembered and bragged about by men going into the army and having families of their own.

"You disbelieve in the Bible," Mr. Herman said.

"I didn't say I disbelieved in the Bible, Mr. Herman. I said I believe in the story of the exploding sun." There were good stories in the Bible. My dad made a slingshot, four strings and a pocket, that he said was the kind that David used and the kind that Dad himself used. I could never make it work. I used my forked stick with inner tube rubber bands and killed Goliath anyway. "I don't believe the story in the Bible about the creation of the world is the way it happened, Mr. Herman."

Junior Charles whinnied and drummed the top of his desk.

"Quiet there," Mr. Herman said.

"Do you believe in the cave-men or in Adam and Eve?"

"I believe Adam and Eve was cave-men," I said.

"Do you go to Sunday School?"

"Congregational Church," I said.

"And you disbelieve in the Bible?"

"There stories that are stories and there stories about how things happen. Cain't you see, Mr. Herman?"

Mr. Herman turned suddenly to Patty across the aisle.

"I believe in the story of the exploding sun, Mr. Herman." Pride and pleasure flooded through me. Patty was actually worth rescuing from a burning house.

Judy Moss started crying. "You *know* you're going to hell and burn, Michael. The both of you."

That she even used the word hell that way caused silence in the room.

"Do you go to Sunday School, Patty?"

"Sometimes. We live way out on Grey's Creek, Mr. Herman."

"Do you read the Bible sometimes?"

"My Ma reads it sometimes."

"You believe your ancestors were cave-men?"

She said, "Some of them are about that bad." Even Mr. Herman smiled.

"*Why,*" he said, "do you believe in the exploding sun?"

She glanced at me before she leaned forward and said, "I got a rock at home you can see where the fern was in it, Mr. Herman."

But Patty and I were outvoted 22 to 2. Mr. Herman had the votes, and now he had the question, the right question.

He was looking at me.

"Do you believe in God?"

It had never occurred to me that that had anything to do with it. That was exactly what Patty asked him. "What's that got to do with it, Mr. Herman?" Mr. Herman was paused midway in the aisle. I recognized this as a deadly serious

question. I was sure that I believed in God and I couldn't see
that it was any matter when the important thing was to save
this story that was as good as Captain Blood.

"Yes," I said, "I believe in God."

Judy Moss hit her desk. "How can you, Michael?"

"The Bible is God's Word, Michael," Mr. Herman said. He
was serious now. "Do you believe in God, Patty?"

"Yes, I do, Mr. Herman, but—"

I started talking. "No, Mr. Herman," I said, "I believe the
story of the exploding sun is right—" and I was possessed by
a moment of sixth grade statesmanship "—but I believe God
caused the sun to explode and then caused everything else
that happened." Patty grinned and Patty tossed her hair and
it was tossed for me. "Yes, it happened the way the story says
it happened, but God caused it to happen," I said.

Mr. Herman waited a second watching me and then he
pointed into the seventh grade one two three four five six
seven and the answers came back the Bible the Bible the
Bible the Bible the Bible, all the way through the seventh
grade. Billy Petersen laughed as if I were the dumbest boy
he knew and said, "The Bible." Larry Dickinson wagged his
head as if my follies were without end. "The Bible," he said.

"We settled all that last year," a seventh grade girl said,
"and it didn't take any time at all," as if that made them
much smarter than the sixth grade.

Russell Sutherland was leaning over his desk in the very
back corner of the eighth grade and doodling with hard
strokes on a pad of yellow paper. He always wore a soft

brown suede jacket zipped halfway up that glowed all fuzzy with sunlight. He didn't see Mr. Herman point at him.

"Russell," Mr. Herman said.

Russell looked up. "I believe in the exploding sun," he said.

Mr. Herman became the storm standing still again.

"You changed your mind," he said.

"I changed my mind," Russell said.

That changed the faces of Larry and Billy.

Russell was the oldest boy in the room, fifteen, the easiest and the most handsome. It was a mark of how pretty Patty was that he paid so much attention to her. I never could help liking him, but I didn't like it that he had changed his mind. "You'll change your mind back when you get in a foxhole, Russell Sutherland," Mr. Herman said.

"Maybe," Russell said.

I said, "*Remember Pearl Harbor!*" I timed it just right. There was a lot of laughing.

"If it was a election," the same seventh grade girl said, "it'd all be settled now."

"Let's vote on it, Mr. Herman," Judy said.

Mr. Herman did not seem to notice her.

"I'm not running for President," I said. Patty laughed.

"Anybody can be President," she said, "if they're borned in this country."

Mr. Herman turned to me. "You believe that God caused it?"

"Yes," I said.

He turned to Patty. "Yes," she said.

He looked across the room. "Sure," Russell said.

Mr. Herman gave the science assignment for the next day to the sixth grade, about stars. The exploding sun was a part of our coming year.

Mr. Herman took the bell off his desk and started ringing it out in the hall, it was recess time. I banged my dinner bucket on my desk and took out a big yellow apple. "Want half?"

"O.k.," Patty said.

I cut the apple in half on my desk with my jackknife. We drifted eagerly out the door eating the halves, chattering all cold and hot. Russell stayed back. Russell didn't make a move toward her. Lower grade girls were playing jacks on the steps. Patty hopped off the bottom step into the hopskotch and went through it perfectly and back and threw her head down with her hair and long green ribbon flying before me. She was laughing. I was laughing.

Then the girls went with Miss Dakeman who was carrying a volleyball under her arm and pursing her lips to her whistle. The boys in our room went with Mr. Herman to play football. He suddenly turned and passed the football to me and it rumbled back and forth in my arms but I caught it.

"You're going to get your bottom tanned," Larry sang.

We didn't have time except for only a few plays at recess. Russell Sutherland stayed in back of the privy with another country boy—smoking, I imagine. It was the last play when Mr. Herman looked at the watch in his pocket and blew his whistle. Creeper Wilson broke loose running with the ball even though everybody was walking off the field. I ran after him hard and harder and I was catching up. The tackle was thunderous to me and the ground was hard.

Even Creeper said quietly that it was a good tackle.

Everyone said it that quietly and looked at me.

Patty and I ate dinner together on the merry-go-round pushing it slowly with our feet along with a lot of other boys and girls. I was frightened at the kidding I was going to get for it. She talked about her rock where you could see that a fern had been in it. When she put on lipstick after eating, it started a jitter in my belly. Sure enough Mr. Herman looked out over the sixth grade after the noon hour and everyone knew something was wrong. He slanted down the aisle tugging an endless white handkerchief out of his back pocket. He caught the back of Patty's head with one hand and muffled her face in the handkerchief and wiped off the lipstick. A cold feeling smoothed through my belly and legs.

Russell Sutherland was studying hard over his desk.

I was a couple of empty feet away from her, and she did not ask anyone for help with her eyes. The rest of the afternoon I couldn't help looking at Mr. Herman's back pocket stuffed with the handkerchief with Patty's lipstick on it.

It was three-thirty when school was out. Soon the old black would sweep out our classroom. I wondered if he ever lifted the top of my desk.

I killed time on the steps and watched Patty get on the big

yellow country bus and Russell too. But Russell sometimes drove to school in his family's Ford pickup.

"I'll bring you the rock," she said.

4

I was supposed to see my brother Timmy home but I didn't want to and he didn't want me to either. I went through town with Billy Petersen taking turns using my slingshot and making rooftops flutter with sparrows and starlings. Billy Petersen was the meanest boy I knew. Billy would stick a firecracker up a dog's ass, and once he soaked a cat in gasoline and burned down Suter's barn. Billy would go out with his BB gun and shoot birds nobody was supposed to shoot—bluebirds, robins, song sparrows, cardinals, wild canaries, red-headed woodpeckers, thrushes, bluejays, red-winged blackbirds. The incredible string of birds that he'd bring back would anger and scare me, he was so calm about it. There was a methodical something in everything Billy did. If he caught a sparrow in a barn or a chicken house, he could experiment all afternoon in ways of killing it slowly, a feather a wing a leg at a time.

I told him you can't eat sparrows and starlings. Billy said he'd seen a bullfrog big enough to eat in the pond in the pasture behind his house. I said let's go. I forgot all about the torpedoes I was going to buy with the nickel and went straight home and got my BB gun and skedaddled before

Mom could come out of the bathroom and put me to work.

The best thing about that bullfrog was that he was big enough to eat. Froglegs. The worst thing about him was that he could nudge his head up among the black mud lumps without making ripples. We followed him around and around the pond taking turns with my BB gun. We had to keep an eye on the whole pond. It must have been fifty times that we hit him with BBs. "He'll float up when he's killed," Billy said. I was worried that he might sink, all those BBs. It got so worrisome I thought that grownup stealth was needed, so I crawled out into the pasture on my belly and elbows and then crawled back toward the pond in the general direction of the bullfrog, with Billy crouched on the other side of the pond signalling me with his hands. The bullfrog was there by a mud hump with just one tall eye above water. I moved the BB gun slowly to my shoulder. I aimed right, and I pulled the trigger right, and I hit him right in the head. "I hit him right in the head, Billy! I hit him right in the head! I killed him, I killed him!"

"He come up?" Billy asked, coming around the pond to me.

"He's sinking," I said.

I started poking with a stick where the bullfrog disappeared. It was dreary.

"There he is," I said. I pointed at the bullfrog's head out in the middle of the pond.

"My turn," Billy said.

We stalked him until the water shimmered a black mirror.

EENIE MEENIE MINIE MO

It was sundown, and cowbells and cows were hunching around the shed at the upper end of the pasture near the college where Dad taught. The nigger was up there driving the Humphreys' cows into the shed for milking. Every mud hump in the pond was dead black. Pretty soon it would be too dark to shoot. Now Billy stood right over the bullfrog's head poking above water. That frog was never so dumb for me. Billy aimed so I thought he would never shoot and there was a pent-up yell in me. He shot and the bullfrog just rolled over next to a mud hump with his white belly turning up. I grabbed him out of the water lest he come alive again and held him by one webbed foot up high and his head swung down to my eyes. I jumped and shrieked and yelled. Billy tried to be calm the way the grownup hunters were. That bullfrog was full as a beanbag with BBs under his skin. "Let's cook him on a fire outside," I said. "Let's go and ask our moms."

Billy went with me, and I went with Billy to ask our moms. It always seemed to work better that way.

Mom clapped her hands. "My stars alive!" That was good to hear when she opened the screen door and there I was holding up the bullfrog. It turned out Reverend Harkness was there for supper. Billy and I had to go into the living room and show the frog to him.

"How nice, Michael," Reverend Harkness said. "And you killed him all by yourself."

I said, "All by our own selves."

Billy said, "I shot him."

I said, "Billy shot him the last time. We both shot him hundreds of times." I was staying back out of range of the smell that came from Reverend Harkness and trying to make my eyes move away from the mole on his cheek near his mouth. Dad shifted in his chair, cleared his throat, and told me the frog might drip on the carpet. Mom asked me where Timmy was. I said aww-w Mom I don't know, he's o.k. She gave us some cornbread and two apples and grease and cornmeal in waxpaper for frying the froglegs. "You hear me now about getting home, Michael Dannhauser."

Billy's mom said o.k. too as if there was nothing good to be expected of us anyway.

"Something's dead in your house," Billy said.

I didn't say anything. He didn't go to the Congregational Church.

Billy and I ran into the pasture behind his house and started making the fire by the pond. I tried striking a piece of flint on the big blade of my jackknife but I could hardly get the sparks to fall into the dry grass that I'd wadded up. When they did, I'd get a thin line of smoke and it would go out. I pointed out a couple of charred spots in the dry grass but Billy wasn't impressed and struck a stick match—he had to try three times—by dragging it on the seat of his overalls.

I stood three stones on the edge of the fire so the skillet could rest on it and wiped the grease out of the waxpaper into the skillet. Then I took the package of cornmeal and rolled the froglegs in it and put the hindlegs and front legs in the pan. We thought there might be a little to eat on the front legs too. I said, "Where do bullfrogs go in winter?"

Billy didn't say anything, pretending he didn't hear me. "They burrow in the mud on the bottom and hibernate," I said, "so they won't freeze." He should have listened in school.

"Big Words," he said.

Froglegs are supposed to have a wonderful taste, a little like chicken and a little like fish. We turned them with a twig every two seconds. "When are they done?" I asked.

"When they're brown," Billy said. "Daniel Boone eat everything he shot," Billy said.

"Daniel Boone shot what he wanted to eat," I said.

"That's what I meant."

"Then whyn't you say what you meant?"

Billy said it was his shot that killed the frog so he should have both hindlegs and I should have the front legs. I told him it was my BB gun and I'd hit the bullfrog many times too and I was the one that saw the frog the last time. He ate one hindleg and one front leg, and I ate one hindleg and one front leg. That was a satisfied and powerful feeling looking up at a few stars coming out and sucking the last bit of meat off the bones.

"You think Mr. Herman's going to whip me?" It was the only way that I thought Billy might give some appreciation for what I'd done that morning.

"You think you're awful smart," he said.

I was waiting for the Big Dipper to come up so I could trace the handle and find the North Star. About this time the nigger would be going up the path through Ransoms' yard after getting Humphreys' cows and driving them into the shed and milking them. He would be moving around the silence of everyone on Ransoms' porch. He'd shift something from under his arm and touch his hat and give a shuffle of greeting. Mr. Ransom would rock a little in his chair and then say something too.

> "Eenie, meenie, minie, mo
> Catch old Big Words by the toe.
> If he hollers make him pay
> Fifty dollars every day."

I pretended harder than ever that I wasn't hearing Billy. "Billy, you think all niggers is poor?"

"Niggers eat coon meat all the time," Billy said.

"Possum, too," I said.

"Sweet taters," Billy said. "Niggers don't like things brought at the store."

We hauled ourselves to our feet and faced the sound of a cowbell and the gentle sound of a cow drinking on the other side of the pond. We pissed on the fire to put it out. I pissed longer than Billy, and the steaming smell was satisfying, with little streaks of stars wobbling in the dark pond.

5

Billy left the skillet in the grass by the backsteps for his mom to find in the morning. Larry Dickinson was standing on top the tire swing that hung from the locust tree in Billy's front yard, holding onto the hairy rope with one hand and pumping a little. My brother Timmy and little Al Suter were straddled up in the tree dropping the curly brown pods on Larry. "Bombs away!" They giggled. Larry was good at pretending not to notice. A pod waggled on his hair and another on his shoulder. He kind of hunched his butt and pumped the swing and the pods slipped off without him looking up.

"We just cooked our supper ourselves out in the field," I said. Billy was picking his teeth with a splinter and trying to stay calm. He lasted about three seconds.

"Froglegs," he said.

"We killed him in the pond," I said. "We hunted him all afternoon."

"I killed him," Billy said.

"We shot him again and again and Billy got the last shot," I said, "with my BB gun."

"One frog aint much to eat," Larry said.

"Froglegs taste like chicken and fish," I said.

"Eenie meenie minie mo," Billy was saying.

"Mr. Herman catch old Big Words by the toe," Larry said.

"You think Mr. Herman's going to give me a whipping, Larry?"

"Anybody disbelieve in the Bible ain't worth whipping," Larry said. "The both of you." He meant Patty and me. He started teasing me. "Cain't see how she could keep herself moving with all them fellows around about her," he said.

I wanted to cry and kill and whimper and bust things.

"I don't even know where she lives," I said.

"Lotsa guys do," Larry said. "Russell does."

"I don't," I said. I was miserable.

"Eenie meenie minie mo," Billy said again.

"Catch a nigger by the toe. That's the way," I said. "If he hollers make him pay, fifty dollars everyday."

I was eleven and they were fourteen and I was lonely. I said, "What do niggers do at night?"

"Niggers go into little black holes at night," Larry said.

"Niggers prowl, they're indivisible," Billy said.

"Naw," I said, "that's only sometimes."

Billy's mother laughed in the rocker on the porch, not a good laugh. She was lonely, Mom said, with Billy's dad volunteering in the mountain troops in Italy. I heard Junior Charles' stomach making noises. "You hungry, Junior?" I was miserably trying to get just one guy on my side so I gave Junior the rest of my apple and told him I'd get him some bread at the house and maybe peanut butter. "I ain't eat nothin' all day long," he said. It made me feel so good all of a sudden that I almost went to pieces.

It was near enough to Halloween for such a prank to take hold of my mind. Billy's mother was rocking on the porch in that awful tight way of hers so I couldn't tell about my plan in the yard. I went out onto the road all the way to the ditch on the other side. There I started hishing and whispering and gesturing and saying that there was a big blacksnake there. That brought them all running and picking up rocks to throw at the snake.

"Ain't no blacksnake here," Larry said.

"Shhhhh," I said.

Billy said, "Where?"

I said *shhhhhhhh*.

I told them my plan about the nigger and about my arsenal of fireworks and my cattails soaked in kerosene.

"Where you going, Billy?" His mother was standing up and holding the porch post against her cheek.

"Nowheres, Mom," Billy said.

"Up to no good," she said.

Timmy and Al Suter stayed giggling farther behind. They wanted to be able to run if Larry took out after them.

I started singing "Where have you been, Billy boy, Billy boy, where have you been, charmin' Billy?" I was glad to be able to tease him. "First we gotta get my cattails and crackers," I said.

Billy wanted to use the BB gun. "You cain't do that," I said. "You don't cain't put out nobody's eyes."

I smelled the wet chicken feathers in the bucket by our backsteps before I saw them—Mom killing and frying a chicken for Reverend Harkness. Junior Charles carried out the gallon can of cattails and I carried out my load of fireworks in the cardboard box. I let the screen door ease shut and tiptoed up to the stove to get matches. I heard them talking in the living room and I felt Reverend Harkness' smell in the lighted doorway. I hoped he wouldn't make the fireplace smell. I got a handful of stick matches from a box on the stove and a fistfull of white bread for Junior and I jammed the jar of peanut butter under my arm.

"That you, Michael?" It was my mom.

"How were your froglegs?" Reverend Harkness said.

I didn't go into the living room. I couldn't see him.

"They were just dandy," I said. "Froglegs taste a little like chicken and a little like fish. I'm going out, Mom."

Dad said, sort of cautious, "Don't stay out too long."

Junior dipped into the peanut butter and spread it on the bread with his fingers. I was nervous and told him to hurry and put the jar in the grass by the bucket of chicken feathers.

We pow-wowed in the haymow of Perkins' barn, where sometimes we threw ourselves out of the hayloft door flapping our arms and trying to fly, slamming down on the mountain of manure and straw that Perkins shoveled out of the barn, and one night I tried to fly again and again and again.

I told my brother to stay at the bottom of the ladder leading up to the haymow, and Al Suter at the top where he could relay any message, to make sure no one eavesdropped. Timmy said I was always doing this to him and it was only when Larry told him how important it was, that he stayed down there. Larry kept saying importantly that there was a part of that old black he wanted to take away with him. I didn't know what he meant, and he wasn't explaining himself, and nobody else knew what he meant either, and that was the way he liked it. "My Pa told me what," Larry said. He was lying back on a slope of hay and flipping his jackknife down his side so it stuck in the floorboards where Junior and Billy and me sat cross-legged.

"Your Pa know about this?" I said. And I was sharp. I was mainly emphasizing the secrecy because it was impossible for his Pa to know. Larry reached kind of languid, kind of hunched, down his side, without sitting up, and pulled the jackknife out of the board by his foot.

Junior sat with the gallon bucket of cattails between his legs and the stalks snuggled between his cheek and shoulder chomping up the bread and peanut butter. I hugged the cardboard box of fireworks because I was afraid Larry might try to take over.

Mainly our plot was hatched by Billy and me. He was mean enough and I was imaginative enough. Junior Charles was giggly. Little Al Suter was dropping handfuls of hay down on my brother. I was glad when we left the haymow because the haydust was tickling my nose and I was the one saying that everybody had to be quiet and not cough and not sneeze.

I told them we had to crawl across the field on our bellies all the way to the old black's shack. Larry Dickinson said that was just shit. I said he'd better or he couldn't use one of my roman candles. Larry said that was shit too. I told him if he was going to cross the field standing up where everybody could see him against the stars he had to move far up the field away from us. He did go way up the field. It made me feel good. Everybody else understood the necessity of crawling on our elbows and bellies. I pushed the cardboard box in front of me. Every now and then I would lay my cheek on the ground and feel the silence.

Larry Dickinson was in the dirt lane waiting for us. When

we got close to the black's shack even Larry was stooping
over. I parceled out the firecrackers, the roman candles, the
rockets, the sparklers, and two cattails a piece. He tied our
handkerchiefs across our faces. Each one of us picked a shed
—a ramshackle chicken house, a privy, a pigpen shed, a tool
shed—and came up behind it. You could hear all around the
little scrapings, twangings of bobwire, not loud, the creak of
a damp board, the tossing of a coffee weed, little noises in
the night noosing up around the shack. One window was
rosy gold with the light of a coal-oil lantern. The electric
lines didn't go as far as the old black's shack.

I was tight as a wire behind the pigpen shed, and there was
something like a hummingbird in my stomach. I peeked
around the corner at the rosy window and made sure none
of the blacks was on the porch or in the yard. The pigpen
shed shook against my side when the two hogs hunched
around in it. I tried to strike the first match on the seat of my
jeans and couldn't. I had to fumble on the ground and find a
piece of old fender crumbling with rust. I lit my first cattail.
Yellow flame swelled up, huffing smelly black kerosene
smoke in my face. That was the signal. My breath came
sweaty behind the white handkerchief. Cattail torches flared
around behind the sheds and our howls and screeches
rammed through the flames and the night toward the shack.

It was the black's woman that first stooped over in the
window, and then the black himself looked out over her
shoulder. And then, in a wink, a scream, they disappeared. I
expected the door on the porch to fly open and the black to

bust out and try to beat the tar out of us. Instead the light in the window went out. The shack lumped up darkly. Now the woman was yelling, an eerie muffled yelling. "Chil'ens, chil'ens!" For a second I thought she meant us but then I knew she meant her own kids that never played with us. I didn't know what she was doing with her kids but already things were not going the way I thought they would.

We stopped yelling.

They stopped yelling.

The cattail torches huffed out their yellow song. I was cold, the same as when Mr. Herman wiped the lipstick off Patty. There was my brother and Al over behind the chicken house waving their torches up high and watching snatches of flame fly off, like they were in their own backyard. A terrible racket of wings and clucking was going inside the chicken house. Kerosene seeped down the stalk and over my hands.

I cut loose my mightiest yell and dashed over the dusty yard and planted my cattail in a crack of the steps. Up on the porch the clapboards and the white porcelain doorknob came boom into my eyes. I darted back to the pigpen shed.

"Shitfire and hallelujah, Michael!" Larry shouted. I heard my real name from him.

I was sure the black would come barreling out but he wasn't doing anything he was supposed to do. Billy Peterson yelped behind the privy. I wondered how it smelled back there. He lit a roman candle and aimed red balls of fire and streams of sparks at the back of the shack. He kept one hand across his eyes against the sparks. Somebody was trying to climb out back there. That's what we'd agreed about the roman candles. I stuck my last cattail in the ground and held a two-inch cracker to the torch and the second the fuse hissed I lofted the cracker over the shack at where Billy was firing and somebody was grunting. There came the gunshot clap and something like a fist hitting a windowpane but not breaking it.

Now everyone lofted two-inch crackers. Sharp flashes and all kingdom come busted loose around the shack. Larry Dickinson gave a yell that triggered a waterfall in my blood. He flew over the yard with his cattail torch stuttering flame and everybody screamed to stop throwing crackers and Larry went right up to the house and everything was all terror and daring and heat. He held something to his torch. There was a white sputtering, a handful of sparklers. I thought he was going to plant them in the ground, a ring of sparkler fire around the shack, and I envied him the idea.

Then he heaved them up onto the old shingled roof, and my feeling shriveled as he threw another handful under the house. He tossed his torch right against the wall by the door and howled back to the toolshed. The torch hit just before the door opened.

It wasn't the black.

It was the woman.

She was vast and ragged in the doorway with the shadows of the torch mumbling over her. I wanted to run up and throw myself down and hug her legs, and look up and say, "Hello."

"Masters," she was saying, "young masters."

Firecrackers. Roman candles. Rockets. War whoops. Bright flashes bumped and jumped around her, and balls and streams of fire streaked and criss-crossed everywhere shattering on the shack and dripping liquidly. A flash knocked right against her and her head jerked back and she grabbed her left forearm. "Masters, masters," she was saying, rubbing her forearm.

Then, as if she'd just noticed it, she stooped over and picked up the cattail. A huge black smear went up the wall, and crumbling coals silvered the edges of the clapboard. She brushed at the burning places. She was saying something about mercy and forgiveness. "They just chil'en, Joshua," she kept saying, "they just chil'en."

We never got to see the black come out of the house. We never got the chance to make him try and chase us away. Out of nowhere a black car skidded on the road and doors were open and men reaching out with their legs before it even stopped. They threw themselves flat on the ground by fence posts. Sheriff Walt Jeffries, dressed in white from head to toe, crouched by the radiator of the car and fired into the air. It was louder than any firecracker. The other men fired into the air too. That was a lot of noise for the town of Wilson. The Sheriff was shouting for us to come out with our hands behind our heads.

I suddenly threw away my cattail and turned to run, and ran right into the belt buckle of a man who was taller than any man had a right to be on a dark night. He clapped me against him and swung and bumped me into the yard in front of the porch. *"Kids,"* he was yelling, *"kids!"* Powerful flashlight beams mashed against us as men came out from all sides with handkerchief-masked kids struggling in their arms. Junior Charles was the only one not present with us circled about by the men near the porch steps. "Kids," the Sheriff said.

He put that pistol into the holster on his hip.

"Kids."

Then he jerked the handkerchief off my face and it hurt the back of my head. "Michael Dannhauser," he said, and threw the handkerchief on the ground. I started trying not to cry.

"What do we do with no-good pups, Harmon?"

"We put 'em in a gunny sack and throw 'em in the creek," Harmon said. It was gangly old Harmon Harris holding me. I'd heard Harmon was worse than Junior Charles a few years before.

Three or four little fires were licking about on the roof. "Jesus," the Sheriff said. "Joshua, where's your well at?" No answer. "Where in hell's your well at, boy?"

" 'Hind the house, She'ff Walt," Joshua said.

Two of the men jumped after Joshua going behind the house.

There was a lot of silence from the woman and the men.

The two men jogged back, one with two buckets of water and one with a ladder under his arm and a gunny sack slung over his shoulder Joshua sloped behind them faster than I'd

ever seen him move. A man shinnied up the ladder with the
soaked gunny sack. His foot punched through the roof down
to his thigh and he just stayed there with the other foot
bunched under him and thrashed away at the little fires with
the wet gunny sack. When a bucket was passed up to him, he
side-swung the water over the roof.

The Sheriff pushed the flashlight beam right into my face. I
had to close my eyes and twist my head away. I wanted to
scream that I was sorry sorry sorry but the scream was tied tight
in my throat. "Never no cause to bother about color in my
county," the Sheriff was saying. "What's your daddy going to
say, son? You put no thought to your daddy tonight?" I
wanted to blame somebody badly but it was my brother and
Al Suter crying and blaming me.

The Sheriff flicked the beam from face to face.

"Well, well," he said, "Larry Dickinson."

He shook the light in Billy's face. "You, what's your name?"

"Billy," Billy said. "Billy Petersen."

"Homer Petersen's boy?"

Billy nodded, reluctant.

"Ain't this just the kind of thing you want your mom to
write overseas about?" The Sheriff let the beam move from
Larry's tennis shoes up to his face again. "Old enough to get
into trouble is old enough to know better, Larry Dickinson."

"Yeah," Larry said.

The Sheriff fast switched the flashlight to his left hand and
slapped him. "What'd you say?"

"Yes, sir," Larry said.

The men were stamping out the cattail torches and searching around for any other fire. Junior Charles just wasn't anywhere. I didn't know it then but he slithered right under the pigpen fence and went into the shed with the hogs. That's dangerous. Hogs eat people sometimes.

The woman leaned with her forearms on the jambs of the doorway, as if she were keeping the house upright, and her two kids poking out behind her skirts. The little girl with tiny spikes of braids and red ribbon all over her head picked up the charred cattail torch and held it, very curious. It was the only thing that I could blame and so I whined at the Sheriff asking him why the kids didn't come to school as if that was the reason. "You're just more curioser than you know how to handle, *ain't* you, son?" He started whacking me over his knee. "You *know* better," he said. "Now you sit down here, all of you." He crowded us onto the running board of the car.

Two men from up the lane were standing up on tiptoe in back of the car trying to see over it. The Sheriff did something then that somehow made sense to me but I couldn't put it into words. He shouted and laughed and fired the pistol at the ground near Joshua's feet, and Joshua jogged up and down. The two men behind the car laughed a little too.

Then the Sheriff squatted before us and talked. I mainly remember the badge on the left pocket of his white shirt with pens and pencils clipped around it. The badge was heavier and bigger and more elaborate than anything I ever got with boxtops.

Then my dad walked around the car.

I went sick and cold and quivering.

I could hardly believe it when the Sheriff gave out a really jovial, "Hi, there, Jerry." And Dad was saying hunh and giving little grunts. "Michael," he said, as if I hardly belonged to him. "Timmy." I didn't even try to smile.

Timmy ran to Dad's side and stayed there.

Dad and the Sheriff talked by themselves with Dad holding Timmy's head against his thigh. The negroes on the porch and us kids on the running board watched things being straightened out. "They just chil'en," the negro woman called. "They just chil'en, Sheriff Walt. Just chil'en, Mister Jerry." It was just one more thing to hear that the woman knew my dad's name. I found out later that Dad offered to put a new roof on the place and have any damage fixed up. I saw him push a five dollar bill down into Joshua's shirt pocket too.

"What you been up to?" It was one of the men come from behind the car grinning.

"Nothing," we said.

"Yeah," the man said, "sure seems that way."

The running board was cold on my bottom.

"You go with your dad," the Sheriff said. "You two," he pointed out Larry and Billy, "going to take a long ride with me."

I jumped to my feet. "They wouldn't a done it if it hadn't been for me," I said.

"Michael," my father said.

"It ain't nobody's fault only my own!" I said.

"Michael," my father said.

I didn't know it but the Sheriff was only going to drive them the long way around and give Larry and Billy a good scare. Dad said over his shoulder to the negroes, a little uncertainly, "Goodnight."

"Night, Mister Jerry."

I waited every step for him to say something but every step he didn't, across the starry field. It was the same way the year before when he caught me in the pool hall. There wasn't going to be any spanking, but something was seething me inside.

Pieces of my old box-kite were shivering black in the dead side branches of the oak tree in our backyard. It got stuck there just before school started in September. I didn't mention the jar of peanut butter in the grass by the bucket of chicken feathers.

All Mom said was,

"Michael, Timmy, for crying out loud, whatever on this earth—"

Dad nodded at me. "Michael says it was his idea."

Timmy was crying and saying it was my idea too.

"Hush up," Mom said. Dad took Al Suter home.

"We'll see about that tomorrow," she said. She shunted us down the hall. "Now get to bed before I beat the living daylights out of you so you can get to school," she said.

I moved my legs strangely under the covers, and looked at the ceiling, and listened to Timmy who was lying on his back too. I let my hand hang over the side of the bed and hold the rudder of my Wheaties plane between two fingers. I twitched it back and forth. I went to sleep without making up a story about Patty.

6

I did wake at the same time in the morning, and I nearly didn't recognize Joshua walking along the dirt lane fence because a deputy was walking with him, and it was an overcast day. Mom and Dad that morning held something back and silently said something else to us all the time. They would have liked to have known about the exploding sun. I ate the oatmeal and raisins, all of it. Then I was hunched up on my elbows lying on the living room carpet reading the *Globe-Democrat* and counting how old I was and whether the war would last long enough to find use for me. I was breathing through my teeth because Reverend Harkness' smell seemed to linger in the room.

In front of Kinder's grocery the Sheriff stood on the sidewalk with his arms folded, as if I were unknown and unimportant to him. He always dressed in white. Joshua was somewhere inside the store.

Billy's mom had beat Billy silly that night.

Larry's lip was cut and blue where his pa hit him.

Patty showed me the rock she brought and I traced where the fern had been in it. I tried to smile but felt I'd known and lost the rock a long time ago. Mr. Herman strode down the aisle and suddenly the yardstick smashed on my desk. He did the same thing to Larry and Billy but kept them waiting. Miss Dakeman did it in the fourth grade to Timmy and Al.

Noonhour Mr. Herman locked the door to our room and lined the three of us up in front of his desk. He asked us what did we think we were doing last night. And everytime he slammed the yardstick on the desk I tried hard not to let the shock of it make my eyes blink. "Nothing," I said. I no longer had any urge to ask him why the two colored kids didn't go to school.

He made us drop our pants on the floor around our ankles and bend over with our elbows on the desk. When I felt myself naked and trembling below my shirttail, I wanted to cry. He made me fold my arms on the Bible and put my forehead down. He whipped Billy first, and Billy started crying almost immediately. Larry made Mr. Herman believe that he was trying to hold out and then started crying. It was terrible the way he made me wait and listen to them. Then I couldn't stop the tears going down my cheeks but I made no noise and I tried to rub the tears off on my sleeve but I couldn't rub fast enough and they streaked the black cover of the Bible. Every time he hit me on the bottom a cry knotted up.

Mom and Dad would never know about the exploding sun. They would never know about this either.

Larry and Billy would not call me Big Words again for a long time. It was dirty and lonely and cold with them out on the playground. Timmy and Al shied away from me because

Miss Dakeman hadn't whipped them. It wasn't until the end of the afternoon that I started wrinkling my nose when I came near Junior Charles, trying to rescue some barest bit of pride. He just grinned a little scared, a little sheepish. Larry and Billy wrinkled their noses at him too because by now we knew how he got away. "He tanned you cause of yesterday," Patty said. "Michael, I know he did." It was lonesome the way she said my name. "They just chil'en," the colored woman had said.

The gravel smelled clean and cold from rain after school. I stayed alone hunting around in the marshy fields below the playground because sometimes Patty went that way and I thought I'd seen her. Then, up on the hillside, suddenly, her lipstick was red as the cigarette in her hand was white, red as a sumac leaf turning. Eighth grade boys were trailing after her and Russell in his brown suede jacket was right beside her. She saw me down below, she looked straight down at me, with head to toe pride, and she did not say a word or wave to me. The boys were jumpy and laughing. She was leading Russell as he took her by the elbow and they went, all of them, into a red-sprinkled mass of glistening sumac.

I saw Russell's black Ford pickup parked in front of the school. The bus was already gone. I saw a mop being shaken out of a window of our room. It was Joshua cleaning up.

I went home picking up sticks and throwing them into the streams of brown water rapping through the ditches. It kept my mind off how to hide the soreness in my bottom from Mom. If I threw enough sticks into the ditches one might actually float down to a gully, and down the gully to Gardner Branch, and down Gardner Branch to the Big Tavern, and down the Big Tavern to the Osage River, and down the Osage to the Missouri River, and down the Missouri to the Mississippi, and down the Mississippi and out into the Gulf of Mexico. I saw maps, maps, maps. I wanted maps. I was trying to spell Mississippi right when I saw the stick floating out into the Gulf of Mexico into the spaciousness of the ocean, where huge clouds walked on the air. I was walking on the edge of the sidewalk keeping my balance and throwing sticks in the ditch. I had an idea that Jesus was able to walk on water because he kept perfect balance. I had told my friends that anybody could walk on water if they kept perfect balance. I was practicing.

DALEY GOES HOME

Master Sergeant William Daley's main job on his tour of duty in Korea, so far as he saw it, was marking off time. The first thing he did in the morning, even before shaving, was to draw one diagonal line through the square of the day. The last thing he did before turning off the lights, even when drunk, was to draw the other line.

He never went whoring. He never went outside the barbed wire that surrounded the compound except on dispensary business. He even refused R & R leaves to Japan saying that he was saving money and wanted to stay clean. At the end of this tour of duty he would complete his twenty years retirement, and he had plans. He was saving for a fishing and hunting lodge that was his dream on the Gulf of Mexico, and the tour of duty in Korea was not just a postponement of those plans, it was a chance to finance them, since everybody in the Korean theater drew combat pay. He spent money only on booze at the NCO club where he was popular with his buddies from years of service. Most of the work and decisions in the dispensary he managed to leave to Corporal Warner and Staff Sergeant Francis. They enjoyed it.

On the walls of his NCOIC room in the medics' quonset hut was a big display of photographs of his family, his wife, his two boys, his little girl—picnics, eighth grade graduation, fishing, washing the car, Christmas, birthdays, barbecue suppers, etc. Photos of his wife were stuck in the sides of his mirror on the wall opposite the foot of his bunk. A re-touched portrait of her leaned up in a mahogany frame on the shelf near the head of the bunk. Every night when he looked at the portrait he polished its glass on the chest of his tee-shirt. The only other object on the wall was the big picture calendar that hoarded the crossed-off days—a pretty miss on horseback, under the limbs of a red-turning maple tree, gazing over a rail fence and a golden sunset wheat field.

His room was stacked neatly with hundreds of magazines, comic books, and paperbacks, mostly westerns. He could lie on his back on his cot in his tee-shirt and white army shorts and read these books and magazines straight, one after another, hour after hour. He traded with his buddies for more of the same. Once a month he took a long time about cleaning the .45 that he carried in the Phillipines in WW II.

He might have made it, every day of eighteen months of days, all 547 of them, except for one thing that happened in his first February in Korea, in weather too cold for it to happen. In that weather, in that country, where no American soldier went AWOL because there was nowhere to go, Daley not only went AWOL, but became, in effect, a deserter.

1

The men in Daley's medical detachment stationed in the huge compound of the 78th Engineer Group were all becoming increasingly eccentric through this long and barren winter. Young guys who had hardly smoked at all were now three-pack-a-day addicts, and constantly experimenting with cigars and pipes. Corporal Warner, the Senior Aidman, had a phonograph. Nobody questioned his right to overwhelm the entire quonset hut with Wagnerian opera and Beethoven. It passed the time. Warner had been given a Special Court Martial recently for a drunken night in which he had gathered a dozen charges against himself. It irked Daley first that Warner was a really good medic and took pride in it, and second that Corporal Warner, *draftee* Warner, had presumed to exercise his rights and rejected the Group's rubber-stamp defense counsel, got his own counsel, pleaded not guilty, and came out of the court-martial with a heavy fine but no stockade time and with his stripes still on his sleeves and a fair warning by the grapevine from the frustrated Colonel's office that he better walk a very straight line.

Staff Sergeant Meyer, the pharmacist, was an American Nazi. He hunched on his stool in the closeted pharmacy and constantly read and dreamed upon the books and memoirs and collected works and letters of great Nazis. Meyer took long dallying journeys alone into the whorehouses, and savored conversations with Warner, who was half-German, about Aryan destiny, while Meyer was merely Irish. Meyer flattered and amused Warner. Meyer passed the time. Daley was amused by Meyer too, but fatherly toward him, though Meyer was older than Daley. Daley, with his harsh Irish-born buoyancy, bullied the two youngest guys, Jacobsen and Henderson. Pfc Jacobsen made sure that he screwed *something* every day. Pfc Henderson popped pills in imaginative combinations, using his meager medical knowledge for ways to stimulate and depress his sympathetic and para-sympathetic nervous systems. Henderson's needs for pills put Meyer on the alert to protect the security cabinet in his pharmacy. It passed the time.

Captain Wilson, the doctor, who slept safely in the BOQ, discovered himself as a Kiplingesque figure on Empire's frontier, and persisted after small pickings of the exotic in this miserable Far Eastern City of Pusan. Staff Sergeant Francis, the Assistant NCOIC, inducted from the National Guard, and Pfc Harrison, the clerk, had not been here long enough to find their trade for passing the time. They all worked, fucked, played poker and blackjack, smoked, drank, hard, while Daley marked off the days, and sent money home to his wife.

"Corporal Warner," Daley bellowed from the screening room up front down the hall of the pre-fab that housed the dispensary. "Papasan, I'm busy," the Corporal yelled back. He was just pressing the button on a can of Ethyl Chloride to freeze the bulging cyst behind the ear of a black soldier, who was slumped in faded stockade fatigues on the stool in the Treatment Room. But it was mail-call and if Corporal Warner paid no attention to mail-call, Master Sergeant Daley, when it came mail-call, grabbed his letters and went to his room for the time that it took to read them. Daley barged through the door of the Treatment Room and thrust the sick-call slips and one letter for Warner on the counter by a syringe full of white procaine penicillin with an alcohol pad folded under and over the needle. Corporal Warner did not approve of foreign materials being put on his treatment table. He didn't look at the sergeant or even at the letter to see who it was from. "Look down, boysan," he said to the soldier, who had looked up when Daley came in. Warner cut the frozen cyst behind the man's ear and the large pus oozed out onto the gauze the Corporal pressed there. "Don't get any of that in your eyes," Daley said. It was Daley's rote attempt to make it seem that he was a part of the scene. The Corporal didn't even acknowledge Daley

Daley moved smartly in the sharp hard air on the duckboard walk that led zig-zag to the medics' quonset hut. He felt pushed back by his great huffs of steam. He was already thumbing open the letters even at that pace. There was one from Milly, one from his oldest boy Kenny, and and one from his best buddy Mike Riordan at the post in Texas where Daley had been stationed before Korea. He always made it a point to be sitting in front of Milly's portrait when he read her letters—auburn hair, tinted blue eyes, rosy cheeks, lips wetly parted the way he liked them. She was touching her fingertips to a silver brooch on her breast. He sat on the edge of his cot and polished his glasses on his sleeve.

Milly's letter was lengthy about the kids in school and little Lucy in nursery school and the fishing and hunting lodge they were saving for and the adventures of Kenny on his first bicycle, and the letter was signed Milly in her tall up and down letters, with four big lipstick impressions, one with lips closed and the last with lips wide open, her french-kissing signature she called it and sometimes she hinted more than that. Kenny, in his letter, wrote about his bicycle and school and said everybody and everything was fine but they missed him. He wanted his dad to send him something Korean so he could show it to the guys at school. Daley hit the side of his thigh with plain exuberance. God, he could feel the bike, feel it wobble, as he held it for the kid to get on. The last letter was from Sfc Michael Riordan, Fort Sam Houston, Texas, the big medical training center where Daley had spent four years, his best years in the army, where Milly and the kids lived in post housing now. Mike Riordan was his buddy from the Phillipines in WW II. They even rented a boat in Corpus Christi to go fishing with their families for marlin in the Gulf.

Mike Riordan's letter began with saying that he had spent a lot of time before he knew that he had to write it. As if freezing liquid were sprayed inside his guts, Daley suddenly tightened to sustain the distance on all four sides between him and the walls. *Milly was screwing around. Milly was serious about a guy.* They'd been seen in restaurants in San Antonio, they'd been discovered in the back seat of the guy's car in. . . . "Willy," Mike wrote, "you know I wouldn't do this, unless something's got to be done. You got to straighten her out, Willy. You want me to help any way, I'll do it. Just tell me, buddy. I won't do nothing unless you tell me."

On the cot beside Daley was Milly's letter and Kenny's letter and he spied the last wide-open lipstick impression that was Milly's french-kiss across thousands of miles and her hint that it meant something more. That instant, he saw, in the backseat of a car in a post parking lot, Milly kneeling between the guy's. . . . and the room went up like something tossed from a shovel and he gave such a violent jerk and yell that the cot skidded.

Christ, he thought the next moment. He cat-leaped to the door of his room and looked down the barracks, along all the cots and footlockers and shined boots, past Warner's phonograph on the wooden box by his cot. What if those mother-fuckers heard me? His heart bump, bumped, sapping his breath. There at the far end was Li the orphan Korean houseboy, pretending to shine boots and trying to understand with hesitant smiles what he should do about Daley's yelling.

"Dijobi, boysan," Daley said. "All dijobi."

The boy nodded. The boy smiled.

Daley subscribed to the old Regular Army dictum that what you don't know won't hurt you as enthusiastically as he crossed off days. So it must be serious or Mike wouldn't have written. Goddamnit, Riordan, is it a sergeant or an officer or just a kid? He lifted the cot at the foot with one hand and set it straight and snatched the letters up off the floor and stuffed them under his pillow. He jogged along the duckboard to the dispensary feeling as if he were a nail about to be driven through the approaching door. He wanted to go to work hard. He envied with a sudden dry pinch in his throat Warner and the Treatment Room and all the blood and sewing up and bandaging and medicines and the simple concentration it took. It seemed so long since he had done any work.

God Almighty, he wrenched sideways, stopped short, at the door. He strained his head down and to the side, as if looking away from an intense light, immensely ashamed. He was trying hard not to be pulled down into himself. It frightened him that he should be frightened that he would see Milly and the guy fucking on the floor of the waiting room of this dispensary when he opened the door. But he saw, he saw, the guy's naked, hairy back, and Milly's legs and arms curled around him, moving, moving, her chin in the guy's shoulder, her eyes closed and her face happy and wild and pained. . . . her eyes tinted blue. . . . the eyes in the portrait. . . . Now he couldn't see her. . . . She was either the portrait . . . or she was . . . or she was . . . or she was . . .

Daley stalked into the dispensary announcing that he was going to make the run in the jeep that day to the Station Hospital. The last of the sick call line was trailing into the Treatment Room, the men leaning bored on the walls. . . . "How many for the hospital?" Daley yelled. They all stirred and straightened a little. Four guys were going to the hospital for tests. "I'll have to take the fucking three-quarter," Daley said, meaning the small truck. Daley was rapping out his words. He gathered up Corporal Warner's surgical packs to be autoclaved at the hospital and and was told by the Corporal to pick up materials taken there earlier in the week. His gut went hard with anger at Warner, at his sheer punk competence. He gathered up six tubes of blood wrapped in pink slips for serology. He was stepping fast on the plywood floors. Two of the medics, Pfc Henderson and Pfc Jacobsen, wanted to go along for the ride. "Not enough room," Daley barked. He hit the cold air and took off his glasses to polish away the mist.

In the early afternoon the three-quarter was back at the dispensary door, parked where it was supposed to be, but nobody had seen Daley. The autoclaved surgical packs were resting along with slips showing results of tests on Warner's counter in the Treatment Room. Master Sergeant Tracy of the 563rd Engineers, an old buddy of Daley's, came by after evening chow and asked for Daley and then went over to the NCO club to find him. Tracy came back twice asking for Daley.

But Daley was nowhere around and nobody else asked any questions until that night when, with lights out at 2300, he was not in his room, though a small lamp still burned on the shelf by his bunk. It had been burning all day but not until night did the glow gather the room about it. The medics in the quonset, accustomed to doing without their NCOIC, thought that Daley must be drinking somewhere. Then the Sergeant of the Guard stuck his flashlight in the quonset door and asked whoever was in charge to douse the light.

It was the first time that Corporal Warner ever set foot in Daley's room, among the comic books and photos, in his tee-shirt and briefs. He stood in his Japanese shower slippers on the mat beside Daley's cot. There was a hint of queasiness in his belly, as before a plunge. He let his hand drift to snap off the shaded desk lamp, and looked, not pleased, at the portrait of the woman on the shelf, the re-touching, the blue eyes, the auburn hair, the cheeks, her fingertips resting with light self-consciousness on the brooch on her chest. He turned off the light, and padded rapidly through the chill air back to his cot. "Where the hell is Daley?" he said, to the dark barracks. Immediately, from the humps in the cots, it was suggested that Daley was knocking off a piece of ass at last, having lasted longer in his abstinence than any man they knew, etc.

"Turn on some Wagner," Meyer said.

"Ah-h, Sarge," Jacobsen said.

"Yeah," Harrison said.

"Fuck, yes," Francis said.

They went to sleep with Valkyries pulsing about their heads. . . .

In the morning Daley was not present or accounted for. Strictly speaking he was AWOL. Harrison, the medical and detachment clerk, asked Captain Wilson what he should do. The doctor laughed and agreed that Daley was long overdue, as if it were good for the health and sanity of everyone, and Daley was marked present on the Morning Report. "Tell the sergeant, when he comes in," the doctor said, "that I want to see him." He wanted to see Daley because, in ten days, Captain Wilson was being transferred to the good land of Japan. Another doctor would take over the dispensary and Daley would want to know about it. Already Captain Wilson was making his last raids on Korean culture, with a stack of inlaid, black enamelware tables, trays and boxes by his desk. "And tell Li to crate this stuff so I can send it home."

But on the second day Daley was still not present. Captain Wilson called the whole staff into his office and closed the door and it was the NCOs who said that Daley should still be marked present and accounted for on the Morning Report. "How the hell do I know he's shacked up? Maybe he's dead," the Captain said. "Damn it, if he's not marked AWOL, we can't tell the MPs and we can't find him." The doctor, to distinguish himself from his men, restricted his swearing to damn and hell and shit. He was suggesting that he had been a good guy long enough. "I think I can find him," Meyer said. Meyer took the jeep and rolled up and down streets all afternoon through the whorehouse districts of Pusan but couldn't find Daley.

The next day, "That's it, my friend," the doctor said, and Daley was marked AWOL on the Morning Report and the MPs went out to look for him.

2

Everytime he stopped or slowed for Koreans crossing the streets he tasted the rage. His throat was sore. A force in him

would not let go. Milly. Milly, kneeling . . . fluorescent light
in the post parking lot coming through the window of the car
and making her lips blue. . . . her lips. . . . He forgot there
were four guys bouncing in the back of the truck. He drove
with a deadly exactness, every turn taut, as if spun on a line
of centrifugal force.

He went snap-snap from clinic to clinic at the Station
Hospital, picking up the autoclaved surgical kits and reports
on blood, urine, smear tests. Then he hustled together the
four guys who had given samples of their bodily fluids, and
headed back to the dispensary. He was looking out at this
city that he had hardly seen before. It was stacked on hills
and along the reaches of land around the harbor, shacky and
dirty and cold and hungry, and full of people that looked the
part of their surroundings. He thought of trying to talk about
Milly to someone. He thought of not talking about it. God,
his throat was sore. He rammed the gears into second. I
need a drink.

He was waved through the gate of the compound by the
guard, and the three-quarter jounced to a stop in front of the
dispensary, with the four guys simply left there sitting in the
back. He was not sneaking or hiding, but he went in the back
way walking soft-footed. Only the doctor and Harrison were
there, in the front office, everybody else at chow. Daley
deposited the surgical packs and the results of the tests on
the counter in the Treatment Room. He went fast out the
back door without being seen.

First, he cashed a money order, that he'd bought just the

day before but hadn't filled in Milly's name yet, at the PX.
Now he had nearly $300 in his pocket. He patted his field
jacket and his muffler and rubbed his gloved hands together
and strode out the gate. The guard nodded. Daley hitched a
ride on a deuce-and-a-half and got off near the first traffic
circle on the MSR waving his thanks to the driver. He didn't
stop stretching his stocky legs and singeing his lungs with
zero air until he banged the door behind him in the Orderly
Room of Echo Company of the 563rd Engineer battalion.

Master Sergeant Melvin Tracy, on the other side of the
counter that divided the pre-fab, was twirling the cylinder of
a typewriter to start a piece of paper. "Daley, well, well," he
said, coming sad and loose toward the counter and letting
his hand move out to Daley's hand. "You got the malaria
again?" Tracy was smiling at Daley's breathing and the small
quivers in Daley's cheeks. Daley faked his way through some
blustery buddy-buddy talk and then cut it short asking if they
could go to Tracy's bunk. Tracy paused. Then, "Sure,
papasan," he said. Tracy told his company clerk that he
would be in his room.

When they got there, Tracy said, "You want the door
closed?" Daley nodded. "Something's got you by the balls,"
Tracy said, to make it easier for Daley to talk. "Take your
jacket off, papasan. Sit awhile." But Daley only loosened the
neck of his field jacket. He wanted a drink but Tracy said he
didn't have any booze, meaning he didn't permit his men to
have booze in their quonsets so he didn't have any either.
Daley told his story with the help of only a canteen of water

that he held between his knees as he sat on Tracy's footlocker.

"Riordan should have kept his trap shut," Tracy said.

"What the fuck do I care about Riordan?" Daley said. "Who the hell's wife is screwing around, anyway?"

"So she's a bitch, Daley. So she's a bitch."

Tracy's room was bare, as if he'd just moved out of it, with only one book and a small alarm clock on the shelf by the head of his bunk. Daley shook the canteen between his knees, then shook it again. Booze, booze, booze, if only Tracy had booze, if only he couldn't see, see. . . . Milly. . . . The cat-pacing force would not let go. "What the fuck should I do, Trace?"

"Go back to the 'spensary, papasan. They're all bitches."

Tracy seemed to be in pain.

Daley sucked the canteen empty. "I gotta think. I gotta go."

"I'll chogi over tonight," Tracy said. "Fuck 'em. Let's hang one on." He said it emphatically.

Daley was staring at Tracy's back in the mirror.

Instead of turning left to go back to the dispensary Daley turned right going out the gate of the 563rd. "I need a drink. I need a drink." His throat ached when he swallowed.

He began to move with a certain cleverness. He hitchhiked to the RTO at the Port of Pusan. In a short while, he was talking to a merchant marine guy and knew where the sailors did their drinking. In a half hour he was huffing steam by a tall white board, on which the name The Purple Bird

was written in a column in six languages, near steps that went
down under the street. He would have a few drinks, time to
think. Then he'd get back to the dispensary and see how he
was going to handle this crap.

A shoeshine boy squatted, packed around with layers of
ragged clothing, under the board at the top of the steps, and
another boy was at the bottom of the steps. Their job was to
warn the bar when MPs were coming. A word shot from the
first boy to the second who slipped along the passageway
and hissed it into the bar. "Number one shine, sergeant.
Number hucking one." Daley saw that his quick pace might
not be politic, but he needed the drink, bad. He skipped
down the steps and through the right-angled passageway that
smelled of dank and pickled things. He was on edge the first
moment in the room when he couldn't see anything.

Then there were small tables, small chairs, a low bar in the
back with a Korean behind it looking at him, and a bunch of
tall, blond, big-legged Dutchmen making fools of themselves
in one corner bouncing a girl from one lap to another. The
place was made for foreign business, not GI business, not
Korean business. The fine film of slime on the concrete floor
under his combat boots, and the bare edge-worn tables and
chairs and the damp walls and the lone purple drape over the
canopy of the bar made you know that anything in Pusan was
poor, makeshift, temporary, ready for the next fire or the
next war. "Yes," the Korean bartender said, without looking
up at Daley's face. Daley ordered a shot of straight whiskey,
gulped it. It burned through him like piss through a

snowbank. Brrrrrrrr, it shook him. Then he settled down at a table with another shot and a quart of Japanese beer, Asahi, placing himself with his back to the wall.

It irritated the hell out of him that, when he put his elbows on it, the table was off-balance. His rage was in him, and he was in his rage, a force, a direction, a destiny, unknown, but carried by it, not knowing where, to what satisfaction, what resolution. He had to get back to the states. But Daley knew he could not tell the Colonel the truth in order to get a special emergency leave, he could not stand there and tell it to the Colonel's face. He might stowaway on a ship going back. Not very likely. He might tell Riordan to do whatever he saw fit to scare the guy away. That was just about as satisfying as the sight of Milly between the guy's knees and probably wouldn't do any good. He could write Milly and tell her what he knew. Shit, fucking *shit,* he could not find a way that was not humiliating, and he was terrified by what he saw when he closed his eyes. . . . *What the hell were we saving for? What the hell was all that buying of house and car and kids' education and financing the fishing lodge all about? What the mother-fuck?* There she was, sucking the. . . . He gripped the edge of the table with both hands rigidly and the booze oiled out in ripples over the shot glass.

It was the woman who found him.

She said her name was Jane.

"Just plain slant-eyed Jane," Daley said, with a loud laugh. She understood what he said. She pressed the skin back at her temples straightening her eyes. She stuck out her tongue and twittered it. He roared with laughter again. It came out of him like a cannonball, and then he felt grey and shaky, needing comfort. "Buy me drink," she said. Oh, man, he thought. He bought her a drink. When the bartender, who never looked into anyone's face, brought the drinks, Daley picked hers up and tasted it. The bartender was offended and looked away toward the door. Plain Jane was offended. It was gin and tonic all right, in the middle of the winter. "Me no work-ee this place," she said. "He frien'," she indicated the bartender. "Me no work-ee." Daley roared again. "You work," he said. Jesus, he felt ugly and wanted to break things. That was what happened when he spread his hands on his chest. It seemed hard and flat and empty as a boiler. He wanted to break it. It frightened the shit out of him.

They began drinking. They even danced a little.

It was Plain Slant-Eyed Jane who hauled him out into the night. "Close now," the bartender said, his smile going away as he shut the door behind them. "Where go? Where you go?" Plain Jane spoke distinctly holding Daley's arm with both hands. She was cold. "I go with you, jo-san. Take me home," he said. He bumped uneasily against her.

"What name your place?"

"Take me home," Daley screamed. She became quiet and certain in the dying away of his scream, with people hunching by them, past curfew. Daley was quivering.

"You want go me?"

"Ne. Dijobi, jo-san. Ne. I go you."

"Shortime?"

223

"All the fucking night."

"O.k., sergeant." He was carrying a pint of bourbon. . . .

Daley toppled onto the pallets and mats on the warm floor of her room. He lolled on his back, he couldn't get it up, and let her do what she wanted. He had no idea how long she worked at him with her hand and then he just went to sleep. Sometime in the night he groped awake and took her head, she was asleep, and pushed it down into his crotch. He was sure that wouldn't work either but it felt mean and satisfying to make her try and he was thinking of Milly as he squinted down at the top of Plain Slant-Eyed Jane's black hair. He wondered where his glasses were. But he was surprised and she got on top and a few seconds after he came he plunged into a spiralling sleep.

He woke in the morning light in the room with a contentment that proved more seductive than his rage. When he moved his head, his hangover was godawful. She was gone. He slid around in the thick covers and bumped the pint and drank and lay back with his eyes closed until the burning hummed through him. Then he hunted in the covers for his glasses and put them on. There was nothing on the walls. Nothing. He wasn't going back. From one minute to the next, one hour to the next, one day to the next, he decided he wasn't going back to the dispensary. He wasn't going back and feel that heat from all those people with all their ideas about him and Milly.

The panel on the side of the room was shuffled to one side and Plain Jane came in on her knees, in a very loose white gown, putting down a tray. "Chop-chop," she said. "Number one." She smiled. There was tea and things in covered dishes on the tray. Goddamn her, plain slant-eyed Jane. When she asked him if he wanted egg or anything American, he tensed against puking. Tea and rice, that was fine. He drank a little tea, ate a little rice with his fingers, not much. He was drinking the bourbon again. He patted his paunch and his stocky thighs. "I got lots to go on," he said. But Plain Jane, pleased that tea and rice was fine, was saddened that he didn't eat much. He gave her a ten-dollar bill, MPC scrip, more than the going rate for one night. She folded it solemnly and stuck it under the gown in her brassiere. "Comupsomida," she murmured. She did not smile or look at him for several minutes. He found out later that she gave the money to her mother who managed the household, and the mother bowed low on her knees whenever Daley went past her into the room. There were some kids in the house too, but he never got it straight.

He didn't want to stay with Plain Jane during the day. He wanted a bar. So he began finding the native bars and cafes and came back to her at night. With good instinct, on the second day of his AWOL, he tried to stay a jump ahead of the MPs that he was sure were coming after him. He paid shoeshine boys to watch out for him, and he began to develop a second-guessing radar for when the MPs were turning the corner and coming toward him. It got to the point where the steep back streets were visited two or three times a day by MP jeeps. Out any available back or side door he

went, or quickly out the front and around the corner. He had
no shame or hesitation about wading through family quarters,
or even crawling into private rooms. Sometimes there was
even a window to crawl out of, or drop out. The gooks were
scared of any American soldier, even if the whole Army
apparatus was hellbent after him, so Daley was free to come
and go. And come and go he did from bar to bar and back to
Plain Jane's, for two weeks.

Then he was made aware that CID interpreters were out
asking questions and offering a reward. MPs searched houses.
They knew that he was alive and in the area. They would get
to a bar and find that he had been there only minutes before.
Sometimes within an hour they would be in another bar that
he had also left just a few minutes before. Plain Jane said,
"Why you run? Why you not go back?" And yet she was
worried about him and yet she was always there. His pants
became bunched at the waist as he lost weight. "Why you no
chop-chop? Food hav-a-yes. Michengai. Chop-chop." Sure it
was crazy not to eat so he gave her money and told her to
just be there anyway.

Then there were a couple of days when he didn't know
where he was.

Only because he could no longer walk the MPs finally
caught him the first time. There would be the second and the
third time too. They caught him crawling, frost-bitten, so
weak he sprawled within a few steps of yet another bar.
Koreans in the street simply watched him curiously or
fearfully and hurried away. The MPs did not arrest him and he

wasn't taken to the PMO. They had different orders. "Come on, Sarge. Up you go, papasan." His frozen hands were shaking so badly he couldn't pick up his glasses from the ground. An MP did it, and put them on for him too. They pushed him into their jeep and took him straight back to the dispensary where, for several days now, an argument had been going among the officers of the Engineer Group.

What was to be done with him?

3

Captain Wilson was already transferred with his Kiplingesque needs into the more likely land of Japan. The new doctor Captain Weisman was a different fellow. He told his men that this NCOIC whom he had never seen would get the toughest court martial possible as soon as they got their hands on him. There was no reason why Master Sergeant Daley should be treated differently from any other soldier.

Pfc Harrison the medical and detachment clerk, because he handled the phone and the records and messages, had made the most of becoming a sort of detective in search of Daley and Daley's motive. It was Harrison's first try at passing the time. Daley was traced from the outcry that the houseboy Li heard in the quonset, to the PX, out the gate, up to when he left Master Sergeant Melvin Tracy at Echo Company of the 563rd. But Master Sergeant Tracy said that he had no idea why Daley went AWOL and there was no way for Harrison to know that Tracy hoped, when the chips were down, that Daley would come up with a better excuse.

But Captain Weisman was thorough and secretly suspicious that he, as a Jew, was Daley's reason. Warner and Harrison were detailed to search Daley's room. They sawed the lock off Daley's footlocker with a hacksaw and Harrison read through old letters. Warner paced the room asking himself where he would hide things. The tinted blue eyes of the woman in the portrait followed him and he turned the portrait face down on the shelf. When he jerked the blankets off the cot, letters and envelopes fluttered out from under the pillow. He grimaced at the lipstick impressions at the bottom of the wife's letter, and then read a letter from an Sfc Michael Riordan. "Well, that's it," he said, handing it to Harrison. "Boy, that's it," Harrison said. They gave the letter to Captain Weisman who shook his head and touched the bridge of his glasses with one straight index finger, as if this man he'd never seen smelled of weakness and incompetence that was morally offensive. Then the Colonel, the Group Commander, was shown the letter. There was a general satisfaction and relief, not that it got them any closer to cornering Daley. Harrison talked with the MPs and heard about Daley's hairbreadth escapes. "There's goddamn near a battalion of MPs after him," Harrison said. That was satisfying too. But the longer Daley was gone the more he became a side interest in dispensary life.

The new doctor was instantly aware of the major problem of passing the time and of the great liberty given to an

ingenious man for doing it. The former CO was hardly in the
air over the China Sea when Captain Weisman began
declaring himself in small and large ways. He made much of
the fact that he too was a draftee and there was no reason
why he and his men could not carve out a passably pleasant
way of life for themselves for the rest of their tours of duty.

Now every day of every year in every Army dispensary a
great many cocks show up in need of treatment—large cocks,
small cocks, long cocks, thin cocks, stubby cocks, tan cocks,
dusky cocks, pink cocks, cocks circumcised, cocks
uncircumcised, cocks dripping with gonorrhea, cocks with
chancroid ulcers, cocks with syphilis lesions, cocks with
warts, cocks with non-specific urethritis, cocks with waving
fungal forests, and just plain worried cocks. It was in this area
of treatment that Weisman found unexplored possibilities for
passing the time. He believed that the foreskin was unclean, a
mistake of evolution, a source of filth and infection, and he
found that most uncircumcised men also feared that this was
so. Immediately, though medical ordinance was against it due
to the supposed danger of infection in Korea, the dispensary
became involved in giving circumcisions. Sgt Francis and Pfc
Harrison found their trade for passing the time at last.

The doctor was eager, the patients were eager, the
neophyte medics were eager. Weisman was intent on training
every medic in the place to perform circumcisions. "Nothing
to it," he said. Warner alone among the younger men was
intensely bored by the new doctor's enthusiasms. But then
Warner was a shortimer, going back to the states in a couple

of months, and walking such a straight line since his court martial made his eyes tired of the interest in everything.

Now the circumcision of a grown man is a bloody thing. The rite began to be performed almost everyday at the dispensary in the relative privacy after sick call. Some of the finest cocks in Korea literally went down the drain. But circumcision itself was not enough, because Captain Weisman was a man who fancied himself the crusader of good causes and the destroyer of false taboos. Circumcisions, abortions, hysterectomies—anything that connected sex and social cause, he was there with medicine or knife. In addition, he preached that the best way to avoid disease and stay in good mental health was to have a steady shack, and he would personally give any man's shack a periodic check-up, treatment and abortion if necessary. Into this changed scene the NCOIC that Captain Weisman had never seen, made his first appearance.

In the front office by the waiting room, Jacobsen, Harrison and Henderson were trying out Cuban cigars. Meyer was leaning with his elbows on his pharmacy counter reading an account of Goering's last days and waving away the smoke that drifted from the cigars. Nowadays he wrapped innocuous bookjackets around his Nazi works. He felt intensely justified in having a Jew for his CO and huddled down into himself, while Weisman was amused with Meyer because it challenged his fair-mindedness. Down the hall in the doctor's office Francis was taking off the daily lap of foreskin under the doctor's supervision. Warner was in the Treatment Room

loudly humming the Spring Song from the first act of
"Die Walküre". . . .

Two MPs struggled through the door into the waiting room
with a man handcuffed between them and back kicked the
door shut against the booming icy air. The usual thing would
be the MPs bringing someone who needed treatment or
examination. The medics didn't know why they were staring.

A concentration camp could not have been more effective
in reducing Daley. His uniform was immensely baggy and
bunched around the belt, and the filth was a part of his skin
and cloth and hair. He hovered between the MP's sharp
uniforms that sparkled with brass and braided green loops.
He was trembling so steadily a hum seemed to come out of
him. But in his eyes, which were vivid in his dirty face, there
was a kind of quickness, awareness, cleverness, not missing a
chance. "Harrison. My clerk. Pfc Harrison." Daley named
them all. "Jacobsen. Henderson. Sergeant Meyer." He was
sardonic as far as his shaking lips would allow. "Daley,
Daley." Meyer repeated his name with a huddled, attentive,
motherly concern.

One of the MPs said, "Where do you want him?"

Harrison rushed to the doctor's office. Captain Weisman
stood cool and careful in the face of the announcement that
Daley was here. He told Harrison to put the NCOIC in the
back room. Daley was guided down the hall between the MPs
with Meyer tenderly holding him upright from behind. Daley
glanced into the doctor's office where a man was spread
upon a table with a great bloody mess around his groin and

Sergeant Francis was sawing a long black thread up and down in the man's cock. Daley shuddered profoundly, as if certain that what he saw were, worst of all, an imagination of his own. Captain Weisman, at the foot of the table, with his hands on his large hips, watched Daley with a chilled face. On the other side of the hall in the Treatment Room Warner was filling a syringe holding bottle and needle up to the light. Now it was Warner who started, the Wagnerian aria snatched from his throat. "Sarge," he said. Daley shivered out the words. "Corporal Warner. My Senior Aidman."

Harrison followed the MPs out to their jeep to get their story while the other medics laid Daley on the cot in the back room. The doctor kneeled by the cot and began examining his NCOIC with a well-drilled calm. Daley's cheeks twitched when the stethoscope touched his chest and he was trembling so violently that the cot was shaking. Everyone in the dispensary crowded in the room and the doorway. Sergeant Francis was left alone to sew up the cock of the man on the table in the doctor's office. With the blasé smile of morphine, the man was asking Francis what he should do if he got a hardon. "You won't," Francis said. Daley was stripped, bathed, by Jacobsen and Henderson, who were decidedly shy of washing the body of their sergeant. Then he was given on the doctor's orders a shot for DTs, intravenous feeding of glucose solution, and a sedative. Jacobsen and Henderson were alternately posted to guard the door of the room and make sure that Daley didn't crawl away.

Now the argument began in earnest among the Group

officers about what should be done with him. Captain
Weisman wanted to give him a court-martial as tough as the
Code of Military Justice would allow. In Army slang, he
wanted Daley hung. But the Group officers were wary
because Daley was a Master Sergeant, because he was RA,
and because the morale of the RA NCOs would be badly
affected if one of their members, with otherwise such a good
record, were so degraded. They said that any man who
committed himself to the Army should be permitted one or
two major blow-ups, if his record were otherwise
commendable. The punishment should be no more than
company punishment, withdrawal of pass privileges, nothing
put on his record, no stripes taken away, no dishonor.
Weisman, however, was the CO, the official initiator of
charges, and the charges would be drawn up by him. He was
just as strong in saying that the letter of the Military Code
should apply to Daley as well as any draftee. He was saying it
publicly and gaining much admiration from many of the men
in his dispensary.

When he first came to Korea, Corporal Warner might have
agreed with the new doctor about punishing Daley. But after
a year's duty he too had blown up and gathered a stack of
charges against himself, from resisting arrest to drunken
driving, to driving without a tripticket, to being in an off
limits area and out of uniform, all in one night. The Group
Commander, who now wanted to spare Daley, had wanted
Warner "hung" as an example case. "You did right, Corporal
Warner," Daley said, trembling from head to toe on the cot,

and Warner sensed that Daley wanted someone to dissuade the doctor. "You didn't lie down and die. You didn't take their rubber-stamp defense counsel. You fought back. You were the only one that fought back. I'm glad you kept your stripes." Warner was pleased, but Warner was staying on his prescribed straight line, and there was still not much to say between him and Daley. Daley's NCO buddies came to see him and closed the door of the room to talk strategy. Master Sergeant Tracy always left the room more sad and cautious than ever. It was Daley, without the help of anyone, who resolved the issue between the Group officers and the new doctor.

He did not ask for his mail and it was not given to him.

His rage returned with his strength.

After three days of treatment he was able to walk. He asked Jacobsen to take him to the latrine. It was reasonable for him to wear his field jacket and gloves and muffler even though the other medics, without bundling up, danced from the back door to the latrine, pissed, and danced back again. When Daley took his piss and came out of the latrine buttoning up, "Look at that over there," he said, pointing out and away. Jacobsen turned to look, and when he turned back around, Daley was gone. It was flabbergasting that Daley got away with it.

The Officer of the Day was notified and the huge Engineer compound, fenced by doubled barbwire with a trough of barbwire on top and paced by guards, was searched from one end to the other. It was not believed that Daley could get away. But in two days the reports came back from the MPs that he was in the native bars again, elusive as ever. "He'll be busted to buck private," Captain Weisman said. "There'll be nothing but dust left on his arm." The Captain's eyes really flashed.

4

Daley had timed it just right and when Jacobsen looked where he pointed he dodged around the corner of the nearby pre-fab, turned the next corner and put the building between him and Jacobsen. He slipped into the motor pool, into a rank of dump trucks, and climbed over the back and into the bottom of an empty truck that was just starting out. With this force that drove him, that had to be followed, he was capable of instant right decision. In the crusted depths of the truck he was banged and bounced but it went through the gate slowing only for the guard's recognition, then sped down the MSR. When it slowed for traffic by the Fire Station whorehouse area, Daley jumped off. He waved at the truck whose driver had still not seen him, and went to find Plain Jane, slipping a ten dollar bill into his glove. He had no plans, only the need and awareness of booze.

Again the MPs were in the streets and in and out of the bars. He acted from one drink to another, from one bar to another, back in the routine of being carried by the raging force that packed him from place to place whatever way it could get him there. Plain Jane was leading him home at night.

MPs came right into their courtyard. "No speak-ee, no speak-ee," he told Plain Jane who hurried into native Korean dress, rather than Western, to head them off. Daley climbed onto the roof and lay on the steep slant of the tiles holding onto the peak with his hands. The narrow street dropped more than fifty feet so the MPs down there couldn't see him and the ones in the house did not even consider that he might be on the roof. No one was more astonished than Plain Jane that they couldn't find him. When he crawled back through the window, she shrieked.

He began to hallucinate.

His rage went in every direction.

Milly came and stood by his pallet, in her baby-doll nightie, holding a panful of cold white grease with charred bacon bits stuck in it. "Bitch, bitch," he screamed. She was holding the pan so he could see in it, that she was ashamed and he was accused, and the white grease and the charred bacon bits slipped and began to flow over the edge. . . . "*Is that what we were working for?*" . . . hordes of snakes roared through his legs and under his arms. He could hear Milly saying his name, "Willy, Willy," but he couldn't hear a word from Plain Jane who threw herself upon him and tried to burrow through his thrashing and quiet him. The walls spiralled inward. . . .

Again he got so unsteady that he could not always walk or run from the MPs. Again he was paying two or three shoeshine boys at every bar to watch the streets. Again there were times when there was no other way except to crawl. He was crawling on all fours with Koreans simply moving away from him in fear and wonderment and he realized he wasn't going to make it. There was a hole in the side of the street. He inched backward into the sewer, and Milly was with him in the sewer. "Bitch, go away, bitch." The ooze of shit came halfway up his boots. He couldn't smell it. He understood that it couldn't get at him. He held onto the rocks at the opening as if onto the edge of a life raft. That was the only way he could stand on his feet. He watched shiny-booted MPs go by.

Then he was crawling, and to him it was as if he crawled between two mirrors—crawled on the surface of one mirror that stretched out endlessly with another mirror just above his head that also stretched out, crawled between them, with a flashing reverberating. . . . That was the way the MPs found him, tossing his head, with his eyes rolling white, and both lenses in his glasses cracked and filmed with filth.

This time the MPs radioed the PMO and the PMO called the dispensary. They were still under orders not to arrest him. Corporal Warner took the jeep to get Daley. He was excited and proud for the experience. It seemed to him that Daley was the only man in the area who was doing something that had to be done. Daley was still crawling around, as if blinded, inside a circle of MPs who cuffed their gloved hands together and huffed steam. Now and then, when Daley reached the edge of the circle, an MP would nudge him with a booted foot to keep him inside it. It was easy to see why they didn't want to touch him. Daley was a piece of sewage. Corporal Warner had to dump him into the jeep.

The MPs followed them back to the dispensary.

5

Captain Weisman closed the door of his office so the MPs with Warner and Daley wouldn't see Sergeant Homer Francis' steady shack, with only a brassiere on, sitting on the edge of the examining table chewing bubble gum. Daley was hustled onto the cot in the back room, stripped, washed. The same treatment began, intravenous glucose feeding, shot for DTs, and sedatives. But two guards were posted on him this time, and Weisman said that he would have their ass if Daley got away. The argument between him and the Group officers on how Daley was to be punished was stalemated. Weisman thought Daley was nailed now so no one could disagree, but the Colonel insisted that Weisman just get Daley off the booze—wasn't he the doctor, for God's sake?—and then maybe they could make a compromise. The Protestant chaplain and the Catholic chaplain were sent to talk with Daley, separately. Daley only chattered away from head to foot and the chaplains left, separately. "He is resting," the Catholic chaplain said. "Where's the rabbi?" Weisman said, wryly.

For three days Daley lay in the room soaking up glucose and strength. The guards Jacobsen and Henderson, and sometimes Harrison, played blackjack and read Big Little Smilin' Jack pornography books, and beat their gums about their mutual interests of drugs and ass. When Daley needed to piss, one walked in front and another behind him. Daley was hard and silent and wouldn't talk with them. On the third day they fed him three good meals. At midnight Pfc Henderson opened the door with a canteen cup of grapefruit juice, and Daley was gone. "Sarge," he said, in a sort of whimper. He gazed around the little room, kneeled and looked under the cot. Daley had vanished. Henderson immediately popped a benzedrine, and washed it down with the grapefruit juice. He was feeling the good smooth jitter of the benny when he phoned Captain Weisman out of bed at the BOQ and reported the disappearance. There was a stuffed silence in the phone. Then Captain Weisman said, strangely, that he was not superstitious.

Again the compound guards were alerted. Again the dispensary was searched and all the pre-fabs nearby. Again the compound was ransacked. Again they couldn't find him. Men searched the room and marvelled. Every one of them looked under the cot, sometimes twice. There was only an old stove-pipe opening near the ceiling, covered with a loose flap, and that opening was meager. Warner measured the width of the square hole with his hands and compared it with his own lean hips. He was really proud of Daley. "Look," he said, "I'd lose some skin," and that started everybody to shaking their heads. Daley had become wondrously thin in the past few weeks.

Daley's second escape got the doctor called on the carpet

by the Colonel where he was told that he was in the Army and had better start proving himself to be an officer capable of commanding men. Weisman's demands that Daley get the same treatment as any other soldier were not even politely ignored. He was told to shut up, he couldn't even keep a shaky little alcoholic under lock and key, and the Colonel was shaking when he said it. Captain Weisman, in turn, found himself insensibly chewing out Jacobsen and Henderson. It was Daley's revenge.

The Colonel stared at the stove-pipe hole with none of the pleasure that Corporal Warner showed. How was this one indomitable AWOL to be stopped? How were they to discipline him without embarassing the loyalty of the Regular Army Master Sergeants who knew each other intimately from Korea to Frankfurt? Worst of all, right now, how were they to catch him again? And if they caught him for a third time, where could they put him, so he would stay put until they made a decision that satisfied all contingencies? Captain Weisman sensed that it would be a good idea to shift the blame so he mentioned his minor psychiatric training and suggested that Daley was suicidal.

The MPs received no reports of Daley in his old haunts. Their patrol boats began dragging Pusan Harbor for his body.

Daley always escaped in such simple ways that no one else would even consider them. This time he stood on a chair and dropped his bulky field jacket out of the stove-pipe hole and then skinned through it himself. It was then that he did again what couldn't be done. He timed the pacing of the guard along the compound fence and simply climbed over the doubled barbwire and over the trough of barbwire at the top, picking up a few small cuts and congratulating himself on having his tetanus shots. He still had some money. He was in good shape. He stayed with Plain Jane that night only, and then shifted to Yong-Do, the big dome-shaped island connected by a short bridge to the mainland city.

With only his rage and a bottle for company he crawled under a dock area where men, women, children, nobody knew how many, lived with their tiny smoky fires heating blackened cans of rice. They peered at him with none of the fear and shame of the gooks in the street, but he cared not a damn and they let him shrink up by himself. They were all black with dirt and wrapped in rags, and only their eyes showed clean in their faces. He was right that the MPs would not follow him, even though the garbage and filth was frozen hard.

It was different under the docks because he didn't have to run from them. He could drink. He could let the rage, that was so stern and sweet and so insatiable, take and carry him. "You go away, bitch," he said, as if she did not frighten him, as if he'd had enough of her. But Milly was here, there, everywhere, maybe suddenly sitting on her knees with her hands in her lap close by, angry or ashamed in a way that accused him. Or she was covered with blood. When she was covered with blood, she was silent, without eyes.

He came out in the busy daytime to buy his booze.

A woman died an arm's length from him one afternoon of what he thought was pneumonia. He didn't bother to move away from her. A little gook kid, boy or girl he didn't know, rags tied thickly around it, whimpered and pushed against the woman. Faraway through the opening under the dock a green and white MP patrol boat inched across the harbor with the stillness of distance. By the time the distance was dark and prickled by lights, the woman was silent. The gook kid just sat there in a lump. The demanding glimmer of the eyes in the little face wrapped in rags caused Daley to make the costly effort of kneeling and pressing his ear to the woman's chest. Nothing. "Angry as hell," Daley thought, dreamy with cold and booze. "Thinks its mamasan's asleep. Half the mother-fucking city lives this way." He took the pint out of his pocket and measured its contents with his finger shaking against the bottle. He decided, slowly, that it wouldn't do any good to give the child any of the booze. For fear authorities might come for the body he moved away as far as possible under the docks.

He lost his glasses and had to squint hard when anything came close to him. The first sign of a change was when he wanted to be with Plain Jane again, not sexually, but something in him, something deeper than cold, was chilly, as the wet March air itself. Feeling his way along railings and the sides of buildings for support, he crossed the bridge into the mainland city. In a crowd in the first traffic circle he patted the spare tire on the back of an MP jeep and thought it was a good omen. Plain Jane was dressed up for the bar business when he crawled into the narrow hallway of her house. He squinted up, at bright red lips and blue shadowed eyes, and then fumbled numbly in his pockets for money. He slumped asleep right there at her feet with his hands in his pockets.

For two days he groveled in the pallets on the warm floor, drinking less and less, eating large hunks of rice with seaweed streaked through it, and he liked the seaweed. Plain Jane went out with a note on which he'd lettered GRAPEFRUIT JUICE and came back with several big cans from the black market. "Sergeant, crazy taksan michengai sergeant," she said, in a detached tone, running her fingers through his hair. Oh, God, it felt good, her holding his head and running her fingers through his hair and to hell with her tone. The third day he woke with the chilly place in him warmed at last.

The force, the rage, was diminished, diminishing, even gone. He wondered what day it was. Hard as he tried he couldn't get Plain Jane to understand that he wanted a calendar. It was amusing when he thought of going out to the bars to find a calendar. Then it amused even more when he realized that a calendar wouldn't help him at all. He didn't know how many days he had been gone. He was worried whether it was more than thirty days, whether he was, technically, a deserter. The only thing he could do he thought was to get his uniform cleaned and pressed, his boots shined, and surrender. Plain Jane sent one of the children in the house with his OG uniform and his boots, hat and field jacket to a little shop that tried to make a living cleaning and pressing GI clothing. She understood that he was going back,

and he was barely able to tolerate her sad smile. He was
working on the last can of grapefruit juice.

It was imperative, as an honorable gesture that would
stand in his favor, that he be able to surrender before he was
caught. It would not be very useful as a gesture to surrender
to the doctor back at the dispensary. He wanted to be in the
hands of the RAs anyway. The Provost Marshall's Office was
the place. The middle of the day seemed the busiest and most
likely time to get from here to there. For the first time he was
scared of being caught and uneasy about making a mistake.

Late the next morning he gave her all the money he had in
his pockets, about 4 dollars and some change. It meant the
end of any chance of going back into the streets. "That ought
to about do it, jo-san," he said. It was a sunny, chilly, early
spring day and the kids, that he had never got straight, all
Korean, no GI mixture, were shrieking in the courtyard
playing a sort of peek-a-boo with a cloth they draped over
their heads. Then he said goodbye to her. "Comupsomida
very much," he said. "See you in the funny papers." Plain
Jane said little and she was still wearing the loose white
gown. She came no further than the doorway, not quite in the
sunlight. "Comupsomida. You come back, sergeant," she said.
There was that smile again.

When he walked away from her he was nagged by a
desolate whimper in his belly. "Go back and hug her." Not
native custom. He looked at the amazing shine on his boots,
then doubled his fists in his pockets and continued his brazen
stroll to the PMO, with the thin, exhilarated, cautious feeling
of a man who has been in a sickbed for a long time. He was

glancing right and left to keep away from MPs who might recognize and arrest him before he got there.

Koreans were crisscrossing the streets in continuous movement. "I ought to hitch a ride." He hailed a Quartermaster three-quarter on the MSR and rode right to the steps of the PMO. "Don't do anything I wouldn't do." the driver yelled at him. Again he was nagged by the wish that he had hugged Plain Jane.

Sharply uniformed, glittering MPs were coming and going in the waiting room. With a sort of hide and seek triumph Daley stood before the PMO desk that came up as high as his chest. It just so happened, as it was always happening, that he recognized the desk sergeant from a tour in Panama and another tour in Germany. Sfc Perkins shifted expectantly behind the desk and looked down at Daley without recognition. "Master Sergeant William Daley reporting AWOL," Daley said. Daley knew how to make the right appeasements. "I aint forgot that I wear a uniform, Perkins." Daley stepped back from the desk and stood so Perkins could look him up and down, the uniform gathered in fistfuls around the belt, but clean and pressed, the boots shined. Perkins would be giving this testimony on his behalf.

"Christ, Daley," Perkins said, "how did you do it?"

7

Daley had been absent without leave for more than thirty days, but the days were not counted continuously so he avoided the charge of desertion. The Colonel, tap-tap-tapping his everlasting riding crop on his thigh, visited Captain Weisman and told him how to write up the court martial charges. With the promise that Daley would be transferred north to Inchon, out of sight and out of mind, Weisman consented to a Summary Court-Martial, rigged all the way, in which Daley would lose one stripe. It was formidable for a Master Sergeant to lose a stripe, and easier to move from buck private to Sfc than from Sfc to Master. But it was the most serious and least degrading punishment the Colonel could figure out. The Colonel himself would sit as the court.

The court martial was simple and snappy, pre-determined and done by rote. Daley was court-martialled the next morning and on orders to be transferred to Inchon that afternoon. Nobody wanted him to have the slightest chance or temptation to take off again. Daley came out of the court-martial into the company of a host of his buddies waiting for him, all sergeants. They walked with him to the dispensary to get his orders, to say their goodbyes, and to make sure that he didn't take off again.

"You lose that, Corporal Warner, and you lose something," Daley said, pointing at the stripes on his sleeve where one rocker was cut off.

"Sarge," Warner said, "how did you do it?"

"I'll tell you how." Daley was really angered by the Corporal's voice and he jammed a finger against Warner's chest and said *anything you have to do, you can do it.* "I'm glad you kept your stripes, Corporal." Wherever Daley stood,

now in a uniform tailored to fit him at the door of the clerk's
office in the dispensary, he was definitive, lean and tough and
caustic, and there was not the limberness of any dream about
him. "Pfc Harrison," he said. Pfc Harrison handed Daley his
orders and a fistful of mail, six weeks of it.

It was early afternoon in the quonset hut. Everything was as
peaceful as the starry specks of dust in the blocks of sunlight.
Daley sat on the bunk that he had not slept in for weeks
while Tracy and two other sergeants walked around the room.
Li the houseboy was stacking up the vast number of comic
books, magazines and paperbacks. "You want them, Tracy?"

"Sure," Tracy said, with just a tinge of covetous
satisfaction.

"Put in this box and this box, boysan," Daley said.

Daley put on his second pair of glasses, as carefully as one
of the old letterwriters squatting on a mat on a streetcorner of
Pusan. By the postmarks he saw that Milly's letters became
more and more frequent, plastered with kisses on the back.
Milly . . . Milly . . . she was strange and distant. He couldn't
see her. He took her portrait and stuffed it into his duffel bag
without looking at it. There were two letters from Riordan.
"The washbasin, boysan," Daley said. The houseboy held the
washbasin solemnly while Daley burned Riordan's letters
without opening them. The sergeants in the room watched
uncomfortably, silently. "Riordan," Daley said to Tracy. Tracy
was the only who knew, he thought. Tracy nodded
without comment.

First Daley read the two letters from his oldest boy Kenny.

He could see Kenny, but still strange and distant. Well, if Milly was whoring around it wasn't affecting the kids. He read her two cablegrams before he read her letters. She was worried sick she said. She wanted him to use the overseas phone at the PX. "Not fucking likely," Daley snarled with a laugh, and the men in the room glanced at him and then looked away. He could imagine himself talking to her while her lover, whoever he was, sat at a table just outside the booth. No, she would get the call at home—he might talk to the kids. No, he wasn't going to call. He would write her a few lines in a couple of days. The return address would show him to be Sfc Daley. She might wonder about that. Riordan, you sonofabitch, you got me busted.

He scanned Milly's letters for any information about the kids and about the house, and he was not ashamed of the strangeness and distance. Everybody had flu back in February. There was an odd piece of folded up paper in one letter and it came as a shock into Daley's hand. It was a nursery school drawing from little Lucy and Lucy told her Mommy to tell her Daddy that the drawing was about a man and a woman and three children and a house and railroad tracks, yellow, green, and brown crayon, with orange crayon streaks. Daley showed it to Tracy. "My daughter," he said. The other two sergeants looked over Tracy's shoulders and asked Daley how old his daughter was. "Four and a half this month," Daley said. He folded the drawing up and put it in his breast pocket and buttoned the pocket. He read what Milly wrote about the fishing lodge. . . . he wished he hadn't burned Riordan's letters. No, baby, I'm going for thirty. Not for any fishing lodge. RA all the way. That, he realized, was the one decision he had made. There'll be another war, he thought. I'll get that fucking rocker back.

He laughed aloud as he jerked all the photos off the walls and stuffed them willy-nilly into the duffel bag. Then he lifted the calendar off the wall, and glared at all the days he had not crossed off in February. He held the calendar up and swung it around for the other men in the room to see. They were appreciative of his humor. He tore off the month of February and tossed it into the wastebasket and there was the virginal month of March. He was staring at that picture of the pretty miss on horseback under the red-turning maple tree looking out over the rail fence and the sunset wheat field. It made him suddenly remember the time when he shoved Plain Jane's head down into his crotch, as if it were as faraway as Milly. Then he saw the little gook kid squatting by its dead mamasan under the docks.

Folding the calendar, he creased it tightly several times and then wadded it and tossed it into the wastebasket. "Got everything, Willy?" It was Tracy speaking. Daley looked around the room and nodded. Tracy shouldered the duffel bag and the other two sergeants carried out the footlocker. "Here, boysan," Daley said, giving Li the houseboy two one dollar bills. Li danced out of the room with a big smile. "Comupsomida," he yelled. There was only a navy blue flight bag left for Daley.

Warner showed up in the doorway saying that the

three-quarter from the motor pool was here and ready to take Daley to K-9 airport. "Anything I can carry, papasan?"

"Oopso," Daley said.

Warner turned to go out. "Corporal Warner," Daley said softly. Daley was stooped over the flight bag on the floor pulling out his old .45. "Je-e-e-e-e-e-sus-s-s," Warner said. For one stark second he didn't know whether to run away from Daley or toward him. Daley stood straight and, as if saying the Pledge of Allegiance, pointed the .45 at his own chest, with the mirror behind him and the flight bag on the floor by his feet. It was the way a CID sergeant, a buddy of Daley's had done it a few months ago. "Shit," Daley laughed, "did you think I was going to do it?" He put the .45 back into the flight bag and zipped it shut. Warner was gnawing one side of his mouth. "Let's go, boysan," Daley said.

Captain Weisman and Sergeant Francis and Pfc Harrison were collecting another foreskin in the doctor's office so they were not present in the parking lot. Sergeant Meyer moved about busily, helping pile Daley's duffel bag and footlocker and boxes into the back of the three-quarter. Daley once again came up to Warner and extended his closed fist as if to give Warner something. Warner was afraid of a joke and put out his hand gingerly. "Just to let you know, Corporal," Daley said, spilling several capsules into Warner's hand. One glance and Warner knew the capsules were little yellow nembutals. "Oh, fuck it, sarge," he said. Daley was gone in the back of the three-quarter with his buddies and didn't wave or look back.

Warner waited until Meyer was hunched on his high stool
in his pharmacy brooding over Daley's departure, with a copy
of the *Papers of Franz von Papen,* wrapped in a Taylor
Caldwell bookjacket, turned on its face on his thigh. Warner
rapped on the counter. "I think you ought to check your
security cabinet, sergeant." He started counting the
nembutals one by one onto the counter.

"What the hell have you—?"

"*Twelve.*" Warner looked up.

"The shitass," Meyer said.

He unlocked his security cabinet and counted his
nembutals and indeed twelve were missing. "The shitass." It
was Daley's last escape on them. It was his way of saying that
he could do anything he wanted to do. He could even stay in
the Army for a total of thirty years. "The fucking shitass,"
Meyer said.

"Bet he never gets to Inchon," Jacobsen said.

"Bet he runs into a bottle before he gets there."

"He better get to Inchon."

"He said he's going for thirty. Gung-ho. Mother fuck."

"He's all burned out. He'll get there."

VISIT TO MY GRANDFATHER'S GRAVE ALONE

At last I got to go to my grandfather's grave alone.

I came back from Mexico with a fine full beard. I expected a hilarious reception at my grandmother's in Missouri, and tickled the tip of my tongue on the corners of my mustache thinking about it. She lives by herself in town now. But her wild and warm welcome, though tempered by grief, has not yet aged. It is still anticipated with a goodly dash of tremulousness.

We lived, when I was a boy, barely twenty miles away, and came to their farm often. Nevertheless grandmother always acted as if a visit from us were some cosmic surprise. We piled out of the car into the air that shrilled with her crying to granddad, if he wasn't in the fields,

"My stars, dad, why you'd never guess who's come visiting!"

My heated giggling seizures intensified as she came humping urgently over the yard to meet us, with the side-dip body-swing rhythm that accommodates her rheumatic leg.

I remember distinctly, when very young, being mashed against her broad legs somewhere above the knees and below the hips. Then came the time when her hands leaped out and planted my head in her belly, and she stooped and hugged me but good Brrrrrrr with tearful exuberance climaxed, on release, with a big whooping laugh. Up to a point somewhere below her breasts I had little idea of my rights as a person, and I submitted breathlessly and helplessly. About the time when I was nearly as tall as she, around eleven or twelve, I began scheming to escape her splendid greeting, which I considered very akin to enduring a creek-baptismal every week. But if not quick on her feet, she was quick with feelings, and I was not successful. "Aw-w-w, grandmother." I struggled and vainly shortened the ordeal by a second or so.

Grandmother met us carried headlong on the surge of her unthinking motherly passion. She was as lucky to survive as those on whom that mill-race passion opened.

My granddad came forward with style.

He came securely tall behind her, relaxed and strong, down the path through the yard up to the gate under the big oak tree, with his hands in the pockets of his overalls or under the bib. He grinned in a way that never teased or writhed in me, the easy affection all in the words and the manner. In summer the in-reaching green of the land back-dropped his approach. In winter the bleak land isolated his height. For when I remember him, I remember the land.

Old American farming methods brought the Ozarks into an ugly, gullied, dusty, shacky, superstitious ruin by the time of the depression. And yet farmers continued planting corn on a land where you cannot take a step forward or backward or to either side without going up or down. And they continued plowing up and down hill, and going right when they should have gone left, and going up when they should have gone around. The Ozarks grew younger and greener as the years passed, as grass and ponds and forest replaced the gullies. And my grandfather's hair stayed mostly dark, young too I want to think, until the day he died at seventy two. He was a leader. He could inspire. But first and last he loved working the soil himself.

I remember the clear June nights, and the June afternoons, and granddad sitting in the split-hickory rocking chair under the persimmon tree, on a gentle height in the yard, with all his generations distributed more or less around him, on the grass, on the broken concrete porch, near the lilac bush, by the pump. His garden, from which came much of their fresh or canned food, lay stripped out behind him in rows of varying shades and heights of green, and no fence separated it from the yard. Watermelons and bottles of beer and pop bumped about with cakes of ice in tubs. Children ganged up for the ice-cream freezer's rigorous ritual, turned the handle until it stuck, and then backed away before the tongue-in-cheek teasing of uncles whose great grown muscles ground the handle round and round again. Then came the contest. One uncle after another tried the handle until it set solid.

This abundance occurred in the depression. They drew a

magic circle around us kids and somehow they managed a feast everytime relatives came home from cities, or even from nearby, and eventually we all came home from cities. Our talk was close around granddad in the night vastly filled with the singing of tree-frogs and crickets, and the jolting churrings of katydids. His despotic benevolence, his serious, tense, or funny presentation, his way and manner in talking politics or telling stories, his laughing scorn, spellbound me.

I hunted the public library. I came up with every book and pamphlet available on soil conservation. I read them right along with Shakespeare, Zane Grey, and my father's history books, the books that were all around my childhood.

In terror of death in his middle fifties granddad went from church to church trying to believe in the Christian terror. But Deism was traditional with his people. They came to Missouri from Virginia through Kentucky, preserving the deist faith as more backward parts of the hills preserved archaic forms of the language. He couldn't overcome his inborn common sense.

He could believe in the land.

I came fully armed from my reading to those family night talks. I came with deadly seriousness, the words of the pamphlets used as a code between him and me. I talked of terracing. I spoke of the Nixon type and the Broad-Base type with nearly professional familiarity. I talked of contour-plowing, watershed control, forest management, deep and shallow plowing, ponds, grass and cattle farming as opposed to grain farming, wildlife conservation, multiflora rose, and a host of other things.

Sometime around here came my granddad's remark, "John and me, get a little Ford tractor, and *we'd* farm some land"— delivered with that particular tongue-in-cheek intonation, understated exaggeration.

I listened from my new-won position. And the talk varied from politics and farming, to horses and hounds, hunting and fishing, to neighborhood happenings and ancestral anecdotes. There was much eccentricity to emulate in these stories.

At twenty-eight, arriving from Mexico, I was certain that my full beard would excite a memorable exuberance in my grandmother. I grinned with the thought as I walked from the bus station to her house, through the dry, austere sunlight of September.

I bounded onto her porch through the spyrrhea that shook dryly. Through the screen-door I saw grandmother, in hazy shape in the living room, already hit by the sight of me and my beard. I swung open the screen-door, strode up beside her, and the screen whanged shut behind me.

Me and my beard grinned down into her incredible glee. Her glasses flashed when they caught the light just so. She is short. She does not look fat. She looks perfectly shaped. She glanced up at me and then doubled over with laughter, her back broad as a table. She glanced up cautiously again, as if the beard might have providentially disappeared, and then doubled over laughing again. Above her rheumatic knees, she is remarkably agile.

For the first time she seemed stopped from hugging me.

Curtains bellied gently by the windows around the room and I went momentarily barren thinking that her hesitation meant I wouldn't receive the usual overwhelming welcome. She folded her hands across her belly and bent gracefully back, her way of standing and talking to anyone six feet tall. She was squinting up at me as if the sun came over my shoulder into her eyes, looking for any opening where she could get through the beard to me. A grin was tweaking her lips. "Now where am I going to kiss you, John? That awful thing on your face."

I stated, "Most women like it."

"Well, *I* don't." She whooped with laughter, pounding her knee.

She looked slyly up toward me. She grabbed my head with both hands and jabbed a kiss onto my cheekbone above the beard line. *"There,"* she said, as if even at this age I was still contriving to escape her, and again had failed.

We settled down with coffee in the kitchen. Her talk is run-on, ranging the daily happenings of seventy years. The subject suggested by everything is her life with granddad, or everything is suggested by it. Now that granddad is dead she has come into her own with her men grandchildren. She is tuned nimbly to those natural rhythms in story and listener.

She was cooking while talking.

Her hands guess everything. She has never used a measuring cup. She could bake a thousand angel-food cakes in the wood stove on the farm without one cake falling. She complained that every angel-food she tried in her

blaring-white gas stove collapsed. "Seems like me and that
old wood stove just knew what to do. Oh, John, I'll tell you
we worked hard. All the children. All the work. Dark to dark.
Cooked with my hands and feet, they used to say." She
laughed. She demonstrated. She kicked the oven door shut
and reached in the same movement onto a shelf.

Electricity came a little late after much political coaxing
from my grandfather and others. Grandmother was sixty-five.
But she was happy when all those fiercely white promises
filled her kitchen. "We got everything new," she said, "and
dad sometimes used to complain it didn't taste the same." He
missed the pungent strength in smoked ham, thick bacon,
and sausage. With the deep freeze, the smokehouse became
a storing place for musty-rusty odds and ends.

Grandmother's threshing-day dinners were laid out in
enormous and excellent variety on big tables under the oaks
and maples. Those times of hardest work asked community
help and were made easier by celebration—threshing,
haying, quilting, canning, berry-picking, butchering. I sat on
the fence, on the edge of November, with my uncle who
always shot the hogs in the pen. He seldom contributed any
more work than the neatly-placed bullet. My granddad
leaped down into the pen and stuck the shot hogs, the blood
squealing across my sight. The long carcasses were hung by
their hindlegs from a tree, and then scalded and scraped until
white. Black kettles and barrels steamed luxuriously. Misting
guts rode in the tubs. There was bustling everywhere. The
most delicate meat, brains and such, was cooked and

feasted that very day. They worked hard, they wanted to work less. Now they miss that particular rapport, and maybe work less.

Grandmother's angel-food frustration rubs the wrong way against the important memory of herself in her youth. She courted a final social judgment with her cake's lightness and height.

"Grandmother," I said, barely tongue in cheek, "you must have cooked about sixty thousand meals."

Her usually quick response started, and then slowed with awe at herself. She said, "Oh, John, we worked hard."

She spoke of her good garden that year. "Oh, good corn, good tomatoes, good little potatoes and peas."

She wanted tomatoes for dinner. Dinner means the noon meal.

I went out to the garden, where the last little tomatoes glowed in the thick dusty sprawl of vines on the ground. I tested and picked the firm ones. They bulged with round sun-soaked heat against my cradled arms.

I was sitting beside the table and salting a tomato.

"They're good that way," Grandmother said, "right off the ground, when they've been resting in the sun."

She watched me and my beard eat.

When she laughs, her whole body joins in.

"Why, if you'd been stark naked with that awful thing on your face, I wouldn't thought a thing about it, I'd gone right out in the street and brought you in."

She feels her own life in her grandchildren. But death loves her mind too, and with people her own age, she often feels it.

That afternoon, Walter, her older brother, who lives across the street, came to tell her that a relative had just died out in a town near the Lake of the Ozarks. I had visited Walter earlier in the day so the uproar about the beard was now moderated.

He gave this old news of new death hesitantly concerned with how grandmother might take another reminder. She is considered to be touched with grief in a way that expresses itself unpredictably and disastrously.

She wailed quietly.

"It's out there in the street a-rolling from door to door." She writhed gently and came nearly into a rolling position in the chair while her hands rolled in her lap. "It just rolls from door to door. And it'll come through our door, Walter, sometime soon."

"Yes, it will," Walter said, his voice quick, his seventy-eight year old body lean and stiff.

He might have the deep-gripped stability of a conventionally religious faith. Or, having made the deist's peace with death as the completion of conscious life, he might be only paying lip service to church as entertainment. For those Ozark deists, God was all tucked-up somewhere after the most enormous expenditure of energy in the effort of Creation. Men awake have charge of the world, and death's last place is no larger than the grave. This skepticism sprang, like religious revelations, from the pressures of the imminence of death. One of my uncles once said in a

263

conspiring tone and only men in the car when we drove
away from a visit to the cemetery, "When I die might as well
throw my carcass out there on a ledge above the creek and
let the buzzards get me. You go back where you belong that
way and I don't think it makes no difference at all. You're
dead, you're dead all the way." It is largely the women who
promote and maintain the fervent communal funeral fact. In
the men's attitude there is an allegiance to an ideal that they
are alone, on their own, before the barehandedness of natural
happenings. And there seems to be a compulsion in their very
pulse to return, as dead plants and animals, into the processes
of life. If they bow their heads upon the weeping rail late in
life, it is usually the women who, with the tone of revenge
and welcome at last, have led the way.

Grandmother was crying quietly,

"I don't know why it happens. We worked, we worked
hard, we did the best we could for our children and
ourselves. Now they've flew away." Her hands flew in her lap.
"And it's just all shoved under the ground."

"Why, you know he's waiting for you, Aulty."

"No, I *don't* know," she said.

Beliefs about death were among the chary secrets, to be
tested gingerly. They wearily discussed going to the funeral.
How much trouble? How hot? Who would preach the
sermon? I hadn't known the newly dead relative at all. I saw
that this was my chance to make my four-years-postponed
trip alone to my granddad's grave. Grandmother asked me
several times to go to the funeral with her. I said no, always
suggesting that she go with Walter anyway, since I hadn't

known the relative and I had another mysterious thing I wanted to do. She respected my wishes and didn't press me for an explanation. After an afternoon of sporadic hesitations, she decided to go. It was the bee and the flower, she couldn't stay away from funerals.

At that moment I remembered my gift from Mexico for her. Maybe now I was giving it because she made possible my special trip to granddad's grave.

My gift was a black rebozo, with white fluffy tassels and a white Guatemalan design that alternated ranks of animals and people. Each rank's inhabitants conformed to one posture that varied from rank to rank but never within the rank.

"Why, John," she said, as I spread it over her extended arms.

She tried it on and wore it as a stole. Nicely, very nicely, it accented her round shoulders and lengthened her body, so nicely I decided not to tell her the correct way to wear it. She tilted her face from shoulder to shoulder, inspecting herself. For an awful moment I thought she didn't like it. I didn't know quite what to think when she said,

"John, you sure know how to pick things for women."

Sunday morning late she was ready to go to the funeral with Walter. She was dressed in a flowery blue-and-white dress and a bright white hat, handbag, and gloves. I was pleased at the way her outfit became her roundnesses in spirit and shape.

I was ready to take my aunt's car on my own special trip

to the cemetery. She had moved to Michigan, escaping the sharp-felt emptiness in the life-long familiar around her after my uncle died. I was supposed to drive the car up there to her. So I had the use of it.

Grandmother said,

"I won't ask where you're goin'."

Her face changed with a spasm of grief, as if she really knew where I was going. I worried a moment as Walter worried, what might spring from it. The spasm passed, and she became cheerful again, advising me on places to see. I promised to meet her at the information desk at the dam at 4 in the afternoon.

I drove on the plateau across country to where the road dived steeply through the county seat and down to the Osage river bottom. Here my memories began fitting into places with odd familiarity. It was also exactly the point where something solidly unfamiliar was situated. Among trees on top the hill crouched the small white hospital with the great green-trimmed window almost directly above the road. In there my granddad died. I was a thousand miles away when it happened. I looked up, and there was no person to be seen in the hospital or on the grounds. I saw only the ceiling up through the window and the shutters open, like arms, to the land.

I braked and turned sharply just past the foot of the hill and accelerated across the bottoms. As a child I saw the Osage River and its bottomland as singingly huge. My pulse still sings at the sight of it, but it is now another size, as Beagle hounds are smaller too.

MY GRANDFATHER'S GRAVE

The bridge rose under the car and stabbed into the other side's steep slope. It had been a very dry year. The river's water was daily concentrating, its green going richer and deeper, exposing stretches of sandbars.

I shifted to second and went roaring up into the country south of the river, our family's old home ground, where the hills are dramatically wilder. Here the driving became fun. I swooped up and down hills and around curves and sometimes up into curves and then up or down or straight behind the curves, a sense of the ease of flight, flashing through shade and sun.

I crossed Cattail Creek. Beds of stark stone and gravel lay abandoned by not even a glimmer of water on either side of the short bridge. I winced, thinking of the fish dead. In the hills crinkled yellow edges hotly sprinkled the hard September green. One of my grandfather's first farms was here when my mother was a child.

I reached the highest and most barren point in the county. A forest-fire lookout tower stands stilt-legged there, and the pastures show more outcroppings of blackish limestone than soil and grass. Around and around this point blue-hazed ridges rise into an ever-levelling downward distance. I swooped on a curve down the side of the long hill toward Brushy Fork.

A principal ancestor is buried in one of the old family cemeteries up the slope to the left, now become a pig-pen. He lorded over several thousand acres that commanded the most important natural transportation route in the area, got himself "elected" Sheriff and Tax-Collector at the same time, and charged toll to cross his land. He built a huge house, called appropriately just the Big House, and lived high as the rafters in it. His actions too became legends, a petering-out of his life in the common memory. Besides the achievement of living as a fabulous Ozark baron and contributing drastically to his land's ruin, he erected two nearly ineradicable images of himself, one a great chimney and the other a tombstone spire. Inside the Big House a man could stand upright in the chimney's fireplace. The Big House mysteriously burned down shortly after his death, with whispers of treasure and betrayal about the event. Another ordinary clapboard house was built up attached to the same chimney. In the cemetery his spire dominated the much smaller wife-and-son stones as he wished the chimney on the hill to dominate the land.

My grandfather, his grandson, was orphaned by tuberculosis at the age of four. According to the common practice, he was fed and housed by families who weren't harsh with him, but who got from him what work they could. At age nine, possibly because he was more effectively muscled, the principal ancestor chose to take him back under his roof. I don't know enough of the details to judge this belated beneficence. But I do remember that my granddad was fond of saying, with a laugh and a grand quick gesture, that he was not raised, he just *grew* up. You laughed. You saw corn, a plant more dependent than children supposedly are, springing up magically strong, like the man before your eyes.

MY GRANDFATHER'S GRAVE

One spring we discovered that the tombstone spire was knocked onto the ground among the present owner's rooting pigs. It lay crusted and caked with crumbly pig-sty dirt. Only the base stone, a respectable monument in itself, remained deep-set. My brother and I tried to lift the spire and put it back in place. But human strength could not put it back together again. *Shameful* grandmother thought the way the present owners let the cemetery go to hell. Because by now granddad's family was her family too and she was always urging granddad to buy the plot and keep it up and pretty it up. In his reluctance to respect the old bastard's remains granddad may well have been grudging the old bastard. But mostly granddad just didn't give a damn for cemeteries. For that reason I have always considered this particular ancestral place, with its spire twice as tall as a man, now become part of a pig-pen, more of a monument to my grandfather. I remembered the photograph of myself just back from Korea, standing beside the storied ancestor's spire with my doubled fist concealing an erection. I laughed alone in the car. Its wheels banged on the bridge crossing Brushy Fork. One or two isolated tiny pools gleamed among the stones. I had never seen the country so dry, yet the woods so green.

My fun-driving continued down the rushing dapples on the blacktop road until I reached Barren Fork. It is the largest creek of the three, and strangely named Barren. My eyes were relieved on sight of the big pools, the transparent summer-rich green of gravel-bottomed Ozark streams among feathery masses of willows and the shaggy-trunked sycamores. No current moved. Not a trickle darkened the expanses of gravel and rock that separated the pools. From the bridge, across a field and up a slope, the cemetery stones rested like a flock of sheep among the trees.

I turned onto the sinking-soft gravelled road and the car wallowed noisily with dust clouding the back window in the rearview mirror. I stopped the car near the cemetery gate. I saw the place was empty. With backhanded joy I swung the car-door shut behind me. Like cellophane the countryside crackled underfoot. And it would have burnt that quick too.

With sly-feeling nimbleness I passed stones that marked buried bodies that once walked in the same graveyard to face stones that marked buried bodies that once walked too.

Small weather-blackened door-shaped limestone slabs and hand-sized markers crowd the lower slope, all early settler stones, and mostly for children and babies. Grandmother remembers the names. We had walked there together the spring before. She gripped my arm, pumping for balance, body-swinging on her rheumatic legs, hobbling from grave to grave. She told the stories of some of the names. If I pointed to a name that was not familiar, she dismissed it dreamily as she would wave away a fly, and stooped with sad intensity toward a name she knew.

Now I walked on the upper slope where modern stones and granites flaunt their polished and blockily long sharp edges. I was grinning. I was alone.

It was good to stand before the stone of a man who knew there was no connection between life and death. His red granite glassily faced me, gently and roughly shouldered, earth-colored, as grandmother's sentiment wished it to be impressively. Only he wished a plain stone and plain burial and not to rot in the subsoil with thousand-dollar satin.

It was a very warm, very dry day. A little, a very little stickiness worked in my armpits, crotch, and at the base of my neck. A slight headache pressed on the back of my eyes. I stooped suddenly and checked the narrow depth of his name's letters with my index finger. It was too large. The letters were cut and blackened into the stone. My little finger couldn't probe bottom. On the first simple soft limestones, on the lower slope, the letters stood out and weather rubbed them into near obscurity. The dates on granddad's stone said that he lived seventy two years and some odd days.

I imagined no one in the grave. I had nothing to say to the stone. I had much to listen to in myself.

Grandmother told of his last day upright in the October world. The pain first rode into his chest and danced sharply on his heart in the light before the sun comes up, with the tops of things piling up out of the darkness. His cheek was pressed against the strong hide-smell of the quivering flank of a cow, froth building in the bucket under his milking hands. He fainted forward, crumpling, and the cow's hind legs bumped sideways with surprise. He recovered and closed his eyes tightly, trying to smother the pain. He calmed his own panic by calming the cow. "Hey, boss. Hey, boss."

He finished his morning milking. He came into the kitchen. Sunlight streamed through the pantry window's withered screen of morning glories. Maybe for the twenty-two-thousandth time he tasted that breakfast of fried eggs and ham or bacon, oatmeal, blackberries with cream, pan-fried biscuits with honey or blackberry jam. Maybe he complained again that the deep-frozen fresh meat didn't taste the same. But anyway he ate in the spatter-shadowed light reflected from the big white deep freeze, refrigerator, and stove. Grandmother continued her cooking chores throughout the kitchen. They talked. Granddad emphasized again, as grandmother put it, "that we are not meant to be preserved. We are intended to go back to the earth." It seems that he didn't completely trust his wife. He finished eating, but still sat at the table. They reminisced. And that was nothing new. Her thoughts were on daily preparations. Granddad got up to go out to work. He said, "How about a kiss, mom?" "Why," grandmother told me, laughing, "I didn't think a thing about it. I just flung my arms around him and kissed him right there." And neither was that anything new.

I have tried to sense his leathery bodily heaviness in the work-soft denim as he passed the cellar door on the concrete porch between the kitchen and the smokehouse. His workshoe heels dented the soft earth when he stopped for a moment by the two burning bushes on the edge of the garden. I know at that hour the sun stood one tree high, in the misty morning glow, above the far side of the massive October twist-and-crumple flattening toward the ground in his garden. His nervous fingers, under the bib of his overalls, lightly drummed his chest, sending a message from and into his body. And through the day the message carried bit by perplexing bit into his consciousness.

Afternoon, and he suddenly picked up and drove to town. That might have been another signal, going to see his friends upright once more, at the meeting-place on the dock of the MFA where all the sweet-smelling feed and produce is stacked, with ranks of scrubbed milk cans, cooped limy-smelling chickens, and crated eggs. He talked and teased and went serious with old friends who worked or called there. I remember especially the gentle, rightful laughter of his quick-judging scorn—always a demagogue and always ready to change his mind. A couple hours, and he returned to the farm. He worked by himself in the barn.

In the evening he drove up to the schoolhouse to take my schoolteacher aunt Doney home. She told me, "We walked together across the playground to the car. It was getting dark, John, and I couldn't see dad's face clearly and he was so quiet. We got to the car and he just turned and settled backward against the fender, and gripped his chest." She gripped her chest with her right hand over her heart to show the way he did it. " 'Doney,' he said, 'I've had such a awful pain here all day.' " He spoke over a few feet of air, a doomed distance, to his eldest daughter. And with this open admission he went home in open agony and lay down, no longer concealing himself from grandmother's worst fear. Now, in certain fear, she was with him. The doctor was called.

273

And granddad did not get up on his feet again.

Ten days he talked, thought, pained, and considered his wife and the white walls of the room in the country hospital above the river. Branches brightened by his window. Through their senseless movement he could see the river still summer-rich green, just before the water goes cold and brownish clear. People came day and night to see him. They crowded into the hospital and onto the grounds outside. His charisma almost drew them into the grave with him. But only the family was allowed in his room. And granddad had no answer for the doctor who said there was no chance. But this time it may well have been difficult for him to see where his life left off in the all-absorbing land and nature that he loved. On the last day he called grandmother's attention to a striking sunset over the bottomland. Out of his worst rampant pain, he pleaded to see only one other person. It was the son of a relative who lost his wife. Granddad had raised the half-orphaned boy, attracted to his need as he was attracted to the orphaned land. And he may have been calling to his orphaned self in childhood, orphaned now again. Ten days his blood struggled to get around or solve the coronary clot, as men have always struggled to get around the final block in existence, and have failed, as his blood failed.

In the cemetery I gladdened with every bodily movement and feeling in the sun.

I walked up the slope past the long hard-edged grey stone

of my hunter-horseman uncle. His cunning with guns, dogs, and horses was uncanny. I remembered him lean and grey as the earliest dawn when he came home with the hounds. My aunt had shown me a color photograph of him standing against a bank of blooming peach trees three weeks before he died. I was surprised to see that he had gotten heavy in his fifties. I looked down on the cemetery drive. He was spreading gravel there when the stomach ulcer hemorrhaged. His wife's car, that I would drive to Michigan, that he drove himself, gleamed emptily there now.

I thrilled. I looked over Barren Fork, over the pools where the sky plunged into the earth, at the wild hills where nothing moved but me. A woman on the outer edge of the funeral told grandmother that a redbird sang in a cedar throughout the lowering of granddad's casket and the filling of the grave. It was thought a sign, a blessing, because here with all the noise and a cemetery full of people the redbird, a messenger, stayed and sang.

I looked over the cemetery fence into the rising woods on the hill. There the dry dappled shade shivered stiffly now and then. I moved and looked eagerly everywhere. And apparently I was looking for exactly what I saw. I sat in the shade of an oak in the cemetery's upper virginal corner, just thick rough sod and leaves. If this corner ever saw itself sheared with a shovel or plow, going by the dates on the oldest stones it was over a hundred years ago. Little green shoots huddled beneath the bleached haze of the sod's seeded and dead earliest grass of the year. With the flat of

my hand I tested the sod's resilience. Only the sternest
drouth could blot up its moisture. Below and to the side of
the cemetery the over-grazed pasture was rusty and cracked
with dryness. The contrast proved again my granddad's case,
that, in our country, soil-and-water control is practiced best
in cemeteries.

A big shadow rushed after itself over the ground only a
few feet away. I ran out from under the oak. Up I looked into
the caustic sky. A buzzard sailed there. I laughed. And then
three buzzards cruised over the graveyard, where there was
no carrion to pick. They began circling the pasture. A hawk
skimmed treetops down the hill above the cemetery, making
no noise either, but causing a zipping impression. He circled
faster, tighter, beneath the buzzards. Hard green acorns rolled
under my shoes. A joyful play-act suddenly developed. I
chose two acorns. I tried their weight and firmness and shook
them at my ear. They were solid, fertile.

I bounded down the slope to granddad's stone. I planted
one acorn under his name and one under grandmother's
name with her birth date and the dash and the smooth space
where the death date will be cut. Once the spring before,
when we visited the grave in the family troop, I saw
grandmother staring at her unfulfilled name and her
unbroken section of ground. Her plump child-like cheeks
were twitching. She jabbed out her arm. Her pointing finger
trembled. "Not enough room," she complained, as if the
grave were a special apartment where she and granddad
would reside after death and she'd been cheated in leasing

this one forever. We assured her there was plenty of room. With my hands I measured the plot against her girth to prove it.

I poked the acorns deeper into the tight crevice between the earth and the stone down into the moisture. I wanted them to sprout.

She was fifteen when they got married, sixty-seven when he died. She had never lived alone. After putting granddad under the ground, she refused to sell his farm, but she couldn't manage it either. For two years she became that worst of creatures, a hundred and sixty pounds of helpless spiteful childishness, pleading vengefully by not taking care of her own least bodily need. Her daughters, completely frustrated trying to help her and long past indulging her inexhaustibly querulous whims, talked of putting her away, but only talked. Finally they left her mostly deserted on the farm. Nights and nights she sat in the rocking chair with granddad's .38 revolver loaded in her lap, whimpering with losing herself into the vacancy. In the country darkness outside the house were noises, and her whole soul shrilled with each one.

Silence filled the empty chicken house, the barn, and the sheds. Weeds and grass, growing wild, swept thickly over the grounds and piled up against the sides of the buildings, thrust up through the wheels of rusting machinery, and covered the in-seeking snakes and small animals. The

277

foot-high grass divided as a long blacksnake crossed the yard and crawled up the maple tree to pillage birds' nests. She cannot recall it without closing her eyes tightly, shaking her head and shuddering Brrrrrrr. But she is quick to say that granddad never killed snakes around the barn because blacksnakes solved the rat-problem.

She could not exist in a state of seething siege inside her skin forever. Her rheumatic legs are very bad, and she must stay on a cane or on someone's arm and be careful where and how she sits so she can get up again. Once, nearly a hundred yards away from the house at the privy, she fell and couldn't get to her feet again. She lay bawling helplessly in February cold, calling to neighboring farms for help. It is a wonder to me that her powerful voice failed. She rolled over onto her belly, on the ice-hard ground, reached out and grabbed the stump of a weed. She pulled herself along the ground by the stumps of weeds until she reached the house. There she lifted herself by the remaining strength of her arms onto the elevation of the porch, and got her legs under her. She says she just sat there thinking.

She started going outside with a flashlight to verify the source of the night noises. One time she heard someone haunting around the back of the smokehouse. She went with the revolver to the kitchen door and listened. She made up her mind. She opened the door and hobbled straight out into the darkness, jouncing and swinging from leg to leg, managing her cane with one hand and pointing the revolver with the other. She challenged the haunt. She fired the revolver and listened to someone running away, a noise pat-patting away a long time into the night. This bizarre upsurge of courage didn't make her daughters, my mother and my aunts, any happier. They were convinced she was crazy, hearing things.

This time it was she who indulged them.

They said lots of people had this grief to go through and didn't take so long about facing up to it. "You wait till you have it to go through," she said, "and then you come and tell me I'm crazy. Never knowed what it was to live alone. Never in all my life." Her tone yearned upward, imploring forgiveness of someone.

She revived with the redbud and dogwood in grief's second spring, started helping herself and let herself be helped by others. She sold the farm, severed herself from the soil which he worked to support their life together as it could not support her longing to continue that life. She moved into town. She was not on her feet so much. Like a huge aching tooth, the rheumatism receded into her knees.

For a while, she competed with any funeral that occurred in the cemetery. She connived someone into driving her there, where she conducted her own repeated ceremony before granddad's grave, piling up the flowers as if she were the widow of her first afternoon, as she will always be. She embarrassed the other funeral even more with wild condolences and passionately bewildered philosophizing on children, hard work, life, love, and death.

At night she lies on her back in bed. "And I remember all my life with dad. I go over and over things. And I study, and study, and study." It is a good word for what she is doing.

She is trying to figure out why it is all shoved under the ground.

Once she woke with shadows running across her walls and light flaring against her window. It was the neighbors' garage on fire, shooting up into the blackest zero night of January. She doesn't remember getting out of the house. Next she remembers standing outside in her nightgown, hollering over and over again,

"Children, get up, you're burnin' up! *Oh,* children, get up, you're burnin' up!"

She could call granddad home to supper across seven hills. She had no trouble waking the neighborhood. And they put out the fire. Grandmother said that the way the younger sleep, a fire would have to come up and grab hold of them in bed before they would know it was there. She saved not only the houses, including her own, but most of the garage too. And it wasn't until the excitement was over that she saw that she had done it all without her cane. Her seventy-two-year-old rheumatic legs responded to the sting of adrenalin. She basked in their gratitude for weeks.

Grandmother always addresses a group as "Children."

Granddad always addressed a group as "People."

It disappointed her that she didn't die in her seventy-second year as granddad did. It seemed a misappropriation of nature's inconsiderate beneficence.

A lizard dashed around the base ledge of granddad's stone. A striped flickering thrill leaped through me. But the lizard was not what I wanted to see. And now that I thought about it, I hadn't seen a single snake of any variety crossing the road, mashed on the road, off the road, or in the graveyard. Such an absence is extraordinary in the Ozarks in summer. Many years I couldn't walk in a field or down a creek without the ground splitting beneath my feet and rushing away in every direction. It would have pleased me to see a big blacksnake wrapped over the grave. I remembered childhood's fond fear of him. I went looking.

But my curiosity was going wild with feeding itself in the new finding of old familiar things. On the slope toward the gate, instead of a snake, were big hickory nuts. Several were drilled through the husk and shell by squirrels. Hunting and fishing are missed when away from home, and a squirrel twitching brightly on a branch would please me too. I spied a hole among the lower limbs in the trunk of the hickory. I lobbed nuts, got the range, and the hole quickly overflowed. It wasn't deep enough to keep a squirrel.

I husked three nuts. I hefted a hand-sized rock and went grinning back to granddad's gravestone. I cracked the nuts on the head of it, one two three. But my gut gave a tremble as if before blasphemy, as if the head of his stone were his head. The kernels were shriveled, no more meat in them than in two wrinkled pieces of paper pasted together. They bitterly puckered my tongue and the insides of my cheeks. I spat, sputtered to clean my mouth. It had been a very dry year, enough deep moisture to keep the leaves green, not enough to fill out and sweeten the meat in nuts. I worried for the acorns that I had planted beneath their names. But I had tested the acorns' weight and fertile firmness well. Very carefully I brushed the nut-debris off the stone's head so no one would notice.

I returned to the upper virginal corner of the cemetery. A greatening release of energy demanded movement. I walked. I tried the sun. I tried the shade. I was exuberant remembering my sadness.

In New York the letter arrived from my mother telling me in scattered phrases that granddad was in the hospital and she and dad were going down to Missouri. In a pay-booth in the Bronx I placed a long-distance call. Everything went fine and snappy to within 20 miles of the farm, and then the connections became a jumble. I could just about have called Tanganyika and got one clearer. The operator translated my mother's shouting, saying they would have to drive to town and I could call to the central phone office. This was done. And then my mother told me that granddad had been buried a few hours before I called. "John, it's been very warm, and we had to get him under the ground."

I walked awkwardly in a park in the Bronx. The pines got darker than the settling dusk, and even the park seemed wild. My feet broke on the blades of grass, on the body of man. I pointed out myself in the pine with five needles in a cluster, the one with three. I watched the shapes of the leaves, the style of the bark and guessed the names of the deciduous trees. I saw the first-shedding cottonwood. Seeing the heavy park sod, surprisingly wild and luxuriant, as a long flow of hair catching bright leaves, I cried. I reviewed the land.

MY GRANDFATHER'S GRAVE

On his death-bed granddad bequeathed his watch to me. I cherished and shared his reverence when the land was worked as a creation and preservation, as a first concern.

The watch fitted in the pocket next to his belly. It ticked above his groin. He took it out in the field. It lay gleaming in his hand, while the big sun shimmered above the oily red clods. Given to me, the watch would tick the time of his special concern, across the land that goes beyond my life too.

It was a long time before grandmother gave me the watch. She couldn't bear to lose one thing that belonged to him. She kept it with his things in a little chest in her bedroom. Sometimes she opens the chest, and studies these left-over things of her life with him. And sometimes it seems cellar-damp grieving and worshipping.

I walked out from under the shade of the huge oak into the open sun, swinging myself in my limbs, down the slope from the raw disordered eminence of the cemetery to the trimmed and well-kept lower slope. I passed his stone. A tearful farewell feeling came and went, like the buzzard's shadow. Body and bone down there walked the lush bright hills of June with me, picking blackberries, and teaching me that work is a steady passion. In our buckets the sky shimmered until the beaded full-juiced berries buried the sky.

I skipped quickly from name to name on the old blackened limestones. I glowed with awareness of all my senses, my physical strength and nimbleness. I vaulted over the fence

by one hand on a post. I was the only name in the graveyard
so capable.

I crossed the crackly field. Its weeds rasped my shoes.
Masses of cockleburs caught and rode on my cuffs and
tangled in my socks. I headed down to Barren Fork.

In a pool above the bridge I was baptized for the third
time. It is a fancy of mine that they suspected me of inborn
heresy. I was coaxed out up to my neck by an itinerant
Baptist minister, in too-clean overalls only up to his waist in
the water, urged by the noisy holy cries from the crowd on the
bank. He placed one hand in the small of my back and
the other over my nose and mouth, intoned the ritual, and
flipped me, clothes and all, in well-nigh hysteria, angry and
afraid, underwater.

Now I searched around the main pool directly below the
bridge. It contained a jumble of greyed-out logs jutting every
which way. A most likely place, and no snake. The stretches
of dry gravel separating the stagnating pools still made me
wonder. Everyday the evaporating pools shrank around the
concentrations of fish. Suckers, hogmollies, punkin' seeds,
flashed their sides in dull throes toward the sun. But the
water's smell exhilarated me.

Imaginations of woman and children, an expansive sexual
feeling, rose and overrode all other feelings beside the green
gravel-bottomed pools where the fish heliographed their
suffocation. At the deepest pool, I stripped and left my
clothing spanking white on the rocks. I used to go barefoot
from April to November. Now my feet cringed and curled on
every rock. But when I stretched out into the water, its

freshness surprised me, and I swam with ease. Shadowy
groups of fish disintegrated on my approach, darting away,
and zinging between my legs, but never touching me. I
imagined a woman stepping gingerly into the pool, her arms
lightly crossing her breasts, and swimming with me.
I remembered granddad's desire that I show him a
great-grandchild before he died. I hurled sparkling showers
into the sun.

When I returned to the cemetery, the lizard darted from
the grave into the nearby pasture. Above the pasture the
hawk still circled. It was very likely that soon the lizard would
enter the processes of the hawk. I saluted the lizard.

This time before his grave there was nothing to review but
the clear present. As he had transferred transcendent
concerns to life, to the land, I had transferred them to other
things too.

Then I wondered with what humor he might have greeted
my full beard. I laughed aloud before the stone.

I had one more chance to see a snake on my way to the
car. I wanted to see it near the door, right under the car, the
door by which I would leave. I wasn't lucky. Later I talked to
a man who said the general ten-year drouth and this very dry
year in particular had drastically reduced the snake
population.

I met grandmother at Bagnell Dam, above the white water
that thundered from its base. She laid her hand rigidly upon
my forearm and pumped for support in getting out of

Walter's car. Her talk buzzed with dreamy criticism of the funeral, the flowers, the nicety of the sermon, the tone of the preacher. She was forming it around her own body in the casket someday. It twisted her face unpleasantly. And the cloying sweet smell of tuberoses clung to her clothes and dulled the liveliness of her blue-and-white flowered outfit.

Then she said dimly, as if just realizing that a living body stood beside her,

"Where you been, John?"

My special trip, completed, no longer needed special protection. I told her.

"Oh, if I'd knowed you was going there —!"

She looked down suddenly as if the rest of the sentence were broken to bits on the ground around her. Her springing surprise made me unsure about my earlier feeling that she knew where I was going. But it is not her custom to leave sentences unfinished. The shock blew away her deathly absorption.

We drove over the country talking happily together and making lively visits. All that time she didn't say one word about funerals or granddad.

And I knew, as he knew, that when my death happens, it happens to others, never to me.

ECHO

Nobody knew but the four of us, the husband and the wife, and my wife and I. He would have to greet me or his friends might wonder what was the matter.

When I saw them in the yard, I took a breath on the dusty road and then came through the iron gate that clinged behind me. Bernie glanced over the yard and shifted in his lawn chair and crossed his legs and talked more seriously to his friend Arnold who always wore large motorcycle sunglasses. Arnold sat with his knees up on the edge of a white-washed truck tire out of which, behind his back, zinnias erupted. Their shattered September petals brightly speckled the white washed tire. Michele was perched on the edge of an orange crate, tucked and leaning forward, as if she might touch a point in the air. Her green shift hung on her. It seemed thin. She smiled faintly at me. She had to.

Bernie did not say hello to me. That greeting is too stylized, and requires meeting of the eyes. I didn't speak a word. I nodded at Arnold and simply sat on my heels near them and plucked a grassblade and began chewing it. I was not asked by anyone what I was carrying wrapped in brown paper about two feet long and damp on one end.

Bernie talked steadily, about hunting. The plums were dark and the apples rosy-spotted above us in the fruit trees that surrounded their starched white house. It was a time to talk of hunting.

I chewed my grassblade and looked at Arnold letting him know I was not troubled by whatever he was thinking behind his sunglasses.

Bernie knew that I knew more about hunting than either of them. He turned with a sort of gruffness and asked where it would be best to go hunting right now. He meant squirrel hunting. He was doing pretty well. Arnold tilted his head back as if he had to see over something to see me through the glasses.

I pulled the grassblade from between my teeth and pointed toward the hills over the railroad tracks that ran, tattered with weeds, along their land. I said that over those hills and down in the hollows, in the timbered ridges by the creek, there were plenty of squirrels. "All right," Bernie said to Arnold, "let's go."

"It'll be just right in an hour or so," I said. They did not ask me if I wanted to come with them.

Bernie heaved himself up, looking down at Michele as though he were being called away by something important. She swung her long thighs pressed together toward him, smiling with a timid suggestion of docility, showing her small teeth. She let one hand go from holding her knees and moved a finger cautiously along her cheek to free a wisp of hair. Her sunny hair was scattered over her shoulders and down her back. It twinkled the way of all the winey things of September. Bernie was looking down at her, she was looking up at him, and both their souls were looking straight at me. So were Arnold's eyes behind the sunglasses.

God, how I had wanted her. She was skinny and limber and her light movements and her light fingers carried away my breath. She wore her hair up in a bun in public then. Now her smile with the little teeth and her hair down and her complexion roughened by lack of sleep or starved by fear for the blood of love suggested something not so clear as that one night. God, god, it had been so sweet, why did she have to tell him?

"Are you going?" she said to him.

"I think we'll go now," he said.

"Well." She clasped her knees and rocked a little.

He was indicating that it was absolutely necessary for him to trust her with me. Bernie and Arnold got their guns from the house and went over the railroad tracks and up into the hills where I had told them to go. He had been a good friend of mine.

I ached in my legs, I was still squatting on my heels and staring at the hills. Now was the time for my gift wrapped in the brown paper. It was a sort of final statement for that stark sweetness that haunted me as intensely as my betrayal and hers haunted Bernie. But the gift was to teach her something too. A trim, white narcissus in September. I had dug it up whole, and I wanted her to plant it again.

Michele was leaning toward me, hovering on the edge of the orange crate. When I looked at her, her smile faded. She watched me.

I was bitterly satisfied that no one had heard about this thing from me. I had never asked her why she had told him. Every time I had seen her since then I had joked with her, and we talked about other things, other than what our souls, looking at each other, were thinking.

"I have something for you," I said.

"Oh." She rocked slightly and smiled. "What is it?"

"Let's find a place for it first."

"O.K."

She moved ahead of me under the plum trees around their house. She lifted her hands behind her neck and lifted her hair and let it fall just at the moment she passed from shade into sun. And then she stretched, as if waking in the sun. And my soul answered as it had answered before. I let her move more ahead.

By an old wagon, that had not been used in a long time, the end of its tongue drifted into the ground, Michele turned toward me. We were in the shade of the lilac bushes around their garden, which was grown up in stiff yellow weeds. She feared that I would be harsh with her, and her words were more breath than sound.

"What is it?"

I unwrapped it, the white flower first, and then the green

stems and the fat black dirt. "Oh," she said, "oh, it's—" stretching out with her delicate fingers—and she would not let herself say anything common in appreciation. "Oh," she said, gaining time, and then smiling, "it's a bit of the pale spring sun. Oh, pure and alive." Holding the flower so it rested on her fingertips, she put it to her cheek, and swayed a little.

I was smiling. I wadded up the brown paper and tossed it into the wagon. "You have to plant it again," I said.

"O.K.," she said slowly, looking around, "right here."

She knelt and dug in the moist hard dirt in a sunny spot by a lilac bush. "Kneel beside me," she said, "and let's do it together."

I squatted beside her. I made no other move. "No. It's yours," I said.

She grabbed my hand and awkwardly tried to make both our hands pat the dirt down around the flower. My throat ached at the touch of her and the swelling started in my crotch. She was so easy. And it was out in the open, in the sun between the coarse September lilacs and the old wagon, in clear view of the white house and the yard where the lawn chair and the orange crate rested under the trees. This was where she would want to do it, right here, nowhere else.

She pretended to kiss me, just a slight kiss in thanks for the flower, and the memory came, the excitement jumping in me and in her, our lips trembling and jerking, shock in our eyes, a simple party kiss. Lord, lord, I wanted her hand and her long light fingers the way I remembered.

I said, "No, no, it is yours, for yourself, you must plant it."
Still squatting she turned suddenly and her dress knocked
over the narcissus.

"Help, help me." She was trying to pat the dirt around the
flower again, and grabbing at my hand. And there were
echoes from her, and answers from me. And how she
managed it I don't know but she was struggling with me—
"Help me, help"—and she pulled me off balance onto the
cool hard ground. And her whole long body, so beautifully
accidental, pressed and moved against me, and her pleading
pale blue eyes said it was not happening, I did not have to
think it was happening. But I saw the flower knocked over
again, and I tried to raise myself and reach for it, telling her
she must plant it, she must plant it herself. But our bodies
were long and moving against each other on the ground. And
it was the moment, when I must give in to her, or lift myself
and leave, and I would not lift myself and leave until she
planted the flower.

I glanced down the length of our bodies into the yard,
where, abruptly, Bernie appeared, walking briskly off the
road through the gate under the apple trees, his rifle held at
ready across his chest. Arnold with the sunglasses strode just
behind him, his rifle crooked in his elbow. "We've changed
our minds," Bernie called.

Afternoon light skittered through the treetops. Shadows
were things without end. In the next moment, looking
straight through the trees across the yard at us lying and
struggling together between the wagon and the lilacs, Bernie
let go a sort of groan. "Oh, my God."

ECHO

Michele leaped up, and spun around to the other side of the wagon, where I couldn't see her. Bernie was running toward us, his rifle held up across his chest. And suddenly he threw, shoved, batted the rifle away. When he reached us, the contradictions in his fury did not permit him to do anything but suddenly sit down on the woodpile near the wagon, staring at the ground.

Michele was standing carefully on one side, stirring slightly, with her hands clipped together down in front of her. "For God's sake," he yelled, looking up directly at me for the first time, "won't you ever leave me alone?"

He had sought to kill me the night she told him in the spring. Now I tried to say something. What was there to say? I tried to gesture with my hands. What was there to gesture? He was beating his fists on his knees and yelling. She was standing so quietly, swinging gently on her hips, as if waiting for everyone to leave so she could comfort him. Not quite smiling, not quite showing fear, she even seemed a little proud of Bernie, with an aura of protection about her like the light on the flower that lay by the crusted wagon wheel.

With his face stuffed with indignation Bernie stared at the ground between me and her. He hit his fists hard on his knees. "Will you go? Will you go, now?" And what would he tell my wife, the mother of my son? She would clasp our little boy between her legs. . . .

Arnold drifted forward with his rifle cradled in his arm. When I looked at him, he still said nothing, only raised his head. And what did he think, what would he say?

A cry of anger shook in my chest. And then I went

suddenly gentle with pity and fear. I wanted to speak. I wanted to gesture. I moved here and there, I moved toward Bernie sitting on the woodpile. He screamed toward Michele's legs, but at me, "Go, go!" And Michele stopped rocking on her hips, and lifted her hand nervously to fiddle with her earlobe.

She was watching my back as I went away. I was sure Bernie was still watching the ground. And Arnold watched everyone behind his sunglasses.

JESSE HAD A WIFE

When anyone asked, "How you doing, Jess?" he said,
"Oh, I'm keeping myself alive."

Jesse sat this spring morning, in his undershirt, no belt on
his jeans, with one bare foot stretched out on the concrete
battlement of the porch of his rooming house. People passing
on the sidewalk below saw only Jesse lounging up there
with his leg stretched out and his hands stuffed in his armpits
and his long dreamy gaze and his chest moving when he
itched his shoulder blades on the brick wall. But Jesse had a
thick rubber band hooked around the first two fingers of his
left hand.

When the people down on the sidewalk passed on by,
Jesse unfolded his arms, aimed the paper wad, and fired—
man, woman, old, young, Jesse did not discriminate, some
little kids got it too. And he wet the paper wads to put weight
and sting in them.

When whoever got stung yelped and looked up and
around, there was Jesse sitting there with his arms folded

and his hands bound in his armpits, in the sort of silence that follows a rifle shot. Jesse was in his thirties, Jesse was solemn. Sometimes, when they looked up so sharply puzzled, he would speak directly, "How do you do," with a polite jerk of his chin.

So the people passed on. "Fucking kids," they might say.

Three times this morning, and Jesse had not missed so far. His targets always looked down the gangway by the side of the rooming house for kids who were too accurate to miss and too clever to be seen. And many was the time that Jesse could have hit them twice, but that would call attention to himself.

"Shitfire," he breathed, when he hit a fancy willowy young woman right in the ear. Her grocery cart jerked and celery and oranges spilled onto the sidewalk. And, yeah, she yelped, she really yelped, and knocked her sunglasses askew when she jerked her hand to her stung ear. She wore white shorts and a white blue-trimmed pull-over, and she was tanned from the thongs of her sandals to her sun-streaked brown ponytail. She lived in the houses around the corner, the ones with the white shutters and the old black iron railings. And furthermore she was angry, and it was all too good to pass up.

Jesse unlimbered himself and skip-shuffled barefoot down the steps, fast enough to scoop up one of the oranges still rolling on the sidewalk. "Ma'am," he was saying, rolling easily toward her, with tongue in cheek shyness, popping the orange from one hand to the other.

"Did you see them? *Did* you see them?"

With a sweet snap of indignation she said it, like tiny glass snapping in her mouth. And now the tiny glass in her mouth snapped again and again.

"What's the matter, ma'am?"

"What's the matter? What's the *matter*? I've just been—"

Then she got confused. She stooped over to whisk up the celery and her round ass in the tight white shorts winked at Jesse. Jesse gave a low left-eye wink back.

She darted after the oranges.

"Can I help you, ma'am?"

"Thank you," she said, "thank you," her indignation burning her breath to a heavy whisper. "That's a lesson. Not ever this shortcut again. Thank you."

She looked over the weeds at the cobwebbed casement window of the rooming-house basement. "Where *are* they?"

With a pop shrug of his shoulders, Jesse dropped the orange from about two feet up into the sack in the grocery cart. "You O.K.?" With all the warmth and courtesy of his soft voice, he knew just how much he could help this woman.

"I am O.K."

Jesse gave a polite dip of his chin.

And she picked up a rock to throw it and her willowy legs and arms swung in flashes of sun and shade. The rock tittered from wall to wall down the gangway and skipped out into the backyard of the rooming house—a yard of packed dirt, damp newspaper, bottles, and tin cans. "You won't get another chance," she hissed heavily to the empty gangway. And she meant that she would not take this shortcut again.

"Can I walk you a ways?"

"Thank you, no. Thank you. I'll manage." She bumped out each word, and Jesse did not have the feeling that her eyes saw him behind the sunglasses.

She rushed away with the grocery cart jumping in sharp clatters on the uneven cracks of the sidewalk. He pulled the good thick rubber band out of his pocket and fired a paper wad high after her, a single speeding snowflake in the sun. It hit in bushes behind her. Jesse hooked his thumbs in the top of his jeans, and played his big toes on the sidewalk and liked the feel of the moist grainy concrete on his bare feet. That sweet round ass in the tight white shorts, swinging away from him, Jesse gave it a left-eye wink.

Well, that did it. That started the morning.

He wrapped his hand around the ball of the gatepost going up the steps. He tickled one of Mrs. McAlester's tattered white petunias drooping out of the porch box with his big toe. His hips were loose, his arms were swinging, and he was lightly flapping his hands on the rail, the post, as if every object were the top of a small boy's head. And Jesse was smiling, shaking his head, clucking his tongue.

Jesse turned the doorknob in the same smooth motion of slapping it. There he stood in the dim dust-sour hallway and snapped his fingers just to remind himself of what he already knew. There, in the array of thirty brass mailboxes that stretched down the hall to Mrs. McAlester's door, was his name on the nearest box—Jesse Woodson—and the last name was scratched out. Carey. That had been his last name.

JESSE HAD A WIFE

Jesse Woodson Carey. He had scratched the Carey out with a razor blade at 2 A.M. one night when he came back from his job of sweeping out the ABZ warehouse. He'd known since he was a kid that his first and middle names were the same as the first and middle names of Jesse James. No one that passed him that night in the hall asked him what he was doing scratching out his name. Even Mrs. McAlester the landlady didn't mention that she had noticed.

Jesse never locked the mailbox anymore. He just flipped up the flap, winked at the little cobweb twinkling in one corner, and let the flap drop, all with the soft slapping style that made him grin.

He caressed the top of the newel post and the moment he started to pull himself into his slow gallop up the stairs Mrs. McAlester's door opened. Her skinny, wrinkled face poked out. "Oh, Jesse?"

"Yes, ma'am." He was poised attentively with one bare foot stretched three steps up and the other still on the hall floor.

"How'm I going to cook you dumplings if you don't shoot me some squirrels?" She laughed. It was their one joke. "Everything all right, Jess?"

"Everything's just dandy," Jesse said.

"You're good people, Jess."

And he knew she was watching him go up the stairs.

The worn sandpapery carpet tickled his bare feet. He climbed two and three steps at a time in the slow gallop that made him feel that he was rolling downhill, up to the third floor, where he ambled down the narrow hall with his hands pop-popping a rhythm on both walls.

He snuck the key into the lock and hunched his shoulders into the door. It jumped open, shaking the air. Jesse put his hand flat on it and smiled at the sudden stop of its shaking. And he locked the door and hooked the chain. This morning was just beginning.

Jesse's room was clean and neat, and no one but Jesse kept it that way. Every dish and cup was washed, sparkling in the red plastic rack on the board between the sink and the stove. And the shining on the white stove wavered as Jesse moved around the room. The mirror above the sink was so pure and deep he said he could stick his head in it and look around, or flash an S.O.S. all the way across the city, like he did with the ABZ warehouse lights every night. The bed was made, a clean pink blanket turned back army-style and tucked under at the head. The black shoes for Jesse's bare feet rested by the iron leg at the foot of the bed.

He paid a little more weekly for this front corner room with its three-windowed half-dormer overlooking the hospital parking lot and the big shopping center and its parking lot beyond the hospital fence, with the green AMOCO watertower standing stilt-legged above the buildings faraway.

With a slicing precision now he pulled the shades all the way down on the two windows to each side of the center window, then pulled the center shade down half-way, and pushed the window up to meet the shade. He grinned at his chill and trembling fingertips as he tucked the pull-string with its little circlet up into the hem of the shade.

First he made himself a cup of instant coffee. "Da da dee da," he was humming, wiping the sprinkle of coffee powder off the red-and-white checked oilcloth, then folding the washcloth to drape it over the faucet.

With the cup in his left hand, he picked up the armchair with the other and swung it handily into position facing the window. He stationed the cup on the radiator right under the window. Spinning on one bare heel and pumping the other leg jubilantly in the air, Jesse clapped his hands and opened his mouth to loose a silent yell, as if he were standing on one foot on top of a flagpole.

From a shelf high in his closet, he brought forth a blanket-wrapped bundle. He carried it in both hands above his head, the way the King of the Gorillas carried off women.

Jesse unwrapped the blanket on his bed and took out, the barrel in one hand and the stock in the other, a lever-action .22 rifle with telescopic sight. He snapped the rifle together. He dabbed at the lens with green toilet-paper. He raised one foot onto the bed and aimed with the cross-hairs right between the eyes of a suddenly massive auburn-haired Jesus above the head of his bed. "And I could too," he said, with such a sudden surge of jubilance that he again pumped the air with one leg, turning on the other foot toward the window.

Jesse propped his feet on the flanges of the radiator and scrounged down in the chair testing the view. Mrs. McAlester had not provided a screen, and bugs came in at night and flies during the day. He gazed over the hospital parking lot and into the shopping center, the supermarket, the liquor store, the bakery, the restaurant, the gift shops, and the dry cleaner's sign flashing FAST FAST FAST FAST ONE-DAY SERVICE.

Holding the rifle with the butt on his hip, he sipped the coffee, and it was so stinging hot he jerked forward letting the coffee run out of his mouth back into the cup. He worked his mouth to work away the blistered feeling.

Then over the whirling shimmers on the backs of cars in the hospital parking lot, he spied, through the wire fence, a hurrying woman with a wide floppy brown hat. Jesse eased the coffee cup down onto the radiator, taking his time. He put the rifle to his shoulder. He hunkered and squirmed into the right grip.

The wire fence and the woman moving on the other side of it sprang up in the telescopic circle. The cross-hairs came to rest, with butterfly sureness, just under her left shoulder, a pretty orange kerchief bunched around her neck. Jesse felt his breathing, the firm chill of his fingertip on the trigger, and moved the cross-hairs to lead her just a hair—

Click!

"JESSE WOODSON STRIKES AGAIN." He waved his hand and printed off a banner black headline in his mind. He worked the lever action just as if there were a shell in it.

He watched the woman walking with the same jostling hurry on the other side of the fence as if he were seeing her through shivering water. Jesus H. Christ, they were all wearing shorts, and with such a wobble of the ass. He blew her a light kiss in salute as a hospital building came between him and her.

Then Jesse made a cameo out of a fat woman in the sight —also wearing shorts, shoving a grocery cart out of the supermarket and tilting it over the curb down into the parking lot. A little girl sucking on half of a raspberry popsicle tagged along after her. The cross-hairs touched home right on the opening of the little girl's middy blouse—

Click!

Jesse clucked his tongue solemnly and said, "Come one, come all, JESSE 'CLICK' WOODSON STRIKES AGAIN."

Then he picked a bald man, embracing great sacks in his arms, barging out of the magic door of the liquor store. Jesse fenced the cross-hairs on the sweaty top of the forehead above the face that looked astonished at getting through the magic doors in time—

Click!

And Jesse murmured, with the flutter of headlines in his head. He sipped his coffee, it was just right now, but needed more sugar. He took his time about getting up and sweetening it, holding his rifle all the while.

Then Jesse got him a nurse, an old one, coming around the rear of her car in the parking lot like a sailboat making a turn. *Click!* Next—*click!*—he bagged a Korean doctor—all the young slant-eyed doctors in the hospital were Korean— standing under the Emergency Entrance sign smoking a cigarette fast, puff after puff.

Then a flicker of willowiness swung Jesse's gaze over the fence into the shopping center parking lot—white shorts and white blue-trimmed pull-over.

She jumped up to meet him in the circle, still wearing her sunglasses, her brown ponytail tossing as she glanced back over her shoulder. "Hey," Jesse breathed, "you're dead. Play fair."

Sweet round ass in tight white shorts, she sidled between two close-parked cars toward the bakery. The cross-hairs played tag with the white button above the zipper of her shorts.

Jesse felt a fine radiance of sweat, his cheek sticky on the stock. He tasted the thought that there was a box of shells in the closet. "Still mad, ma'am?"

Click!

Right where she lived!

That was enough. That was enough for one day. His breath rumbled richly and quietly in his chest. "Five," he blew out the words, "and one sweet round ass in tight white shorts. That's your limit, buddy boy." He whewed, fluttering his lips.

He couldn't wait one moment longer. He leaned the rifle against the radiator.

He unbuckled and, bracing his feet against the radiator, lifted his ass in the chair and pulled his pants all the way down around his ankles. He spit a big gob on his hand and made it with himself, slow, long, and smooth.

He called up the memory of the skinny colored girl that he'd met in a bar a couple of weeks ago. He couldn't bring her to his room so he talked her into taking a shortcut down an alley where he hoisted her up on a row of ash cans and bent over her, looking straight at a NO PARKING sign a few feet away on a power pole. She made the ash cans and that alley ring. Now the nigger girl changed around and mixed up with the sweet round ass in tight white shorts that winked at him with the cross-hairs playing tag with the button, and both women started doing exactly what he pleased and what he pleased was everything.

He stood up suddenly and, bowing his legs to lower his height, aimed. He let it jump through the window and his legs were vibrating good.

He buckled and zipped up quickly and eased his head out the window to see where it might have hit on the sidewalk or on someone he hoped. No sign of it, and no one on the sidewalk either way. He slapped the windowsill, snapped his fingers, opened his mouth to let go the silent yell, stamped the floor, and ran off another banner headline in his mind.

"JESSE 'CLICK' WOODSON COMES AGAIN."

Jesse tucked the rifle up in its blanket and slid it onto the top shelf of the closet. He was humming and washing the coffee cup in the sink when he was surprised by his face in the mirror. He winked. He was keeping alive.

He swung the armchair back in its place near the head of the bed. When he jerked up the window shades, the sunlight burst on the mirror and scattered over the stove, the bed, the floor, and the auburn-haired Jesus.

He lapped a heavy towel over his shoulder and wandered down the hall toward the shower, stroking out a rhythm on both walls. He heard Mrs. McAlester jittering with the buffer going bumpety-bump from wall to wall down the second floor hallway. It was springtime. He had his rifle in the closet and his rubber band in his pocket. And soon he would go to the bar around the corner, drink a few beers, shoot a few games of eight ball, and shoot the shit with some of his off-and-on buddies and the aged alcoholic whores who dug into the bar with their elbows and hung on for dear life. And then he would take the bus, push the broom, empty the trash, turn lights off and on, off and on . . .

Jesse was soaping under one arm and letting the shower beat on the back of his neck, when his toes winced against the rubber mat.

"Hey," he breathed, "play fair."

And he made a soft cluck with his tongue.

THE OFFENDING PARTY

That knocking downstairs just would not stop. I knew who showed up at three o'clock in the morning and knocked without shame: Mel. Well, well. He was years late. I'd taken his wife away from him but I didn't marry her and she did not go back with him. Clare.

I lay on my side as true as a board under the sheet beside Rachel. She made a sound meaning for me to go downstairs and answer it. I squinted against the itching in my nose under the drifting curtains at the window full of the unincorporated night bellying out to where car lights flickered through the trees on Tumbril Hill. Way in the southeast, Chicago made the sky smoky pink. Lilac air puffed on my cheek. Loneliness fizzed in my belly. I could tell Rachel was angry, but I gave her no sign. "Who the hell?" she said, twisting the sheet away. Who the hell, indeed? I listened to her bare feet shushing the carpeted hallway and then the stairs.

"Who is it?"

The knocking stopped, the door opened, bits of shrieking

came in from out on the road by the lake. Downstairs their voices were hushed and friendly, as if they didn't want to wake a sick child. The electric clock on my end table hummed. Rachel was down there unnecessarily long. Something was serious. I dressed fast.

Rachel wandered back up toward me at the head of the stairs where I was standing impatiently with my shoes pinched together in one hand. I looked over her head at her backside moving away in the gilt-scrolled rococo mirror that ranges up the wall on the middle landing. Red carpet everywhere. She hadn't even bothered to throw a housecoat over her yellow nightie, and she was nicely hazy inside it.

"An old friend of yours is down there," she said "He wants to see you." She managed to pass me without touching or looking at me. "Aren't you going down?"

"No time is too good for my friends," I said.

She eased open the door of the kids' room. "He's your friend," she said.

Royalty never composed themselves on stairs more carefully. I sat down and watched myself in the top part of the mirror putting my shoes on, and the first try I confused my right and left foot. The very walls judged my composure as I stepped down to the bend of the middle landing and I couldn't think of anything better to do than reach out for the head of the post when I looked down where the venetian blind was bunched at the top of the front door and Mel stretched up hungrily with his chest against the glass grinning and waving his fingers. The door was closed.

THE OFFENDING PARTY

No doubt Rachel let Mel talk her into closing it so I would be the one who had to welcome him. I brought my hand away from the banister rail and sniffed for dust. Spider, our black labrador, scratched at the screen on the back porch.

I opened the door just enough for me to stand before him. "Mel," I said.

I could not make my eyes stay steady on his eyes that were so pale and faraway. "Jeremy," he said, "Jeremy, Jeremy."

I saw more of the inevitable out there under the bluish streetlight. God, what a crew, his friends and followers, you could see it at a glance, faggots, lesbians, hippies, sad and terrible with aging, swarming around their old Model A Ford parked, with its door open, right where our little Black Sambo hitching post figures perk up on either side of the gravel path. On the other side of the road our country lake swelled sleekly black down to the huge Schlitz neon sign over the shopping center a mile away where red glimmers whirled in the water. Spider started barking on the back porch. The garage on the side of the house was locked, inside and out, car door and house door, thank God. They wouldn't be taking any rides in our new Volvo forest-green station wagon.

"There they are," Mel said.

"There they are," I said.

They turned handsprings, swung round and round on our hitching post figures, then gathered themselves as if into the barrel of a cannon. A Negro faggot tickled the crotch and patted the cheek of one of the Black Sambo figures. We have many amusing antiques.

It was my immediate feeling that resistance would only make things worse. "Your friends," I said, with my mouth as dry as my wit. They were coming up the gravel path.

Mel kept purposely standing too close to me with the looseness and stuffiness of unclean tweed. Give him a good shake and everybody would be coughing. "We're tired, Jeremy, it's been a long trip."

"Hi, honey," a sleepy-faced faggot said. He went through the door as if powered through a suction tube.

"Take care about waking the kids," Mel said.

"We have two, Mel," I said.

"Tell me about your kids, Jeremy."

They were cramming themselves through the door.

"Son and daughter, Mel."

"How old are they, Jeremy?"

"The boy's four, Mel, and the little girl's almost two."

"That's perfect, Jeremy."

A barefoot fellow in a billowy blue unbuttoned workshirt and farmer's blue jeans with his fly open and no underwear drifted past us. They were all in the house now. The Model A was empty with its door open at the end of the gravel path. The honking boom of a nighthawk plunged above us. Way over the Macphersons' white colonial that peeped with gables out of trees, the full moon took a deep, white breath, as if to blow dust off the top of the house. We have antiques, the Macphersons have birdhouses—pretty little and big many-storied birdhouses hung in the trees surrounding their house. Morning at the Macphersons is something to hear.

God, I was lonely. "It must be wonderful for kids out here, Jeremy."

"Yes, Mel. Yes, it is."

"What do you do for bread, Jeremy?"

Our streetlight shadows stood black on either side of the redwood frame around the glass door while our shadows from the moon leaned faintly under the coach lamps across the ivied sandstone walls. I wanted to say that I'm now brand-name manager, Mel, for a new beauty soap for men that our company is putting out. I wanted to say that we are testing it in stores in New York, Arkansas, Iowa, and California. "Jeremy, I told them that you're my brother. Jeremy, it's good to see you." I wanted to say that I couldn't say the same but I couldn't deny that I was secretly pleased, as the doctors say. I was always the one who was as honest as any four walls.

"So you might as well come in and meet my wife," I said.

The pigmy lemon tree in the big black kettle was still shivering in the foyer where he touched it. You could hear them throughout the house and the refrigerator door slamming and a TV weather report talking about a clear day down in the rec room and Spider whimpering his cowardly whimper on the back porch. A shriek, like a mouse crushed in a fist, came from the living room. It was Rachel, under the arch between the living room and the dining room, with a crewcut butch lesbian in tight white jeans and cowboy belt buckle kneeling before her in courtier-style and kissing the hem of her nightie. The butch had the shortest hair in the gang. She was trying to speak Elizabethan. "If all the night and earth were young, and truth in every mother's tongue. . . ." Rachel's reflection trembled in the glass of the cabinet where the big silver tray stood on its side at the far end of the redwood table in the dining room. There was the dim feeling in me that Rachel deserved it.

A hippie slid down the banister with his rumpled engineer boots flung toward my face and long orange hair floating behind him. He spilled himself off just before he hit the newel post. "Cha-a-a-a-a-a-a-a-ar-r-r-ge," he said. In the living room he gently and entwiningly took the hand of a girl whose brown hair was as long as the big man's white shirt she was wearing down to her bare legs. She was tilting a delicate finger at the Picasso reproduction on the wall above our splay-armed couch and tilting a delicate eye at the hippie. Blue period, boy and a horse. Rachel likes it. My Van Gogh is on the other wall, all sunny and whirling with dark.

"Good God, the *kids*," I said. I lunged up the stairs.

"Jeremy," came Rachel's angry whimper.

I swear people think the only word I understand is my name.

My head brushed the cow-jumped-over-the-moon mobile hanging from the light string in the center of the kids' room. Ralphie was sleeping on his bed against the wall hugging his red robot Champ. Champ really walks. Little Janie was sprawled with both legs sticking out of the slats of her crib. Her pacifier ticked in her mouth. Ivy was stitched around outside the window over the foot of Ralphie's bed, and sometimes little grey-brown lizards climb in the vines and look in upon the children on a sunny afternoon. Moonlight was coming through the screen. The shadows of the cow, the dog, the cat, the dish, the fiddle, the spoon and the moon went dipping and riding around the walls. I kissed Ralphie. I was surprised by my hoarse self-consciousness. "Hello, little boy." I couldn't bend far enough over the crib to kiss little Janie so I touched her cheek and she murmured from head to foot, drew up her legs under her diapered butt. The pacifier ticked rapidly.

Ralphie used to get scared of the quavering boom of the nighthawks. When I leaned my elbows on the window sill, I itched the tip of my nose on the screen, listening to the noise below. The Model A out there under the fluorescent streetlight would be an amusing conversation thing for showing weekend friends around the countryside. I discovered myself humming mournfully. I could call the sheriff but that would let Mel and his followers get their satisfaction.

In the bathroom light that came into the hall I took an old photograph out of my billfold. It was of me and Clare, in full body profile, screwing on a chair. She looked so happy and there was no likeness of me that pleased me so much. I'd never shown it even to Rachel.

I went down the stairs humming, I was so melancholy, I didn't know what until I heard the words, "*I'll be loving you, al-wa-a-a-a-a-ays. I'll be . . .*" I wished I could walk into the tall mirror and up its stairs and into its house and let my image walk out and take over for me. He seemed so capable in his white short-sleeved shirt and his tanned body made trim by handball and swimming.

With her eyelids slid half-closed and her arms still folded Rachel was leaning back on the side of the dining room arch. Mel had his arm braced against the wall beside her. They were not talking. The butch lesbian was kneeling by our big fireplace with her hands prayerful under her chin muttering a sort of Gregorian chant about the beauties of Rachel. The sleepy-faced faggot in a black jacket was picking his way dog-fashion over the rugs under the dining room table with a pewter soup spoon in his mouth. Good pewter. Teethmarks.

Rachel sullenly stirred her hips, and her bush and bellybutton came out clear against the translucent nightie and then, as she moved, were hidden in a yellow cloud. It was enough for me to watch it as calmly as I could.

I'd hardly ever said a word about Mel to Rachel. I don't think Rachel even knew his name. "Rachel, I want you to meet the old friend that I've talked so much about."

She tried to stir her hips with that sullen taunt again and she almost cried because she couldn't.

"Nothing really between us," Mel said, coming to shake my hand. "How are you, Jeremy? You do seem well. And you do have a very pretty wife."

I said, musically, "Thank you," dipping my chin.

"How do you do," Rachel said. She gave me a quick glare as if lightning convulsed behind her eyes.

The faggot with the pewter soup spoon in his mouth

emerged from the side of the redwood table and growled and nuzzled between the legs of the orange-haired hippie and his girl. "You're too much, Jim," they said, looking down at him. Sleepy Face Jim. The hippie was tossing a hundred-and-twenty-year-old pepper grinder up in the air and catching it languidly in the palm of his hand. "It's very old," the girl said.

Mel's hand was bony and dry as chalk in mine.

I felt my back breathe coldly.

"Yes, Mel, she is very pretty."

"Jeremy, you might as well meet Sal." Mel grinned on one side of his mouth. Sal the butch was touching Rachel's knee soulfully and not about to meet me. It was terrifying the way Rachel suddenly shook without making any noise. She kicked the butch with her bare foot, right in the mouth. But the butch bumped out only a muffled sensuous sound and rocked back languorously on the carpet wiping her mouth and smiled cock-eyed up at Rachel. The butch looked at the blood on her forefinger. Then she licked it. "There comes a tide in all affairs," she sighed.

Instantly Rachel dashed around the dining room table and grabbed the pewter spoon out of the mouth of Sleepy Face Jim and the pepper grinder out of John the hippie's hand. John and Sleepy Face gave Rachel the slow lifted eyebrow and smile of pleased offense. The girl, Naomi, reached out and touched the pepper grinder with delicate familiarity. "It's nice," she said. Rachel clutched the spoon in one hand and the pepper grinder in the other against her breasts. Mel

stroked himself from chair to chair around the dining room
table and up to her. "You must understand that they are
lonely," he said, touching Rachel's hand. He was always
touching you. He made a point of it.

Rachel aimed her guttural demand at me. "Get them out of
here, *get them out of here!*"

A stillness came, like the woods after an owl has hooted.

Rachel pressed spoon and pepper grinder to her cheeks.
Whimpering went through her. Mel put his hand on her
shoulder right by the shiny yellow ribbon ruffled through the
neck of her nightie. "Aren't you lonely?"

"Oh, for heaven's sake," she said.

They all came quietly from all over the house and gathered
around our redwood dining table with the straw basket in
the center piled with dark-as-blood Indian corn and a wax
jack-o-lantern. They all faced and watched John who plucked
something from his pink shirt pocket. I was in the living room
and not in their circle and I felt, oddly, not physically there.
I had the eerie momentary sense of my body standing in Mel
beside Rachel so strongly that my feet stammered and I
looked around to see if anyone noticed. The Negro faggot,
who was called Sesame, cupped a match for John. John
sucked air and smoke. He started talking with held breath, a
sort of quiet quacking. He did it well and you could see by
the way he stood that he had an everyday pride in it. "This
stuff is out of sight. . . ." The joint went from one to another
until one side of the table was lined discreetly by chests full
of held breath and everyone commented hoarsely on the
quality of it.

Rachel went on whimpering and did not move to get Mel's hand off her shoulder. "Please don't wake the children," she said, "please."

It was Sal the butch lesbian at the end of the dining room table who extended the joint to me. I had to step forward and take it, rather than provoke them, and besides I am not wholly unfamiliar with the grass. "You'll never catch up," Sal said, "you're way behind." They were quick never to let me win. They laughed, up and down the line, chain reaction, together, in rhythm. Even Mel smiled. "Today we give thanks," he said. I passed the joint to Sleepy Face Jim, who murmured, "Thank you, sweet." I wiped off the touch of his fingers on my pants.

Throw them out. But that is not the way I do things. Throw them out? I would drop one throbbing out of a window into the bushes and while throwing out another the first would scramble back into the house and jam his hands in my pants.

John handed the joint to the side toward Rachel but did not look at her. He would be pleased if she turned it down and pleased if she accepted. She seemed not to know for a moment what was in his hand, then she clapped the spoon and pepper grinder on the table. She put the joint to her lips with a hint of her hostess smile. She choked awfully and tears came. "Oh, I do want to," she said.

"Here," Mel said. He quacked through held breath explaining how. She gave him that earnest girlish attention that magnifies men around her and makes me feel feverishly vacant.

"Ah-h," they all said, and drew up around the table, like a drawstring.

Mel took a quickie and said, "Take another."

And another.

And another. And another.

She held her breath ostentatiously. I saw her nipples stiff against her nightie. "Ah, the goodies," Mel said. He pursed the tiny end between his thumb and finger and put it to her lips. She took the goodies too, and yelped and jumped back when sparks fluttered over the front of her nightie. Mel helped her brush them off.

She was the center of their really reverent attention.

Air breathed on my back from the open front door and a fox barked near the lake. Rachel didn't hear the fox. We would usually go to the front door and stand together and listen.

"Let me see your house," Mel said to Rachel.

I don't know what Rachel understood from my smile but the beatific face that she beamed at me made rage ram through my gut. Mel guided her through the swinging doors into the kitchen as if she floated before his hand on her back. Now everybody else went in all directions and I was so empty and melancholy I wanted to run and touch and hug little Ralphie and Janie. It seemed the only thing that would keep me from dissolving into just another mist coming off the lake. I noticed that I was made a little easier by my one big chest full. Out of sight.

It was the kids that worried me.

Leaning on the door of the kids' room, I was playing with

keys and change in my front pocket and staring into the
lighted bathroom. Sesame, with his pants down around his
ankles, was hunched over the sea-green tub. I was aware of
naked dark skin. "All the way, all the way," he was saying. Sal
dipped out some of Rachel's cold cream and smeared it on
the red rubber cock strapped around her hips. I'd only read
about such things. She knelt on the kids' fold-over bench to
get enough height in back of him. "Open, Sesame," she said,
and slid the red cock into his ass. He tightened his elbows
on one side of the tub and his knees against the other,
quivering, and then made an awful racket as she slid the thing
in and out. *"Freedom,"* he sang, just the word, sometimes
falsetto, sometimes deep tenor. I could feel in the shaking in
my gut that I understood for the first time the meaning of the
word "nigger." With one hand reached under him Sal was
plucking just under the head of his hard-on as if it were
a clitoris.

"Grab it, grab it," Sesame was saying. There was sudden
pain in Sal's face, and she wouldn't grab it, couldn't. She
plucked urgently and put her body to driving the rubber
cock. He spat on his hand and grabbed it himself. "Go, go,"
he said, and then he came all over the rubber mat hanging on
that side of the tub.

"Ah-h, freedom," he moaned, and he meant the word
for me.

I jingled the keys and change sharply in my pocket.

They did themselves up and left the bathroom slowly. I
followed them slowly. Sesame slid down the first banister and
flung himself grinning at himself against the mirror. I could

only see my feet in the top of the mirror, but I could see his silly-assed eyes looking up there at me.

I let my breath alone say it.

"Nigger." He didn't hear.

He fluttered his fingers against the mirror grinning at me.

I had nothing better to do so I wended my way out to the street to see their car. Wilted flowers clung in rusted cracks all over it. I patted the head of a hitching post figure. I climbed in behind the wheel with my feet on the floor adrift with tools and carry-out cups and wadded cigarette packages. I knew I shouldn't leave Mel alone with Rachel. I sat there high up in the old car and looked up the gravel path. Every window was lit up, and the great snowy masses of spyrrhea bloom mounted around the base of the house. They were dancing on our rooftop, a flat roof, as if glad for once to have a rooftop, if only to dance upon it. The moonlight was strong. A stark naked fellow jumped on top of our fireplace chimney and tossed his long hair among the stars and shook the TV antenna so it glimmered rapidly. Another climbed on top of our water tank and spread his arms and spread his legs and gave a Tarzan yell. I rested my forehead on my arms on the steering wheel.

"He's seducing your wife."

It was announced so formally.

Never leave Mel alone with a wife. Clare should never have been left alone with me.

"I said he's seducing your wife." It was Sleepy Face, hanging in the car window.

"I thought so," I said.

It was good to hear the harsh laugh come out of his face. He scuttled wildly up the path back to the house.

The best things in life are free.

It would not be good if I tried to open the bedroom door and it turned out to be locked. It would give them too much satisfaction. I got down on my knees on the carpet to squint through the keyhole. The doorknob met my forehead coolly. It was black in there but I heard them going long and slow. Then a womanish moan made my whole body cold and shimmering as jello when you open the refrigerator door. It was Mel.

I walked into the kids' room with the breath of fear in my knees and fingertips. Ralphie was not in his bed and not in the room. Time stretched under my feet. Slat shadows rippled over little Janet in the crib. She slept on her cheek next to her teddy bear. Its wide open pink glass eyes startled me. I bounded through the hall calling Ralphie and down the staircase stiff-arming the wall near the mirror.

"Daddy," he said, pleased with himself and glad to see me.

He was sitting cross-legged, naked down to his pajama bottoms, on the big couch with a sleepily dazed smile. He was pulling at his toes and watching everything slyly. Champ, his red robot, stood faithfully on the floor with his blocky head beside Ralphie's knee. "Hey, Champ," Ralphie urged, "look. Look." I sat down on the couch and put my hand out to steady Champ between my knees. The smoothness of Ralphie's back on my arm was wonderful and made me a different man. "Funny people, daddy," he said. He was so sleepily nonchalant.

Sal the butch swaggered through the dining room dragging the red rubber cock rub-a-tee-dub along the line of chairs. "What's your name, honey?" Ralphie dug his head shyly into my armpit looking sideways up at her.

"Ralphie," he said.

The butch shook her hips. "Let's play, sweetheart."

I was on the point of doing something awful.

"Penis," Ralphie said.

"Touch," she said.

Ralphie giggled.

"It's OK," she said. "It's nice."

Ralphie pulled it down and let it go whanging against Sal's cowboy belt buckle. He said, "Funny penis, daddy."

The butch cocked her eye mournfully.

Ralphie flicked on the switch in Champ's head. Champ grrrrrd and walked his Frankenstein walk about three feet and then turned stiffly and his breasts opened and machine guns came out and lights sputtered. I didn't buy the toy for him, it was a birthday present, and I didn't ask him to like it. I didn't buy that red rubber cock for her either. "Play with Champ," I said. It was the closest I ever came to insulting one of them.

"How nice," she said.

"Champ will play with you," Ralphie said. He really wanted her to play with Champ.

"I always play with champs," she said.

She went away singing "*Cherry Ripe, Cherry Ripe* . . ."

"Wha'd the man say, daddy?"

"It's a woman, Ralphie."

"Woman? A mummy?"

The Champ was marching stiffly three feet here, three feet there, back and forth. "Funny penis," Ralphie drawled. I was working up my courage to do what seemed the only thing I could do. "Let's check the premises, Ralphie."

The place was shambled, overturned chairs and magazines and bits of food everywhere. I looked down the stairs into the rec room. I wasn't going down there.

Naomi, with her man's white shirt pulled up, was doubled up in the black butterfly chair near the bookcase in the rec room. Sal knelt in the shuffleboard triangle on the concrete, nuzzling in Naomi's crotch. A feverish something tumbled in my gut. I tried to keep smiling but they weren't looking up. "Oh, Sal," Naomi said sweetly, "I want to do you, too."

"I'll do the work, honey, I'll do it," Sal said a little urgently, burrowing delicately into the teenage bush. In a moment Naomi went taut and was driving her crotch into Sal's face and pulling on the back of Sal's head. I could hear Sal's jubilance. The TV was going with a report for farmers on hog prices.

I knew now that I had to use the tape that I have upstairs that I sometimes use as a way of ending a party. It's raunchy. We left Champ working his way back and forth in the living room.

None of the invaders were upstairs. "Mommy in there."

Ralphie was watching the white dead-still bedroom door
while I was threading the tape in the closet. "Mommy in
there, daddy?" I turned the volume control all the way up.
"She's sleeping, Ralphie." I locked the closet and put the key
in my pocket. Even Rachel couldn't get in there to turn it
off and there was a speaker over the bed.

Ralphie went on fast feet on the red carpet ahead of me
and scooted up and down the top stairs laughing at the sight
of himself in the mirror. I sat down on the top step. The
tape begins with about half of a Beatles' song and about the
time everybody starts swaying and drumming and snapping
their fingers, it cuts in with old Hit Parade tunes one after
the other.

There was a kind of silence that met the Beatles down
below. Ralphie settled down beside me and laughed at the
sight of our feet in the top of the mirror. "Music loud,
daddy." "It sure is, Ralphie." Then came *Linda*. "*When I walk
down the street, the people I meet blah blah blah blah blah
about Linda . . .*" Ralphie and I descended the stairs stiffly,
pretending that we walked the way Champ walks. John, the
orange-haired hippie, said, "Hey, man, are you serious?" It
was the first time he ever addressed me personally. He
walked jerkily back and forth, as if for the first time in his life
he faced a dilemma. Ralphie and I drifted regally hand in
hand through the house. "*When every breeze seems to
whisper Louise . . .*" "My name's Naomi." She held up to me
a cluster of my own lilac blooms. I looked at her. There
was not much more to say about her. She was alight from
what Sal had done to her and now she hooked her arm in

John's, and gave him the lilac cluster. Champ stalked sturdily back and forth in the living room with his machine-gun breasts chattering light at every turn.

In the kitchen, Naomi opened the refrigerator with a snap. The music was so loud you heard the snap only with your eyes. She snapped off a piece of celery, snapped off a bite and snapped the door closed. She pushed open the screen door with her foot and went out onto the back porch.

There was screeching on the back porch and somebody banging a pipe on the washing machine and the dryer. *"I love those dear hearts and gentle people . . ."* "Turn it off, turn it off, turn it off," they chanted. "Or *else*," a voice soloed, along with the voice in the speakers singing, *"who live in my hometown."*

"You'll never catch up," I murmured, "you're way behind." Ralphie was trying to shout above the music all the time but I wasn't paying my usual attention. *"You call everybody darling, and everybody calls you darling too . . ."* It never sounded raunchier. *"You don't know what you're saying, it's just a game you're playing . . ."* Naomi was holding Fluff by the open guinea pig cage on the back porch and letting him nibble the piece of celery and then taking a bite of it herself. *". . . but you'll find someone else can play the game as well as you."* Now here was the fellow I hadn't seen since he billowed through the front door. Drifty was lolling with his long head of hair back against the wall and his eyes hanging closed and his wrists loose on his knees. Spider nosed his ball up between Drifty's legs trying to get him to play. Then Spider hunkered down in front of his kennel, with SPIDER painted in spidery letters over the door, with his nose on his paws. He watched the ball roll away from Drifty's crotch. Spider waited and then flicked a paw at the ball. Spider is never at a loss. It did amuse me that in some great red cavern of acid an Old Lady of Time might be humming to Drifty some of our music. But then I only know what I read here and there.

The porch smelled violently of gasoline.

Over by the washer and the dryer Sleepy Face Jim was shaking gasoline from a five-gallon can into a clear wine bottle, which Sesame was wrapping in a soaked towel, blinking his eyes against the fumes, and jamming the end of the towel down the neck of the bottle with his little finger. He was simple-minded enough to try and scare me with what I'd seen in the newspapers. I watched with dread and coolness.

The music was so loud I had to ask Ralphie a second time what he'd said.

"What the men making, daddy?"

"A Molotov cocktail, Ralphie."

"Ma'tov cocktail? Daddy, why you play the music so loud?"

"Aw-*wighty*," Sesame said. He had to talk louder than the clear tones of *"Come with me, Lucille, in my merry Oldsmobile . . ."* "You hear about burn, baby,burn?" I looked at him. "You understand?" I still looked at him. "You turn that thing off," he said.

Ralphie gave a hoarse giggle. "Burn, baby," he said, thinking, good little sibling that he was, that the nigger meant

his baby sister Janet. The nigger never got from any
employment agency a smile broader than the one
I gave him.

"Man, you better believe we serious."

"Burn baby Janie all up," Ralphie said. I ruffled the back of
his head. Even the doctors would approve.

"Burn your baby Janie all up, you better believe."

Ralphie said, "After this day I like Janie again, daddy."

"Sure you will," I said.

I said nothing to the nigger faggot.

Out we went into the snowy moonlight in the backyard
among the croquet wickets and mallets and balls. *"I hear you,
honey,"* Sesame screeched inside the screened-in back porch.
I knew he was talking to me. Their shadows jerked back
and forth behind the screen. Naomi, in white shirt, cradling
and petting Fluff in one arm, wandered by the big lilac bush
near one of our raunchiest antiques, the pink plaster flamingo
standing on one leg in a cove of the bushes by the goldfish
pond and the birdbath. "F'uff, F'uff," Ralphie said excitedly.
He ran in his bare feet over the grass to Naomi.

"Is he your guinea pig?"

"Fluff," Ralphie said more carefully.

"He's a nice guinea pig," she said. "Do you take care
of him?"

"Yes," Ralphie said, "I take care of Fluff and sometime
Mommy take care and daddy take care Fluff and Janie," he
took a breath, "take care Fluff too. Janie is just a baby."

Naomi was pleased in spite of herself. "Can I hold Fluff
for awhile?"

"Yes," Ralphie said seriously, "you can hold Fluff awhile."

"I'm Naomi. What's your name?"

"I'm *Ralphie*." He said it with a proud jerk and a laugh.

"Ralphie," I said, "come here." Bits of wet grass were sticking to his bare feet. Naomi was stroking the neck of the plaster flamingo. "You must take great pleasure in these awful things," she said.

This was always the time when I put on my blankest look.

"What awful things?"

She said nothing. I was irritated.

I don't know how it happened but Drifty came through the back screen door without ever opening his eyes and floated, in his big blue workshirt and oversize farmer's jeans, into the backyard, slowly breaststroking his way through the air and then scooping the air toward his body. He was a most compelling sight.

Sesame and Sleepy Face Jim banged out of the screen door.

"Last chance, Charley," Sesame yelled.

I put my hand out to Ralphie. I made no other move.

Sleepy Face Jim lit the match.

They knew just how to bug me the most. Sesame lofted the Molotov cocktail into my biggest lilac bush, right near the pink flamingo. "*Get away*," I yelled to Naomi and crouched and held Ralphie between my knees. It was satisfying the way she stumbled in a hurry and then cowered with Fluff on the other side of the goldfish pond. The house was bellowing, "*Yes, we have no bananas today . . .*" when the bush burst up in one big orange rolling black-wreathed mass of flame, and the heat flashed on my cheek and the lilac bush went to lilac heaven. Ralphie grabbed my legs scared and shrieking. "Burn, sweetheart," I murmured, holding Ralphie against my chest.

Sesame and Sleepy Face Jim stood there as if they were about to plunge into a river, with the light of what they'd done on their faces, under which powered up a howl of awesome glee. "*Naughty* man," Ralphie said, shaking his finger. "*Naughty* man. Spank, spank, spank." They dashed back to the porch with the belief of what they'd done ripping at their heels. A croquet mallet caught between Sleepy Face's ankles. He did a stumble hop dance, and the screen door banged open and closed.

"Bad men, bad men," Ralphie chanted.

I smiled a little stiffly.

"It's OK, Ralphie. It just had to happen."

Now Drifty came down through the middle of the croquet wickets, not touching a one, scooping air and washing his sightless face on the stars. Naomi, on the other side of the goldfish pond, was entranced with the lilac bush simmering down.

I picked up a croquet mallet and started knocking a ball. It didn't feel right because I was using the red mallet on the green ball. Every window in the house blazed with people behind the screens looking out upon the lilac bush. Our bedroom window was dark. The nursery window is on the other side of the house. I did not want to see any dim figure behind the screen of our bedroom. I looked off to where Tumbril Hill bulked up and waited for carlights to move through the trees. Way in the south, the pink of Chicago stayed in the sky. It was a lonesome thing to see. Naomi picked up a mallet in one hand, with Fluff cradled in the other, and knocked a ball fifteen feet through the center wicket. I knew where she was raised. "Not bad," I said.

She didn't answer. She hit the ball again.

The screen door banged.

Sleepy Face Jim and Sesame swung out with the can of gasoline and what turned out to be Rachel's Tampax box. They jerked out the big cotton puffs, dangled them in gasoline, and then whipped the dripping balls of flame into the air. They were falling all around him but Drifty wouldn't have noticed an archangel's sword.

"Hey, man," Sleepy Face said.

"He is somewhere," Sesame said.

I believe in every drop of fire that falls . . .

The lighted windows swelled with Kay Starr singing *The Star Spangled Banner*. Ralphie and I stood solemnly at attention side by side, as we always do, with our family's famous smirk upon our faces. I knew this song was the last on the tape. It was pleasant imagining Rachel's relief in the bedroom. "I want it to stop, daddy." Ralphie jiggled up and down. "I want it to stop."

Sesame grabbed Fluff scrabbling out of Naomi's arms.

"No," Ralphie cried. He ran halfway toward them. I pointed an arm-length finger at Sesame. I told him not to do it.

Sesame liked it that I meant it.

"This your little beastie?" He grinned at Ralphie.

"*Yes,*" Ralphie said. He put up both arms to take Fluff.

"Give it to him," Naomi said.

"Ah, give it," Sleepy Face said.

Ralphie cuddled the scratchy little guinea pig on his bare chest. "Hello, Fluff," he said. Naomi crouched before him. "Poor little guinea pig, poor little Fluff," Naomi soothed, "they wouldn't let you do a really important thing." Drifty dragged his foot through a wicket and it caught and rode on his cuff. I wouldn't have minded at all if he had doused himself with gasoline and become a beacon unto Washington. Even in our backyard.

The war. The war. The war. The war.

The tape ended. None too soon.

Silence came in upon us. The water pump motor was going, pumping water into the tank on top the house. "Let's go, Ralphie," I said.

Ralphie put Fluff back in his cage on the porch.

Janet was crying upstairs. She was holding onto the top rail of her crib and mourning at me. She'd lost her pacifier. I picked it up from the floor, but she clawed it angrily out of her mouth and raised her arms to be picked up. I remembered chocolate cookies in the Hi-Fi closet and gave one to her. She knocked it away. I didn't have the time. She sat down plunk in the crib hitting her little fists on her teddy bear and crying with such red-faced, screwed-up fury she lost her breath. I was halfway down the stairs when Janie's howling came back and then I knew she buried her face in her teddy bear.

Ralphie was playing peek-a-boo on the couch with John the hippie. They were hiding their faces with pillows and Ralphie was shrieking with giggles. John did not look so happy.

"Ah-h, thank you, sir," he said. They all showed the shaky wonder of men who have survived a bombardment. They would never catch up.

I was just in time. I sat down on the ottoman in front of my chair and heard the bedroom door opening upstairs. "Champ still going," Ralphie said. Champ was indeed still going.

Naomi came toward me swift as a sparrow, a stick of celery stuck in her shirt pocket. She knelt and hugged me with her cheek against my belt buckle. "Thank you," she said.

She spun away, saucy.

I turned off Champ's topknot switch. He straightened to a stop.

"She going to babysit me, daddy?"

"Not a chance."

Dawn light filled the windows and dulled the lights and the house seemed smaller. The toilet flushed and died away upstairs. I hoped Mel would use the sample cake of our new soap for men.

Now they were coming down the stairs.

John of the orange hair looked up with one hand on the newel post. "Hey, man," he said softly, "let's split."

I stood up from the ottoman and saw only Rachel's feet in brown flats coming down the steps below the ceiling.

Everybody was standing as if doors were opening for an appearance. She glided down into the living room, no lipstick, fresh face, honey hair brushed, in blue-jean shift, clean, lovely, gentle, certain, graceful, aglow, damn it. She did not seem to see me but I was seeing her.

"Let's split," Mel shouted.

"Let's split," somebody answered out in the kitchen.

They scuttled one by one out of the house. John and Naomi went first, then Sal knocking the red rubber cock against her thigh. Sesame and Sleepy Face Jim went out with the radiance of a cross-eyed saint in their faces. Naomi snapped off a bite of celery. "Bye," she said.

"Bye, bye," Ralphie said.

It took my heart out the way he waved bye bye.

I was chilled seeing that Mel was wearing my old tweed jacket with leather cuffs and elbows and leather trimming on the lapels. He was cleaner now, more elegant, but still heavier than I remembered him in the old days. Rachel hadn't been able to sweat any weight off of him.

"Darling," Rachel said.

She was speaking to me.

She was speaking to him.

"Breakfast." She went through the swinging doors into the kitchen, as if she really wanted to make and eat breakfast. She didn't even say goodbye to Mel. Ralphie grabbed his loose pajama bottoms and ran after her.

Mel was there with his hand on the doorknob. "Jeremy," he said. I walked toward him, smoothly fishing out my billfold, as I would walk toward a caterer I was about to pay.

I edged out the picture of me and Clare screwing on the chair. "Jeremy, Jeremy." I could tell by the pores of his face he had used the soap, but his eyes were still awful and faraway. He hadn't said a word about Clare. He wasn't going to talk to me at all. He was stroking the leather-trimmed lapels with the fingertips of his left hand. It was then that I put the billfold and the picture back into my pocket without showing it. "Jeremy," he said.

"Mel," I said. It released him.

He went rapidly down the gravel path to where they were hanging their somber faces out of the Model A. Mel seated himself by the driver and stared straight up the road toward the Macphersons where there were birdhouses enough for the whole crew.

Just a stranger in paradise . . .

In the kitchen, blue flame poured up under a pan full of bacon white going translucent in the center. Rachel was washing dishes one after the other as if she had to get done on a specified minute or turn into a pillar of salt.

I could tell Ralphie liked the way Rachel was feeling. He was nuzzling her thigh and smiling and easy and slipping his hand in the pocket of her blue-jean shift. "I'm sleepy, mommy."

"I'll put you to bed," I said.

"I want mommy put me to bed." He was definite about it.

"Mommy will put you to bed," Rachel sang, and wiped her hands fast on the towel that hung from the refrigerator handle. "Up you go."

I was turning and pressing the bacon in the pan with a fork

when Rachel came back carrying a saucer full of cigarette butts. "You had to give him my tweed coat," I said. I was smiling.

"You had to play that tape," she said.

That made us even.

I was pleased she'd noticed the tape had been played.

Flies were stuck in the screen of the window over the stove. Bits of color of the croquet game brightened up on the lawn. There was the lilac bush. I saw with a start that the spade faggot's jacket was hanging on the head of the plaster flamingo. What if he came back to get it? I said, "You hear about the lilac bush?"

"I started the fire," she said.

It was a long time since we'd stayed so even.

"Did you take your pill last night?"

"I always take my pill."

Even again.

Good God, Rachel was beating eggs in the blender for french toast. I noticed my palms were chill and sweaty. Spider scratched at the screen door. I was still smiling.

Grease shattered in the bacon pan, all over my hand, and I was screaming obscenities without any continuity. I burned my lips sucking at my hand and jumped to the sink and ran cold water over it and splashed my lips. "Idiot," Rachel said.

She picked up the fork from the floor. The clean privacy of her blue eyes hit me. "Jesus," I whimpered, "the Chumbleys are coming tonight." I went through the swinging doors sucking my hand. Chumbley is our man for buying TV time. He has one glass eye and I was looking into his face right

now. Yet, I was excited; I could feel it in my groin. I thought
I ought to have the guts to go back and screw Rachel right
there on the kitchen floor. Then outside the front window I
saw, *yes,* the blue billow of Drifty moving over our front
lawn scooping air.

I slammed out the front door and rounded the house
screaming every word from "shit" to "motherfuck" and
jerked the nigger's jacket off the head of our flamingo and
came screaming around the house again. *I had to put my
arms around Drifty and guide him.* He'd shit his pants and it
was trickling down his ankles where bits of grass stuck on
his dirty bare feet. Let me say that again. *I had to put my arms
around him and guide him* to the edge of the road between
the hitching post niggers where I lapped the nigger's jacket
over his shoulder. Drifty was naked and hairless and smooth
as Ralphie under the unbuttoned work shirt and his fly
was open and no underwear. He didn't move while I held
him and his eyes didn't open. I had to stand there with him
watching the lake without seeing it until the Model A, with its
foxtail on the radiator cap, came chugging over the rise
by the Macphersons' looking for its lost soul. Then I strode to
the house without so much as a glance over my shoulder
sucking on my hand to moisten it and swinging it in the air to
cool the burn.

Janie was crying upstairs and shaking her crib to get up.
"I'm coming, Janie," I yelled. I went up the stairs three
at a time.

GOODBYE

Behind my eyelids the light goes out. Under Harwood's bed I am beginning to wake. Springs twang. Covers shuffle. Dust sprinkles my cheeks. You can be sure at this moment I allow myself only cautious stretching.

Wooly dust trails hang dimly from the bedsprings. They tickle my air. I tear them away. I roll them into a tiny ball. I aim and flip it. It hits, I hope, the mattressed bulge of his butt.

Now is the *only* time, when under his blankets, that Harwood can be sure no one is watching him. I am listening to his thoughts and feelings. An itching starts warmly between his toes. If you don't know that you have to cross your calves and face your insteps toward each other before you can dig the toes of one foot between the toes of the other, you know that Harwood knows. Anticipation sneaks into his feet. His toes grapple, rub, writhe, promote the itching *and* its vibrant satisfaction.

But the spiteful place in my soul is worse than an itch in

the middle of your back. You can always find a post.

My fingers spread on the bedsprings. They strum lightly. A skinny sound snuggles coldly into his ear. Harwood, a confident sensible man, says to himself, "I only imagined it." My strumming actually stimulates his confidence. And his confidence relaxes him into the process that deliberates into sleep.

But, oh! you should observe the response from another kind of person under whose bed I have lived. I call him Jumpy fondly.

Jumpy hears my strum. His startled senses spring. His reasoning raves with explanations. Someone is under the bed or someone is in the closet or someone is *somewhere* in the room. He crouches under the blanket, his heart rapping his bunched-up knees. He cannot take the chance that the possible someone under the bed will grab his feet. Mightily he leaps into the middle of the room, dashes to the wall and flicks on the light. No one is visible in the room. He fastens all fours and one cheek to the floor and peers back under the bed. No one is there.

He narrows on the closet with tip-toe cunning. He takes up a broom. Not a single board creaks and he grins. He jerks the door open, jumps back, sees *no* legs jutting under the hanging clothes. He jabs the end of the broom-handle into the clothing. It bumps hard against the closet wall.

He checks the windows and doors. All locked.

Then he assumes, in the center of his room, a belligerent stance, with hands on hips, in white shorts laced with holes like worm-eaten cabbage leaves. He compares each thing in the room against his memory. Pictures placed just so on the wall, a magazine with fluttered pages on a chair. Did he open the magazine himself? Or was it the intruder seeking momentary diversion? Jumpy's very thoroughness makes him uneasy. It means that the intruder is diabolically clever.

Reluctantly Jumpy turns out the light. He rubs and stretches his eyes to adjust them quickly to the darkness. He leaps into bed. He lies so he faces all the room. After a few minutes the barest suggestion of a sound occurs again, a strumming on the bedsprings or on the window screens or on the rung of a chair. His mind rapidly reduces the data of noises. But this time memory says, "*No,* no one else is in the room, we checked only fifteen minutes ago." But the mind insists that someone, a highly skilled someone, in the interim *might* have opened a locked window. Jumpy crouches, leaps, searches every corner, comes grimly back to bed.

All these maneuvers, mental and physical, do serve to tire him. Fighting to stay alert on watch tires him more.

In the morning he wakes surprised with rest. He fills with the grateful pleasure of safe light streaming into him.

Harwood is only grateful to his industrious confidence. But Harwood makes living easy. He never looks under the bed.

He makes living too easy. He makes me careless and angry. I am sure if I played on the bedsprings as on a harp that he would only compliment his pretty imagination. Tonight I am dangerously tempted.

He is asleep. I suppress an urge to sneeze.

I turn over and crawl on my belly gently using elbows and feet. I come out from under the bed. I sit on my heels. I could reach and touch the bald top of his head. It is half-buried in the pillow and maybe, just maybe, he is not as buried as I think in his confidence. He is motionless. I stretch. I relieve the cramps in my legs slowly. Otherwise, standing up too quickly, I might topple onto the floor or onto his bed. Even Harwood would not dismiss that as imagination.

I dust my pants, it powders my hands, my soul *screeks*.

It has been a comfort against him that Harwood's maid usually cleans under the bed. I will leave a note for her today. I am always able to find a place to hide before she enters. But sometimes her steady dreamy face discovers me, for instance, squatting on the top shelf of the closet. Dropping broom and bucket, screaming, beating both fists on both thighs, she bounces out of the house and reports a burglar. It is a tiresomely recurrent thing I see. By the time the police arrive I am walking another street. Harwood, informed, assumes, as usual, that the burglar was unsuccessful.

If it is a maid hired for a single day, I risk meeting her at the door. I say I am a friend. I direct her cleaning and my own special places are spotless and waxed. If she tells Harwood that a friend was in the apartment, he checks his roster of social relationships, but always gives up before the end and lets it ride that some friend was in the apartment when he was away. You can see why it was a boon to reside under Harwood's bed after wracking my wits with Jumpy.

GOODBYE

Harwood sleeps mainly without dreams. In a sense *I* do most of his dreaming. And he pays no attention. He is a *senior* vice-president.

I am awake. I walk. I must insist that I always walk in perfect silence on stocking feet. All these creakings people hear, simply the night buttoning up, and only night allows a sound to truly represent itself. I think that is why many people listen to music with their eyes closed. But since most people are securely controlled by daylight schemes, a sound at night, though purely itself, is a trumpeted hint from the unknown. I never make creakings. I admit I make other sounds. But it peeves me that all my sounds are considered omens of danger. Harwood himself listens to music with his eyes closed. Yet he attributes certain sounds, *my* sounds, to his *blessed* imagination. Jumpy is one reaction I know. Harwood another. Neither possesses an adequate apparatus for detecting the meaning in sounds. So they have an unknown life with me and I have a known life with them, sometimes easy, sometimes difficult. *Always* thinking on sounds leads me to this problem of the life easy and the life difficult. I am not enough metaphysically inclined to really trouble my thoughts with this problem. My criterion is sometimes the easier life, the better, other times the more difficult, the more wits required, the better. I don't know why I need both conditions. I know the nature of sounds. I don't know why the others don't. Someday I will die under some fellow's bed and I won't know when he died above me.

My nightly reveries were once sweet to me.

I pad into the kitchen. I open the refrigerator. Yes, the click is loud. It signifies danger only because it is pure. I take a breast of cold chicken, some green beans streaked with white grease, jello, and milk. Cold potatoes are the worst in my experience. But Harwood is concerned about his weight so there is not much cold starch to pall my taste. Hot coffee is all the cooking I can permit myself. Let's say that when Harwood gets up to piss about four hours from now, there I am in the kitchen with pots bubbling and grease sputtering. I have never been trapped in such embarrassment. If he has been drinking, he will get up a couple hours sooner.

It was impossible to make coffee with Jumpy. Almost impossible to eat. My sole escape at times was the refrigerator. I had the major part of Jumpy's food arranged on the upper shelves. That way the lower racks were quickly adjustable. I climbed in and kept a piece of cardboard in the lock. Why didn't Jumpy ever look in the refrigerator? He certainly ransacked the kitchen. Something prevented him from believing that a man would hide in the refrigerator. Children, perhaps. So why did he never suspect that it was a child? He suspected everything else. "All intruders are taller than me," he thought. I waited. My fingertips became brittly numb. I waited until I could tell Jumpy was soundly sleeping by his vibrations coming through the crack in the door. They differed slightly enough from the refrigerator motor. Then my fingers were like sticks and chalk. You can see that the condition of living by my wits is to be endured with discretion.

Yes, Harwood misses the food, and Jumpy too. Jumpy

angrily informs himself that he is wasting time by not buying
more. During daylight Jumpy accuses himself. At night he
accuses the night. Harwood says to himself, "Food is just like
money, you never have as much as you think you have."
Harwood appends sagely that most judgments are extended
into time by hope hand in hand with a certain recognition of
real expectations. Depending on how much hope enters,
the realized results fall that much short. Harwood also knows
that even the most developed human is not free of hope's
sneakily distortive effects. If not achieve results that equal his
estimation, Harwood thinks he can see the reason in the
results. It is peculiar that in daylight Harwood's logic is as
involved as Jumpy's at night. But I haven't minded being
categorized with hope. It means I eat easily. Indeed, I am
becoming padded, dull as a mattress with Harwood's
unwitting beneficence.

    I keep the flame low so it will make good coffee and not
boil too loudly. I pour two full cups. I clean the pot now. I
place it upside down in its proper place on the shelf. I take
the two cups to the head of Harwood's table. I put a saucer
on top of one to inter the heat. I measure Harwood's rich
pure country cream and sugar into the other. I sit in his
stuffed throne-chair. I fit nearly perfectly into his hollows.
From this chair, after a meal, he talks to friends. I meditate.
My two cups stand before me. First I *choose* the one with
cream and sugar. My meditation thickens. It lazily dissolves
my remaining hunger. I clean this cup and return it upside
down to its original place on the shelf.

    I search in Harwood's ashtray. I consider five or six

possible butts. I take, no, not the longest, but the *freshest*, softest one. I accept the second cup of black coffee. Its single taste cleans away the sweet coating on my tongue. My thoughts quicken. If I had to choose between only coffee with cream and sugar all the time, or straight black coffee, I would take the black. *Choice*, I remember, and bitterly burrow with my butt and elbows and back. I change the hollows in the chair just enough so just this once tomorrow Harwood will scrunch around for the *slightest* moment before the familiar comfort fits over his bodily configuration.

I clean this cup. I wipe his table. I bury my pinched thin cigarette butt under the ashes. It is possible that I am now as comfortable as he. But tip-toe excitement in stocking feet always illumines my comfort. In this sense he is the one who lives in dark rooms.

I have about three hours before he gets up for his nightly piss. My work is his work. I don't like to use the name of his firm. Since my residence under his bed his work has improved greatly and steadily. He is more exact, his decisions are more surely founded, they reach further, and he is much neater. At the firm they say that his "sudden blooming" springs from "age and experience." He believes this too. And with a gracious smile, the external symbol of that internal pride, he receives the new plaudits. Now he is up for promotion, to the presidency itself, because the board of directors needs his "age, imagination, and experience." It is *impossible* for me to get any credit. If I leave him, Harwood has what the firm calls a "falling off." In a more poetic response they say he is

"taking a step backward in order to jump forward." When I
return, they say smugly they "knew he would pull through."
And if I choose to leave him for good, they will call his lack
of productivity "senile decline," and say that he was only kept
on the roster because of his "name," or retired with "honor."
All these misplaced names are *me*. I have no name.

Yes, I see he must discover me to recognize me. *Yes,* I
cannot let him.

I escape into work and reverie.

It is usually a little troublesome "getting a grip" on the job
of a new man under whose bed you have chosen to live. First
you must coax your handwriting into an exact resemblance
of his. I filled sheets imitating his signature. It has small
austere flourishes. I traced over all his notes with his pen. It
is important to use *his* pen. In this actually there is no choice.
I can only extend the worth of his work, not change its
character. I can only make it more of himself. Yes, he thinks
it is *he* who has become more of himself. I will not
condescend. I will only smile. For even with my aid errors
still mar the work. I have commented on the analogous
nature of our ignorances. I have also suggested that, though
analogous in nature, the two are *definitely* not the same size.
But again the truth is that we both build upon and build
toward ignorance, and behind our backs, perhaps pressing us
forward, is ignorance too. I have stated that I am not
metaphysically inclined. I grip my teeth together. And while
I smile, while I work at his desk, he sleeps.

If he dreams, it is his promotion, causing an occasional

terrifying expansion of pride in him, a flutter from danger's
internal light. Knowing that I do not know many things, I
think my work may have done him a disfavor. One night
under the bed I will sense his sudden urgent final rhythm.
Blooey, he will explode. And all that stuffy, cottony comfort
and pride will drift in sneezy masses over the room. I am not
sure whether this happening is unlikely or not. Perhaps it is
only my spite that anticipates it. No, this is the one way, that
he die on his soft mattress in ignorance and I on my hard
floor in imitation of his signature, in grander austerity.

I have finished two hours work. I have corrected a dozen
mistakes in his papers, probably added two or three, and in
unsuspicious places I have deposited suggestions that will
advance his firm's advantage. I take long tip-toe pointed steps
through the hall. Perfect timing, there is the first signal, the
twitch of his foot. His knee makes a pyramid. I look down on
his sluggishly inarticulate lips. His brows draw toward the
roman bridge of his nose. He seems considering an *unjust,
unseen* pain. In one minute I would stand in the vista of his
waking. I do not spend, I hoard that minute under his bed.

He turns over. He stretches his arm toward the lamp with
a groan. A click. A long edge of light cuts under the blanket
into the only darkness, my territory. His big knobby
blue-veined feet swing into sight below the blanket. They
poke about hunting his slippers without success. His crawling
fingers stumble among ashtrays, books, and papers, seeking
his glasses on the bedside table. I reach and take a gleeful
chance. I place the slippers within range of his toes. He grunts

to his feet, "Well, it's about time." His feet pause side by side. His ankle bones tempt me. I would tap them and see what reasoning Harwood pursued to explain it. Jumpy, if his ankles were so tapped, would spring not into the middle of the room, but *all* the way to the opposite wall, instantly flatten himself on the floor and peer right into my eyes. All right, I admit that I have tapped ankles a few times, just once lightly, or tapped shoulders, but only when someone else is there too. You should see the suppressed startle when the tapped one turns and sees that that someone else is *nowhere* within reach. But Harwood's feet are within *my* reach. I plant my fidgeting hands under the weight of my butt.

As he goes toward the bathroom, his heels thump, his slippers phlip-phlap. Coffee aromas float dead on the air and nudge his nose. He has forgotten why he flushes the toilet before his piss rattles on the water. Centrifugally the roar plunges down into the center of the night. The night vibrates with renewed stillness. He returns. His slippers' rhythm expresses his impatience toward his bladder's necessity. I *sympathize* with his bladder. He undoes the cord of his bathrobe. He throws the robe over a chair. During the day he hardly remembers that this is the only time when he seems reckless to another's eye. He kicks off his slippers. One sails under the bed and bops me in the belly. I choke. He collapses. The bulge of his butt dives toward me. *Quietly,* with a trembling hand, I put the slipper beside its mate outside my domain.

Now the thought of promotion clings with claws onto

Harwood's mind. He turns and writhes as if to move himself bodily out from under it. My foot *jumps* up and strums the bedsprings solidly. It cuts the promotion off his mind. It leaves him quite still. I am still too. But he contrives the usual conclusion. It smothers wakefulness.

I walk awhile proudly aghast with myself in his apartment.

From now until the final waking the hours always go quickly. I make another cup of coffee, straight black, and take it into his study. I sit in his reading chair. This time my elbows and butt fight instinctively against his molded fit. A book lies angled on the nearby endtable. A white card is slipped like a dagger between its pages. Drinking the coffee and smoking more butts, I read no further than the place marked. *No,* I do not permit him to draw the program for my life. But reading the books that he is reading now sandpapers a certain sensitivity onto my fingertips, enabling me to follow his rhythms and act on his deepest clicks. I rummage through his library the rest of the night reading what I please. It is only habit that I place a particularly good book where he is likely to come upon it.

I catch myself forgetting to wash and dry and put away my cup and saucer. *Any* hint of carelessness jiggles my breath.

I unlock the door. I step onto the fifth-floor porch for a "little exercise and fresh air." Yes, I haunt the backside of his known life and his habits and expressions sneak through my senses. They emerge and I *know* they come from him. I can bear *anything* but becoming him. And I know *exactly* what would happen if he ever faced the maker of most good things in his life. He would not have a heart attack. He would say, "You, sir. Look here, *sir*. Get *out* before I call the police, sir."

I cannot call it *choice*. Two currents move side by side in opposite directions. One is slow and easy, the other swiftly turbulent. I go within and across them. I never know when I will be caught and carried, *zip,* into another direction.

Yes, it is time to re-enter Jumpy's gymnasium. It is time to sweat my spite.

On the porch I fill with clean dawning air. I gaze on the distant skyscraper city, an enormous bed of nails upon which the reddening smoky sky yet seems to rest peacefully as I rest on the floor. I am sweetly sad with the fate of myself and the sky.

I check the apartment. I rearrange and cover suspicions of my presence. My breathlessness rides in my breast again as a bubble atop a jet of air. I look down on Harwood's frowsled greying temple. Combed and shiny those temples will seem strong behind his desk in the day. I whisper,

"Goodbye."

He *hears,* a hint coming across the dawn, a disturbance on the edge of existence. He heaves onto his back, his knee rising and straightening down. On the pillow his head strains against the unseen pain. It is a mere suggestion of what is to come, just as my strumming is a mere suggestion of a sound. At last a warm satisfaction bitterly begins in my belly.

Alarm clocks, in my experience, are very erratic. Five minutes before the hands of the clock grip the set time I retreat under the bed. I stare at square upon square of bedsprings. I have often wished that bedsprings came in patterns of parallelograms, triangles, or circles. I have heard that such bedsprings exist. But I have seen only patterns of squares. The alarm rings.

He tells everybody, he believes himself, that he wakes and hits the floor at the first tingle. But tens of seconds it rattles and rings. His hand gropes, clamps upon it. A snap and he lies quietly.

He throws back the blanket. He swings his legs and hits his feet on the floor. On the edge of the bed he sits in a numb, appalled heap for much longer than he would ever admit.

A couple times, proving to myself and by implication to him how important I am, I have risked taking the alarm under the bed and turning it off before it starts ringing or even seconds after it rings. Then he is late to work. He is disturbed. He suspects that he really, unconsciously, turned off the alarm. Unconscious action is against some principle of his.

His toes creep into his slippers. He sets his glasses on his nose and squinches at the leaping perspective in the suddenly straightened room. He walks toward the bathroom tying the bathrobe cord around his waist. He showers, sings, shits, and shaves. He returns with his hands untying the cord. I lie with my cheek flat on my hand on the floor. It is boring everyday, but I watch because, after all, we are saying goodbye.

I see there will be a speech today. No doubt it is the conference at which the firm will announce his promotion to president. He selects his speech-tie, canary yellow, with the brown tweed suit. Yes, he thinks the contrast aids in training the rows of eyes on him at the rostrum. Never would he wear an outlandish suit. But he is certain that his position permits him to wear around his neck whatever pleases him. A beige button-down sweater tones the speech-tie's savage effect. He opens the door. He turns, hand on the knob, and looks around the apartment. No, he has not forgotten anything.

I close my eyes. I listen to his footsteps walking away into the back of my head. He is heading for a restaurant, no longer aided directly by me. But he carries a briefcase full of good work under his arm.

Harwood knows a man must wait until the "cold light of morning" to see true value. Over his breakfast, while his hand forks food into his mouth, he will read the work and now and then delight will lift his brows. Thus my presence will still fatten his confidence. In the days to come the confidence of the new president will shrink. I am always with him.

Several times I have climbed from under the bed and attempted to sleep on his mattress. I toss and my bones ache remembering their own levels on the floor.

I have four hours before the maid arrives. But today I am going to Jumpy's. I experience a second's writhe of indecision. Well, I will write the note instructing the maid to clean my special places anyway. It is necessary to think that I will return.

A little sleep will revivify and prepare me. I set the alarm. I fold my hands on my chest. My eyelids slide between me and the bedspring squares.

I consider the consequences of goodbye. Its hidden, furry

nature quivers when touched by me. I wonder again why Harwood never, not once, looked under the bed. The answer is always the same. And I confess that life is far more comfortable with a man ashamed of suspecting an actuality, than life with a man who fears what he suspects.

When I return, if I return, I will know that what they call Harwood's "rebirth" is caused by me. I will give myself the pat on the back that should, impossibly, come from him.

I will gird my spirit and trek across the city and into the slums. I will find Jumpy.

I will prove the extent of my cunning capabilities.